METROPOLE

Ferenc Karinthy

Metropole

Translated from Hungarian by
George Szirtes

TELEGRAM
London San Francisco Beirut

ISBN: 978-1-84659-034-4

This edition published 2008 by Telegram

A full CIP record for this book is available from the British Library.

Grateful acknowledgement to the Hungarian Book Foundation for their help in funding the translation

Hungarian Book Foundation

Manufactured in Lebanon

TELEGRAM
26 Westbourne Grove, London W2 5RH
825 Page Street, Suite 203, Berkeley, California 94710
Tabet Building, Mneimneh Street, Hamra, Beirut
www.telegrambooks.com

Looking back on it later it could only have happened because Budai had gone through the wrong door in the confusion at the transit lounge and, having mistaken an exit sign, found himself on a plane bound elsewhere without the airport staff having noticed the change. After that it was impossible to say how far or for how long he had flown, for as soon as the engine purred into life he reclined his seat and fell asleep. He was quite exhausted, hardly having rested the last few days, working himself to a standstill, and apart from anything else there was the speech for the linguistic conference in Helsinki for which he had just now been preparing. He was woken only once during the flight when they brought him his meal, then he promptly fell asleep again, it might have been for ten minutes or for ten hours. He didn't even have his wristwatch with him since he intended buying one out there and didn't want to have to present two watches at customs back home, so he didn't have the least clue how far he was from home. It was only later, once he was in town, that he discovered it wasn't Helsinki and was shocked that he didn't know where he actually was. The passengers had been put on board a bus at the airport. It was dark; a cold and windy evening, or perhaps it was already night and he was still half asleep. The bus stopped in various places and a lot of people got out. Budai had been in Helsinki before but now he sought in vain for familiar buildings or the seafront. At one of the stops everyone got off, including the driver, who gestured for him to do likewise. He found himself at the glass doors of a hotel with great crowds of people pressing past him, quickly separating him from his fellow passengers, and it took him a good while to push through the crowd flowing both ways. The doorman, an enormous portly figure wearing a fur coat and a gold-braided cap, greeted him courteously and opened the swing door before him, but when Budai addressed him in Finnish he plainly did not understand and answered in an unknown language, ushering him into the lobby where the influx of new guests prevented further conversation.

There was a crowd gathered by the hotel reception as well so he had to join the queue and, by the time he found himself face to face with the grey-haired desk-clerk, a man in a dark-blue uniform, there was a large, noisy family – mother, father, three unruly children, plus a mass of luggage – all squashed up behind him, practically pushing him forward with barely disguised impatience. From this point on everything speeded up. He tried to address the receptionist in Finnish, then in English, French, German and Russian, all clearly to no avail since the man replied in a different unknown language. So he showed the man his passport and the desk-clerk took it from him, no doubt to jot down the details, handing him a copper-weighted key in return. Budai had slipped his dollar cheque, the daily stipend for trips abroad, into his passport, and the porter took that too, then consulted his pocket calculator, read off the result and quickly filled out a pre-stamped form which must have been a credit note in the local currency, or so Budai guessed from his rapid gabble. He tried protesting that he didn't want to cash his cheque in now but no one understood him and since the loud and large family behind him were growing ever more impatient, waving documents, the children screaming, and since the desk-clerk was pointing to the neighbouring cash-desk, Budai gave up the struggle, let the family through and stepped over to the next window.

There was a similarly long queue there moving at snail's pace so he took his place at the end ever more irritated, thinking he would have to undergo the same idiotic procedure all over again. The clerk here simply gabbled the same incomprehensible language. Once again he had no time to explain, not that he had any clear idea what it was he wanted to explain nor what language to attempt. The upshot was that he was given a wad of unused banknotes, some bigger, some smaller, a few screwed-up ones and half a fistful of change in coins that he pocketed along with the notes without examining them closely. This was all quite ridiculous and infuriating of course but he had only just begun to speculate on what might have happened. Maybe the weather was bad in Helsinki and the flight had been diverted and that was why they had landed in some other town. But, surely, in that case his luggage would have been returned to him, yet all he had with him now was the little case he had carried on board and had stowed in the compartment over his head. Whichever way he looked the only conclusion he could come to was that he had boarded the wrong flight in transit which meant his suitcase must have arrived in Helsinki without him, though now he came to look for it he could not find his ticket either, nor could he remember anyone taking it from him at the airport. That presented a serious problem since he had left his personal ID and other papers at home, shoving them into a drawer at the last minute, so he was without any documents. But that wasn't what most agitated him right now, that could be sorted out later; what mattered was that he should get to Helsinki as soon as possible. In order to do that he first had to explain to the relevant authorities how he had arrived here and from where, which entailed locating those appropriate authorities who would, most probably, be the representatives of the airline. Unfortunately he had no idea where to find them. The queue at reception was even longer than before so he had no desire to join it again, indeed all the windows were fully occupied, and he couldn't work out which window was for what and where he should go for mere information. There were notices here and there over particular windows along the long desk but he could not make them out, the letters being of some unknown alphabet, as were the captions under the pictures hanging on the walls, the messages of the posters and the text of the newspapers and magazines at the newsagent's counter. In any case he was unable to examine them properly because the lobby was full of the dense, constantly shifting crowd and whenever he tried to stand still he was jostled and swept along elsewhere. So he decided to wait and arrange things by telephone from his room.

The copper weight on his key said 921 so he guessed the room would be on the ninth floor. He found the lifts at the end of the lobby though only three of the eight seemed to be working and each of those had a large group of people waiting by it. Budai would have gone up by the stairs but casting his eyes round for the stairs he couldn't see them and he was unwilling to lose his place in the queue. It took another quarter of an hour before he managed to get into the lift which was so full that there was no room to move. The blue-uniformed lift girl was tall, young and blonde. She called out in her mysterious language, announcing the floors, and indeed they seemed to stop at every one. But as soon as the compartment emptied it filled up again since a whole new crowd piled in at each floor. There was a small, working ventilator fixed to the wall next to the girl yet Budai couldn't help wondering how she could work in such a stuffy, airless compartment with such a constant press of people, working perhaps for hours at a time or on an entire shift. But he quickly dismissed the thought: it wasn't his problem, he was going to be away from here, today with a bit of luck, by tomorrow morning at the latest. He signalled that he wanted to get out at the ninth floor and squeezed out with the rest when they arrived, their places being immediately occupied by others. He met no one in the corridor as he searched for his room, wandering to and fro, counting forward and back in the attempt to locate room 921. There was always a doorway or a junction that broke the sequence and he could not pick it up again. Twice he found himself back at the lift until he finally stumbled on 921 at the very end of a distant branch corridor.

The room was tiny but the fittings were modern and comfortable, complete with a settee, a cupboard, a writing desk, a standard lamp and a bedside reading light. In the tiny en suite there was a shower, a basin with hot and cold running water, a toilet bowl, as well as mirrors and towels. Both rooms were pleasantly warm though there was no sign of a heater: it must have been hidden in the wall. The windows were provided with curtains and canvas blinds and through them, opposite, he saw a tall, wide building, the same height as the hotel, dotted with many lit and darkened windows of its own. There was a single picture on his own wall, an oil painting, glazed, showing a gently undulating snowbound landscape with two pine trees and some scampering fawns in the distance. There was also a framed text beside the door, an inventory perhaps or the house rules, its orthography resembling that of the one downstairs. He didn't recognise the alphabet, knowing only that it wasn't like anything he had noted in passing, not Latin, not Greek, not Cyrillic, not Arabic, not Hebrew, but not Japanese, Chinese or Armenian either: he had taken a quick survey course of all these languages back in his student days. What did stick out, however, was that one or two Arabic numerals appeared in the mass of unrecognisable writing. He took out the money he had been given in exchange for his cheque and found much the same, the writing incomprehensible but the figures under the landscapes and portraits much as usual: eighteen brand new tens, a few ones and twos, and some coins of greater or lesser value. But he felt too drowsy and dull now to continue his investigations and dirty too after his long journey. He took out his bathroom items and put away some of his few belongings.

Fortunately he and his wife had been wary of exceeding the 20kg limit in the suitcase so they stuffed what they could into the zip-up canvas shoulder-bag, including underwear, pyjamas, slippers, the wash-bag, a spare pair of shoes, a jumper, two bottles of wine to give away as presents, that kind of thing ... It was odd how he had failed to seek out his baggage on arrival, though the fact was there seemed to be no opportunity to do so in the rush, in the dreamlike confusion when the passengers were herded onto the bus. But he had a faint memory of looking for something in it, that the suitcase was on the bus with him in the luggage compartment.

He showered and shaved in front of the mirror, put on clean underwear, immediately washing out what he had just worn, hanging his pants and vest on the taps and the shower head. Having done so he tried out the phone. Since there did not appear to be a phonebook or anything like it in the room, he simply kept dialling until he got somebody on the other end of the line. There were in fact a number of voices at the ends of the various lines, male and female both, but whatever language he chose to ask a question in, however often he repeated that question in another language, practically shouting out the word INFORMATION! he was answered in the same incomprehensible way, in a language without discernible inflections, a continual jabbering – '*bebebe*' or '*pepepe*' or '*checheche*'. However he adjusted his sharp ears to the most delicate distinctions, to the most subtle tonal variations, he heard only a kind of muttering or burbling. In the end he slammed the receiver down with a bitter laugh, frustrated that everything and everyone was proving so difficult. In any case, he was hungry and had no idea when he had last eaten. He got dressed, locked his room and set off in search of food.

There was an older woman in charge of the lift now, not the blonde girl, or maybe he himself had got into a different lift, though this was as packed as the last had been. Downstairs in the lobby the grey-haired desk-clerk had also been replaced, but the queue had not grown any shorter. Budai had no more luck with this desk-clerk than he had with the last; it was ridiculous that a hotel as big as this should employ incompetents who could not speak any of the major world languages, but the people behind him in the queue were growing loud and those at the back were shouting and gesturing at him for pushing in, insisting that he should get to the back of the long serpentine row, so, feeling confused again, he put his key down on the desk and moved on.

The crowd in the lobby was just as dense as before, pushing and shoving, and he had to thread his way carefully through to the revolving doors. Once again the fat, gold-braided, fur-coated doorman saluted him, but the street was no less crowded than the hall, its tide of humanity swirling, flooding and lurching this way and that. Everyone was in a hurry, panting, elbowing and fighting to get through; one elderly woman in a headscarf kicked him as hard as she could on the ankle and he received a good many more blows on his shoulder and ribs. The traffic in the roadway was equally packed, the cars nose to tail, now stopping, now starting, making absolutely no allowance for pedestrians, as if they were stuck in some eternal bottleneck, engines continually revving, horns furiously blaring: there was a wide variety of them, saloons and trucks, enormous public conveyances, trolleys and buses, and he was surprised to discover he did not recognise any of the makes he knew from home or from previous visits abroad. Clearly he must have emerged in the evening rush hour and whichever way he turned, now left, now right, the crowd was such that he could not escape but repeatedly found himself back at the hotel entrance. So he turned down a side street, but there too the crowd was dense, the pavement heaving with pedestrians, the roadway jammed with cars: any move he made entailed a real effort. Not that he wanted to go too far of course in case he should get lost and not find his way back to the hotel.

Neon signs were blinking high above him. Most of the shops were still open. They were selling all kinds of things with a very wide range of choice, as the window displays made clear – clothes, shoes, dinner sets, flowers, household equipment, carpets, furniture, bicycles, perfume, plastic items – these, at least, were what he noted. And there were no end of customers, or so it seemed, with long queues inside, some of them extending out into the street. The most crowded were the two groceries that Budai passed on his short journey, a journey he just about found strength to make since the pavement was becoming ever more crowded, the customers who could not get into the shops congregating in the doorways or forming close-packed columns: he had no idea how long it would take to get round to buying something. But the hunger pains were increasingly acute so he was delighted to find a restaurant a little further along, the tables with their tablecloths behind the big plate-glass window, the guests at their dinners, the waiters in their white coats.

Unfortunately there was a queue here too, quite a long one at that, because they only let in as many guests as were leaving so it was rather slow progress. He tried to size up the others in the queue without drawing attention to himself. Some were white, some coloured: right in front of him were two coal-black, wire-haired, young men, a little further off an oriental-looking, pale-yellow woman with her daughter, but there were some tall Germanic types, one tubby Mediterranean gleaming with perspiration in his camel-coloured coat, a few brown-skinned Malays, some Arab or Semitic people, and a young redheaded woman with freckles in a blue woollen jumper, carrying a tennis racquet: it was hard to tell what race or shade formed the majority here, at least in front of the restaurant.

After a good forty minutes of creeping along he too was finally allowed in and left his coat at the counter in exchange for a number.

The tables were all occupied, and it took some time to find him a place near the back of the hall. He asked in English if he might sit down but it seemed nobody could understand him, people glancing blankly up at him from their plates before immediately returning to their food. It was obvious that everyone here was in a hurry but it was another quarter of an hour before the waiter appeared since he was clearly so busy he could not have got to him earlier. He cleared and set the table for Budai, gathering up the used dishes and putting a menu down in front of him, though Budai couldn't make head or tail of the contents. He started to explain this to the old waiter but the man simply shrugged and gabbled something and was, in any case, called away by someone else. Budai tried to address the others at the table. He spoke to them in six or eight languages but without any success whatsoever; they gave no sign of comprehension and didn't even pay him much attention. He was growing ever more irritated, his stomach tense with excitement, but there wasn't even a slice of bread nearby. It was another twenty minutes before the waiter returned with a large and fulsome dish of garnished chicken for his fellow diners but there was no point in Budai indicating his hunger and asking for some of the same for the waiter was called away again and it was impossible to say whether he had made a note of the order at all. In the meantime other diners came and went. The waiter reappeared at the far end of the table with new dishes and clean cutlery and was paid by some but he took not the least notice of Budai and soon enough he was called away to another table. Nevertheless, Budai kept whistling and waving until at last he returned only to rattle on in an annoyed and melancholy manner, his voice heavy with passion, though Budai couldn't tell whether he was simply asking him to be patient or expressing his exasperation and wanted nothing more to do with him. Budai could barely contain himself: he felt helpless not knowing whether it was worth waiting or whether he should do something else. When the waiter returned and once again failed to serve him he smacked his hands down on the table, kicked his chair and stalked off in indignation. He had, of course, to join another queue for his coat, since there was a lot of coming and going, but he barged past them in his fury. He left a small coin for the cloak-room attendant, the old man there possibly grateful, muttering something that might have been a thanks.

Yes, but he had still not eaten and was now incapable of thinking about anything else. He fought his way through the traffic that was just as dense as before, thrusting ahead, using both hands and feet until, at the cost of several more blows and one or two near-confrontations, after an infinitely long half a mile down the road he found himself at something like a self-service buffet. This too was jam-packed with customers who jostled or just stood about but it was impossible to tell what they were waiting for so he stood in one of the queues and waited to see. The queue made pretty slow progress and he found out rather late that it led to a cash desk where people were being given numbered receipts and that another queue beyond that continued right across the long hall to a counter on the far side where the food was dished out. When he did eventually arrive at the cash-desk the woman in the blue coat glanced at him as if to ask what he wanted to order but he was thrown into such confusion that he was unable to utter a word, though naturally it would not have made the slightest difference what he wanted to say as she would not have understood him. The woman addressed him in the strange language he had heard often enough by now and he muttered something in Spanish, he himself being uncertain as to why. In the meantime the people behind him started to grumble, wondering why he was taking all that time, rattling their small change, pushing him and practically treading on his heels so he found himself beyond the cash desk without a receipt. Someone behind him was talking to the woman in blue, and further back the queue was so long with recent arrivals that it was impossible to worm his way back in: they would clearly not allow him to do so, not till he went right to the back anyway. To stand in the counter queue under the circumstances seemed more than useless for not having a receipt he would not be served, but there was no option, his sheer helplessness drove him forward. He queued until he reached the counter where people were handing over their receipts to the person in the white chef's hat to take away the food and drink of their choice while he could only wave his empty hands about uselessly trying to explain why he was doing so. Having no receipt they paid him no attention but attended to the general crush passing dishes of roast meat and pastries over him and around him, right before his nose. He was all but dancing with rage by this time, his arms threshing the air, without any assurance at all that there might be a different outcome if he stood in another queue.

He had just slunk out into the street full of shame for having given up hope of supper for the night when he spotted an old woman on the corner selling roast chestnuts with only some three or four people waiting by the hot iron grill. He was there in less than a minute, but his linguistic skills failed him again, the two dozen languages he could speak or stutter as ineffective as the signs he tried to make with his hands and fingers. He might as well have been talking to the deaf and dumb. He finished up buying all the chestnuts on the stall, some forty of them. He had never bought as many at a time. He gave the old woman one of the smaller banknotes and received some change. He gobbled down the chestnuts immediately, there on the pavement, burning his mouth in the process and grew tearful as he did so. He felt sorry for himself: he had never felt so lost or so foreign in any city. Must get away, he kept thinking. Back to the hotel, grab luggage and find a plane or train, anything not to be here a day or hour longer.

Once more the doorman at the hotel opened the door for him but there was a new face at the desk now. Despite standing in the inevitable queue Budai had no more luck with this clerk than he had with the last. However he pointed to his key hanging on the hook among the rest the man simply shook his head as if slightly bored. So he wrote the number 921 down on a piece of paper, which did the trick. The lift operator was once again the tall blonde girl in blue. He nodded to her but she looked straight through him distractedly, and soon the space between them was filled with more people so he only caught a glimpse of her on leaving.

Back in his room he discovered that his body was covered in blue and green bruises from the blows he had received in the street when fighting his way through the crowd. He was not only bruised but tired and was shocked to realise that he had not accomplished anything and had made no contact with anyone, neither with people back home, nor with the people waiting for him at his destination. Neither at home nor at Helsinki would they have any idea where he had vanished. The strangest thing though was that he himself had no clue, not for the time being anyway: he was no wiser now than he had been on arriving here. Furthermore, he had no idea how he might set about finding out, about leaving, about where to go, about whom to speak to or what procedure to follow ... He had a bad feeling and felt deeply uneasy, thinking he must have missed something or failed to do something, something he should have done but he couldn't think what. He tried the phone again in his anxiety, fretfully dialling numbers anywhere, but it was late at night now, the phones kept ringing and only rarely did a sleepy voice respond and then in that peculiar, foreign-sounding, incomprehensible and indistinguishable language that sounded like stuttering.

Budai's instinct for language had been sharpened by his studies: etymology was his area of interest, the way words developed, their origins. He had had to deal with the strangest languages in the course of his research, both Hungarian and Finnish in the Finno-Ugrian group, but also to some extent Vogul, Ostyak, Turkic, some

Arabic and Persian, and beyond these Old Slavic, Czech, Slovakian, Polish and Serbo-Croat. The language here did not remind him of any of them, nor of Sanskrit, Hindi, Ancient or Modern Greek, nor of High Germanic either, for he knew German proper, as well as English and Dutch. Besides these, he was also acquainted with Latin, French, Italian, and Spanish as well as having a smattering of Portuguese, Romanian, Italian Retoroman and a smidgeon of Hebrew, Armenian, Chinese and Japanese. Most of these he could only read to a so-so standard of course, to the point that they were useful for tracking the development of one or other word, but he knew them sufficiently well to recognise that this language did not resemble any of them. It belonged to a group he could not locate by ear. All he could hear was something that sounded like *edede de* and *gagagaga*.

He removed the framed and printed notice from its nail by the door and examined it with fresh care by the light of the table lamp. But this did not get him anywhere either for whatever templates he applied he had not come across the characters before. He couldn't even tell whether they were characters in the European sense, parts of words as to some extent in Japanese or Chinese, or a series of bare consonants like ancient Semitic and Aramaic. He found the occurrence of normal Arabic numerals disruptive. By now he was so tired he could not think, so having decided to postpone his investigations till the next day, he undressed and went to bed.

Accustomed to reading for half an hour before going to sleep he noticed that there was nothing to read: he had packed all his books, as well as his notes and his speech to the conference, in the other, bigger case. He got up again and unpacked his hand luggage to check but there was nothing there. He felt angry. Why hadn't he bought a newspaper or magazine at least on the plane? He tossed and turned, unable to sleep so eventually opened one of the bottles of red wine he had brought with him. He tried to extricate the cork using one of the blades of his penknife, but the cork broke up in the process so he had to push it back into the bottle. Not being able to cork it up again he drank his way, little by little, through the lot and finally sank into a hazy sleep without a thought in his head.

He woke next morning with a headache: the day outside was grey and dry. He looked out on the street through the closed window. Even from the ninth floor he could see the crowds rolling by, a continuous black stream of traffic and pedestrians. There was something wrong with his stomach too: he had drunk too much last night. He took a long time brushing his teeth to get rid of the foul taste in his mouth. He took a shower, scrubbing his face in the jet of hot water, then rubbed his whole body vigorously with the fluffy towel until he was quite red. He looked in his bag and found a salami-filled roll that he had overlooked. His wife must have packed it as a snack for the journey. It served as some kind of breakfast though it would have been nice to have had some tea as well. He sought in vain for a bell to call for service. Maybe the telephone was there to serve that purpose though he would have to know what number to dial and how to ask the question; in other words he was back exactly where he had been last night ... Suddenly he was all impatience and ready for action. Enough of this nonsense! He had urgent business to attend to in Helsinki! It was the first day of the conference to which he had been delegated, he had to get there, even if a little late, and make his speech. He packed his belongings, put the bag down on the luggage rack ready for departure and hurried downstairs to settle matters once and for all.

There was large group of people waiting at the lifts, before all eight lifts, and judging by the illuminated buttons all the lifts were in use. It seemed to be an even busier morning than usual. Budai couldn't find the stairs on this level either, or at least none of the corridors seemed to lead to them, so he was obliged to join the others in the furthermost queue. The lifts didn't seem to stop on this floor very often, rumbling past it for several minutes without opening their doors. And when one did happen to stop it only had room for four or five people: everybody, it seemed, was going down, leaving rooms on the floor above his. The lifts were crammed by the time they reached here. His queue was the slowest moving of the lot, of course, and a clear ten minutes went by without the characteristic low hum of the lift opening its automatic doors. Thinking it must be out of order, Budai moved to the back of another queue. But no sooner had he done so than it was his old queue that was moving forwards whereas his new queue was at a standstill, and even when the lift did stop at the new queue the indicator immediately showed it returning to the upper floors. It was enough to drive one crazy. Budai's entire body was covered in sweat as he struggled to contain his helpless fury. He felt hot and cramped. Eventually a lift stopped and he reached the ground floor.

There were as many people clogging up the lobby as there had been last night, maybe more. Some stood around in haphazard clusters, others were stuck in long queues, while still others were hurrying from place to place, forcing their way through the rest. Were they all guests at the hotel, or if not, what were they doing here? It was impossible to tell. He struggled through them to the reception desk but it took quite a long time again before he was face to face with the desk-clerk on duty. The man, however, was not one of those he had already met. The only thing he had in common with them was that he too failed to understand a single word, jabbering away himself instead. Budai was so furious he could no longer contain himself: he grew red in the face and beat the counter, bellowing in various languages.

'Skandal. ein Skandal! ... C'est un scandale, comprenez-vous ... ?'

He hardly knew what he was shouting. He demanded his passport and aeroplane ticket; he wanted to see the manager, he called for an interpreter, he raged and threatened, repeating: *pass, passport, passaporto*, now in one language, now in another while ever more people gathered around listening to him. Finally, when the elderly desk-clerk simply spread his hands out in incomprehension, Budai leaned across, grabbed him by the shoulders and started shaking him, screaming at him, waving his hands in front of his face. All this accomplished nothing, of course, since it was perfectly obvious that neither the man nor any of the nearby witnesses to the scene understood him. In any case, there were so many waiting behind him that they too began to grow restive, pressing forwards, each of them preoccupied with his own affairs. It was pointless. The desk-clerk readjusted his jacket. Budai himself grew uncertain and confused. He waited a little longer, looking everywhere, hoping to discover where guests' passports might be stored, at which counter, in which cupboard, but there was no way he could get to the other side of the counter and into the office from here, and he had begun to feel a little ashamed of himself for creating such a fuss. It really wasn't like him. There was no point in making things worse: it would only be more trouble. Nor could the people behind him wait there forever. So, having first mopped his neck and brow with his handkerchief, then, having blown his nose in it, he allowed himself to be elbowed discreetly aside, having achieved nothing.

There were a number of large circular tables in the lobby with armchairs arranged round them and one of them had just become available. He sat down in it and closed his eyes: perhaps this was all a dream, perhaps he was actually in Helsinki or at home, maybe he hadn't even set out from home yet. Or, if he was where he appeared to be, other people would know about it by now, seek him out, apologise and explain, and it would all be cleared up, back to normal. Maybe he just had to wait a minute or two, to count to sixty or, at most, a hundred ... But having done so and looked up, he saw he was still there in the same hotel lobby with heaving crowds pressing this way and that, the printed notices still incomprehensible, the same foreign posters, photographic enlargements, landscape paintings on walls and pillars, the same mysterious papers and magazines at the newsagent's stand, the same men, women, old and young and people of all shapes and sizes. There was a small exotic-looking group close to him now, a collection of church dignitaries of some sort moving through the hall, composed mostly of dark-skinned, bearded ancients in long, black kaftans, wearing lilac hats, highly colourful sashes and heavy, gold chains round their necks: the crowds opened for them so that they might continue their dignified progress.

He forced himself to be calm: he'd not get anywhere at all by shouting and complaining. He tried to put his thoughts in order: firstly, and most urgently, he should recover his passport, followed, naturally, by the ticket for his flight because until he had these he could not get to Helsinki and thence home once the conference was over. He could work out where he was, how he had got here, who was to blame and how he had got into this stupid situation once he had both these items in his hand ... But before any of this he needed a bite since he could hardly regard what he had had so far as a proper breakfast, at least that was what his stomach was telling him. No wonder he was so tense. The hotel was bound to have a restaurant of some kind. He got up to look for it.

He explored the lobby as far as he could, given the difficulty of negotiating the dense crowd and found it very large, some 100 to 150 metres long and about half as wide.

There were shops selling souvenirs and knick-knacks by the walls: he cast his eye over the dolls, statuettes, decorated boxes, bracelets, brooches and baubles, the cameras with unfamiliar brand names and the opera glasses. He even picked a key-ring off the glass counter. It had a fortress or tower motif with some writing underneath it, one of the town's monuments no doubt together with its name, though it wasn't a building he recognised and the writing was no help. Nevertheless, he determined to buy one of these as a memento before he left, to remind him of this crazy adventure, of the night he had spent here.

But he found no trace of a restaurant though he had paid close attention to each corner of the lobby and had even stopped to address one man, repeating the words *restaurant* and *buffet*. This having produced no more than an uncomprehending gaze, he tried to demonstrate his desire to eat by miming and lifting his hand to his mouth. It seemed that the tall, lean man with the hooked nose understood him, since he replied in a loud, sharp voice, almost shouting, asking:

'Gorrabittepropopotu? Vivi tereplebeubeu?'

He might of course have been saying something completely different, his articulation being as peculiar as that of the others. Despite doing his best to listen Budai was not sufficiently expert in this case to note down the phonetic symbols employed by students of linguistics to indicate the most minute distinctions between types of accent and enunciation, though he knew them well enough and regularly used them in his work. Meanwhile the man went on in an unpleasantly harsh voice, almost as though challenging him, going so far as to grab him by the lapels even as he was pointing to something above them, impossible to say where. It would have been good to be free of him now but the man had hold of him and did not let go, bellowing into his face, waving his arms, gesturing, so that in the end Budai had to use brute force to be rid of him.

Later, rather to his surprise, he came upon a set of stairs in the far corner of the lobby. They were wide, red-carpeted stairs with a marble balustrade but they only led as far as the mezzanine, or possibly first floor, where it opened onto a corridor but no further. The corridor itself led to a set of glazed doors both of whose wings were open and hooked to the wall. Behind the door lay a large, vaulted hall, filled floor to ceiling with scaffolding and decorators working away at the distant top, shouting to each other in echoing voices, clambering up and down. In the middle of the hall, in a space left by scaffolding, stood a draped statue or some kind of fountain, behind which extended an enormous serving counter, and beyond that a raised platform with a draped piano, while a mass of tables and chairs lay piled in the corner, all flecked with paint, the floor itself being covered with mortar and rubble. This was, no doubt, the restaurant, but out of service for the time being owing to redecoration. Now he realised what the lean man had been trying to tell him as he was pointing upwards. One of the workmen shuffled over to the door. He was dressed in filthy overalls and carried a bucket, his head covered with a paper hat. Budai accosted him too, using hands and feet to make himself understood, trying to discover where he might find something to eat. The man blinked, mumbled something incomprehensible, waved his hand as if to deny something and described a broad circle with his arm indicating, perhaps, that there were no eating facilities in the building.

This was a peculiarly bad piece of luck, coming as it did on top of everything else. After yesterday evening's unfortunate excursion he shrank from the thought of having to step out into the street again. Nevertheless he still had to eat, and having taken a little consideration, he estimated it to be getting on for noon: even without his wristwatch, his stomach reminded him of the time, the reminders growing ever more urgent. He resolved to keep calm and avoid tension however long he had to wait. Flights usually left early and by now he would have missed the morning one to Helsinki in any case. Just for once he wanted a really good meal and would sacrifice the morning to that end. Having eaten, he could find out about the afternoon or evening flight.

He ambled back into the lobby, patiently waited in the queue for the lift and was finally conveyed upstairs so he could get his coat. Although he had eventually found his room last night he was once again confused by the corridors and it took him a while to locate 921. Once at the door he could hear the telephone so he quickly turned the key and ran inside. But by the time he reached the phone it had stopped ringing and when he picked up the receiver he heard only the same low purring he had heard before ... He wondered who might have been calling him: had someone discovered what had happened to him and tracked him down? Were they even now working out how to get hold of him and take him where he was supposed to be? He sat down on the bed, not daring to move in case they rang again, beating his brow, furious with himself for not having arrived half a minute earlier. However he prayed for it to ring, the telephone remained stubbornly silent: on the other hand, his hunger had not abated at all so having twice gone out into the corridor then darted back into his room to allow the phone a few more minutes, he eventually took a decision and went out.

He handed in his key at the desk downstairs by simply reaching across the long snaking queue: this much, apparently, was permitted to those who did not stand in line. The traffic in the street was not one whit less busy than it had been the night before, with just as many cars and pedestrians and just as much honking, shoving and jostling. He couldn't begin to think where they were all rushing to, what way flowing, from where to where. To work? From work? And who, in any case, were they, and how come the incessant stream? No one paid any attention to him, not for a moment, and if he let his mind wander for a second and did not concentrate he would find himself being pushed so violently that he found himself being spun about, almost falling. He too would have to resort to force, to shoulder and elbow his way through if he was to get anywhere. But no sooner had he thought that he dismissed the whole disgraceful idea: he wasn't after anything or heading anywhere, all he wanted was a good dinner after which he would leave immediately then bye bye! That would be the end of it.

It was cold and dull outside, everything was frozen and the wind was still blowing, steady and uncomfortable. He turned up his collar, pulled his hat down over his brow and set off in the opposite direction from the night before, trying, since he happened to be here, to take better note of his environment. There was a range of old and new buildings along the way, skyscrapers next to single-storey houses, some clapboard dwellings, a few five- or six-storey tenements with peeling stucco walls, another skyscraper all glass and reinforced concrete, then a building still under construction. He was unable to determine whether he was in the city centre, or in some suburb on the outskirts. He paid more attention to the road too and in all the close traffic he distinguished three different kinds of bus: one green, one red and one brown-and-white, as well as trolleybus routes 8, 11 and 137, though he had no idea whatsoever of their routes. He spotted taxis too, if that's what they were: grey, uniform, with a red stripe down the side, and a meter upfront with a little flag the driver could flip up or snap down. He tried waving to one or two of them without success: either there were passengers sitting in them already or, if not, the drivers took no notice of him, having perhaps been called somewhere. True, his waving was a little half-hearted, as if he guessed that it would be pointless trying to communicate with them however he explained or gestured since they would not understand where or how far he wanted to go.

Not far from the hotel he found a small square with the traffic flowing around it and in it a set of yellow rails next to stairs that led underground, where, as ever, a great crowd was pressing down and up. The colour and shape of the rails rang a bell with him: the night before when he was still on the airport bus they had driven past rails like that. Once the traffic lights showed green he joined the black flood of pedestrians crossing the road and was quickly swept into the middle of the little square then down the stairs. It was as he thought: he was at one of the stations of the city metro, a fair-sized oval hall accommodating various lines branching off in different directions with arrows painted on walls and a number of – to him, as ever, incomprehensible – notices of the larger and smaller variety indicating the various routes. People from all points of the city converged here, those arriving, departing or changing trains, those standing in long rows, pushing in, hastening and squirming this way and that: they filled up the place to such an extent it was practically impossible to get through. On top of that, on the opposite platform, he could see an escalator to a lower level that constantly swallowed or spewed forth yet more people. The congestion was so bad that Budai found it difficult to stay on his feet. Nevertheless he tried to make some progress towards an enormous diagrammatic plan of the metro-system he had glimpsed in the distance. Having set out, he found himself caught up in the stream of people heading towards another set of escalators and was swept along by them willy-nilly though he had no desire to travel anywhere, not in this city at any rate. But it was impossible to turn round against the wide flow of a regiment in full battle order, still less to prevent its forward momentum, only at the cost of individual hand-to-hand combat employing knees and fists, and so he fought his way to the edges and broke through to where some others were proceeding in the counter-direction, thereby somewhat easing the forward pressure.

The metro map was behind a pane of glass and gave a diagrammatic sketch of the underground network with various colours to signify individual lines and to indicate various stations and interchanges, the lines dense and generally concentric or radiating as they crossed over or flowed into each other. There was a kind of keyboard underneath, with, it seemed, a button for each station: when people pressed one of them a line was suddenly illuminated. He waited his turn, for here too there was a considerable crowd, then pressed a few buttons at random. There were clearly a number of routes directly leading here, while others required two or three changes, but since the topological map showed only the relationship between the various metro stations and nothing of the streets and squares above, he found it impossible to locate anything, For even if he had been able to read the names of the stations he wouldn't have been able to tell where they were in relation to all the other unfamiliar places in this vast stone-deaf vacancy. The station he was currently at was indicated by a red circle that was rather more smeared than the others because of the great number of fingers tracing routes from it. He was, of course, as incapable of reading the name as he had been of reading anything else and could only make out that the station was located near the bottom left hand corner of the map at the intersection of one of the radiating and one of the concentric lines, and that it seemed to be roughly halfway between the inner city and the outskirts; in other words that he was in one of the south-westerly suburbs. That was if he could safely assume that north was at the top, and so forth.

He went back out into the street: a little further off they were building a skyscraper higher than any he had so far seen. Craning his neck, Budai counted sixty-four floors so far, but there were clearly more to come. An enormous number of people were working on the steel framework and half-completed walls, swarming like ants over the scaffolding, the structure practically black with them, ascending and descending on pulleys that also carried materials, prefabricated components and enormous panels – the proportions of the building inspiring not so much admiration as fear, as if the lot could at any moment collapse around his head and bury him for ever ... But his purpose was not to stand and stare. He went into the nearest grocery and waited patiently like the other customers. And though they did not understand him here either, he refused to shift or give way until they had measured out for him whatever he pointed at. He then had to stand in another queue to receive his cold meat, his butter, cheese and bread, and then in another for some roast fish he fancied. Having only been given a receipt for this he had to stand in line at the till once more. He paid, not knowing how much he had given, put away the change, then stood at the food counter again. The whole process took half an hour.

It was the fat doorman with his gold-braided cap on duty at the hotel again: Budai wondered when the man slept. He received his key the same way by writing down the number 921, carefully storing the piece of paper in his top pocket. He noted which of the lifts was being operated by the blonde attendant – it was the middle one – and he joined that queue. The girl was reading and did not look up as the passengers called out their floors but simply pressed the appropriate buttons. It was only when Budai, unable to tell her it was the ninth floor, touched her on the arm that she looked up. She gazed up at him, blinking once or twice, as if waking from a dream, then the door opened and he stepped out.

They had tidied his room while he was out, swept the floor and made the bed. He found his pyjamas under the blanket and his slippers in the bedside cupboard. He was frightened for a second in case they regarded him as a permanent guest, but he immediately dismissed the thought: after all, it is not the job of the staff to know that, what do they know ... ? He opened his packages and fell greedily to eating, slicing the bread with his penknife and making sandwiches. Everything tasted strange, different from what he was used to at home, somehow sweeter, the meat, the bread, the cucumber and even the fish. He carefully packed away what remained and put it in the window. At last he was well fed, all he needed now was coffee to finish the meal. But he did not feel like making a special trip downstairs for it. He would rather take a short rest. So, with a touch of self-satisfaction for filling his stomach despite all the difficulties, he kicked off his shoes and stretched out on the fully made-up bed.

He can only have snoozed two or three minutes before he suddenly sat up, his heart beating with anxiety. What was wrong with him? Was he mad? They were waiting for him in Helsinki where the conference would be in full swing by now! And he was due to deliver his speech, possibly on the first or second day, and, for all he knew, he might have been drafted onto this or that committee, and they would not understand why he wasn't there. What was he doing here, and, furthermore, where was *here*, what town, what country, what part of the world, what godforsaken spot on the globe? He tried once more to think through the whole impossible set of events: he trusted in logic, in the highly developed power of scientific method and its way of reaching conclusions, and, not least, in his own experience of travel, since he had been travelling ever since his student days. But however he examined the events of the last twenty-four hours he could not work out what he should have done differently, whom he might have consulted, what possible alternatives existed. And while the misunderstanding that had resulted in his being here would, no doubt, be resolved sooner or later, at which point he could immediately leave and move on, he felt somewhat at a loss for now: he was without friends, acquaintances, indeed documents, and to all intents and purposes, utterly on his own, in an unknown city of whose very name he was ignorant, where no one spoke any language that he could understand even though he knew a great many languages, and where he had yet to find anyone with whom he might exchange a word or two.

He tried to piece together such fragments of knowledge about the place as he had so far managed to gather. It must be a large city, that much was obvious, a metropolis, a cosmopolitan city he had never before visited. For the time being he could not even begin to place it on the globe or tell how far it lay from home or in what direction. He might, it occurred to him, have been able to attempt a rough calculation as to the number of hours they had travelled by seeing how much his beard had grown on the plane while he was asleep. But he hadn't thought of it last night when he had arrived and shaved. He was probably feeling a little woozy at the time and now he simply couldn't remember how much hair he had scraped from his jaw ... It was a densely populated city, that was clear enough, more populous than any he had known, though what ethnicity, what colour constituted the majority, was hard to determine going by what he had seen so far. The most conspicuous feature of the place was that people did not seem to speak foreign languages here, none at least that he was familiar with, not even in a hotel as enormous as this, only their mother tongue. And that sounded peculiar, utterly unlike anything else, almost mere gabble. The written version was a vacuous, incomprehensible jumble. Nor was the weather of any help: dry, cold, wintry, exactly like February back home when he left. As for the grocery shop, nothing in the items on sale gave a clue to the whereabouts of the country, being pretty much what was found anywhere, meaning a range of cold and ready-to-cook meats, cheeses, apples, lemons, oranges, bananas, preserves, jams in jars, fruit juice, coffee, sweets, sea-fish and so on. There was no way of telling what was local, what imported. Items of clothing offered nothing different from the usual garments found in the rest of the civilised world, products of boutiques and department stores, differing only in quality, each individual item straight out of some international catalogue, ready to wear. It added up to little more than nothing: it was an equation without known quantities.

What to do? No local body, certainly not the hotel administration, would be likely to know that he had arrived here by mistake, quite unintentionally, otherwise they would have done something by now, returned his passport and so forth ... The passport was another mystery: it was quite incomprehensible why they should have kept it or where they were keeping it since it was normal practice everywhere else to return it once the formalities of registration were over. And where had the grey-haired desk-clerk got to, the one who had taken his passport from him, and whom he had not seen since? Who should he hold responsible? From whom should he request his airline ticket and passport, and to whom should he explain all this and in what language and how? Even now he shuddered to think of the painful events of yesterday morning, of his pointless, idiotic gesturing – and yet he couldn't just leave it like that. How long was he going to spend hanging about here, in a place that had nothing to do with him, on the ninth floor of a strange hotel in a strange city?

He tried to consider methodically where he might turn for help. To the management? To the information desk? To an interpreter, a travel agent, the airline? These ideas passed before him but how was he to locate any of these agencies? Who was there to ask in the dreadful whirl of traffic where no one had the time to address his problems but left him muttering idiotically to himself? They must speak other languages in banks and financial institutions and, possibly, in various public offices, but where to find such places, how to identify them among the mass of buildings, when he couldn't make the slightest sense of the notices on them? What if he sought out a foreign embassy, his own or some other country's? How would he find it and recognise it? Would it be flying the flag at the entrance? He must keep his eyes peeled: surely, if he explored the city systematically, examining everything he passed, continually on the alert, it would be impossible not to discover one. And above all, here in the hotel itself, in such an enormous international establishment, it was unimaginable that he should not eventually meet someone with whom he could talk. The point was not to drift. He had to overcome his natural reticence and awkwardness, to shake himself free of his mental lassitude and extricate himself from this whole dumb episode.

His first thought was to jot everything down in his note-book – he never went anywhere without one in case he had some bright idea on his travels. He should write a brief account, in English, of what had happened to him, where he came from, where he wanted to go and so on, and then add a note requesting the management to act promptly, to help him smoothly on his way or provide him with someone to whom he might explain the situation. He wrote the note and signed it, adding his name and the figures 921, much as a prisoner might give his number, laughing as he did so. He then translated the same text into French and Russian. Once he had handed these in at the desk it stood to reason, plain as the nose on his face, that somebody would understand one of these texts and take the necessary steps.

At the same time he thought he'd try the telephone again and dialled what he thought might be public lines, such as began with

0, 00, 01, 02, 11, 111, 09, 99 and the like, but there was no answer from any of them except, occasionally, a rapid pulsing sound. He was growing furious. Why was there no telephone book in the room? It was the thing that most annoyed him right now and he kept wildly clicking at the phone, tugging at it angrily, slamming the receiver down, bellowing fierce hellos and finally throwing the set down so forcefully it was lucky it didn't break. He had to get a list of names from somewhere. He quickly put on his shoes, calmed himself and dashed out.

His aim was to shortcut the queue and slip his key to the desk clerk as before, but though they took his key, he was pushed out of the way by the crowd before he could hand over his piece of paper and was directed to the back of the queue. So once again he had to stand patiently in line until he reached the desk again and passed the clerk his note written in three languages. The man blinked, turned the piece of paper over and over in his hand, examined his own files, and gabbled something that sounded like a question, but Budai did not stay to listen to him, preferring to disappear into the crowd.

He looked this way and that in the lobby, searching for a public telephone. There wasn't one anywhere, at least he could not find one, though it seemed to him that he had passed one that morning. He went out into the street again where the traffic was as busy as before, sweeping him this way and that so he had to struggle against it, and there it was, albeit a block further off than he had remembered. There really was a phone booth there but it was occupied of course with a tidy queue in front of it. He felt there was no point in waiting for his turn especially because he saw that the list of codes fixed to the wall was long and that the directories themselves were numerous and thick so there was no chance of him removing them with so many people around. He refused to admit defeat though and wandered on looking for another booth as if locating a telephone directory was the most important thing in the world. He took the stairs down into the metro again, and he was right: it was as he remembered, a dozen or so booths lined one of the walls of the station, all of them occupied, the long snaking queues blending with the general crowd. Here too he felt that it was hopeless waiting, but since he was here he determined to study the map he had discovered that morning a little more closely. He ended up not much wiser than he had then, though he did at least establish the name and location of the station and even copied its name and draw its position in his notebook, writing down the characters just outside the little red circle so that he should be able to find his way back to it from anywhere, should he get lost.

Upstairs meanwhile the sky was growing darker and the street lights had come on. It was about this time that the bus had brought him here. That must mean he had spent an entire twenty-four hours in the place. But that was not the most important thing on his mind as he pressed anxiously ahead: he had learned by now to shove, to struggle and carve out a path among the tides of others, like all the rest ... The skyscraper was still rising and there were as many men working under floodlights as there had been during the day. He spotted another diner a little further on, one he had not entered yet, so he peeked through the door. It was a self-service establishment with customers taking ready-prepared dishes from various stands and it was only after having done so that they queued up at the cash desk with their tray. Budai was delighted. The crowd was no worse than elsewhere. This was the first time he had come across something that struck him as a vaguely pleasant surprise so he went straight in. He collected a large range of food: soup, stuffed eggs, a roast with trimmings, some cheese and a slice of gateau – how, after all, did he know when he would be able to have a decent meal again? – and poured himself a small coffee from a machine for good measure. He passed over a handful of change to the woman at the till so she could take the necessary amount, then sat down at the nearest counter and ate it all up. There it was again, that same peculiar sweet taste, as if both meat and egg had been flavoured with sugar.

Near the diner he discovered an unexpectedly empty telephone booth. There was a paper notice stuck to the glass probably to the effect that the phone was out of order but the door could be opened and there were those thick directories in rows, in steel clasps, chained to the wall. He set to work examining them, working out how he could unscrew them, and was fiddling at the screws with his penknife when he noticed that he was being observed by a man in a grey uniform. He wore a short coat and flat cap, a white truncheon hanging from his belt. A policeman, no doubt. Budai remembered that he had no documents with him and that it would be pointless trying to explain what he as doing. He leafed through the book from front to back and vice versa pretending to look for a number or address. The policeman did not move but stood relaxed, steadily observing him. Then Budai had another thought. He stepped out of the booth and went straight over to the policeman. He tried speaking to him in German, English, Italian and several other languages, but was so flustered that he couldn't remember what information it was that he sought: how to get where, whether to an embassy or a tourist office, even what kind of help he needed. Whatever he said the policeman nodded and jabbed at him with his finger:

'*Chetchenche glubglubb? Guluglulubb?*'

That's what he said or something like it then took out a small notebook bound in black, leafed through it in no great hurry and started to explain something while pointing here and there. He spoke slowly and at length then made another gesture, indicating something behind him, pedantically repeating this or that phrase so as to avoid any misunderstanding, though Budai hadn't the faintest clue as to even what the subject was. Finally the policeman jabbed him again as if to ask whether it was all clear:

'*Turubu, shettyekehtyovovo … ?*'

There was nothing Budai could do except open his arms wide in exhaustion and shrug, at which point the policeman saluted and went off. That was enough experimentation for Budai. He was anxious to know whether the notes he had handed to the desk-clerk had found their way to an appropriate person for, if so, they might already have begun to sort things out and were perhaps looking for him, unable to find him. With this in mind he hurried back. For once it was the same clerk at the desk as before, in other words the man to whom he had handed his sheets of notepaper, in fact he recognised him at a distance from where he stood in the queue. But the sickly-looking, sour-faced clerk glanced at him as if he were a stranger and when Budai took the slip of paper with his room number from his pocket and handed it to him, the man put the key down, his face as expressionless as if he had never seen him before. Budai strained to see if there was anything else in box 921 besides the hook for the key but it was empty as the desk-clerk confirmed by spreading his palms. This was so surprising to Budai that he tried once again to explain through words and gestures that he was expecting an answer, some news or information, that there had to be some kind of message, but the man shook his head, carried on gabbling and had already turned his attention to the next guest. It was of course possible that someone was waiting upstairs in his room or at his door, that they might have left some instructions as to where he should go and whom he should see, and that everything would be sorted out. He was about to make his way over to the lift when he noticed a fat volume lying on the counter, clearly a copy of the telephone directory. The clerk happened to be looking the other way. Budai himself was surprised later at his nerve stealing it in front of all those people. He must have decided – his very nervous system must have decided – that whatever the risk he had to have a list of names, that was why he had come down in the first place. It was as if his hands had a will of their own. He stuck the book under his arm as though it belonged to him and calmly walked away with it.

But there was nothing waiting at his door, no notice on the handle, no sheet of paper lying on the threshold, nor in the crack, nor indeed anywhere, though he twice checked the number of the room just to make sure he was in the right place. Nor was there anyone inside, no note, not a scribbled message on the table or anywhere else, however hard he looked. He didn't know how to account for it: maybe his request had not yet been dealt with, maybe they had not done anything yet. Was it possible that, if it came to it, he had to spend another night here? If that were so he would only get to the conference in Helsinki on the second day, and even then only to the afternoon session at the earliest! The thought made him so cross the blood rushed to his head: he was forced to dismiss the thought. The constant running about, on top of everything else, had exhausted him: his shirt was soaked in sweat and he desperately wanted a shower. But in order to do this he had, shamefully, to unpack again, to take the toiletries out of his hand luggage, as well as the washing powder he carried on such trips to give his underwear a quick rinse.

Having refreshed himself a little he sat down comfortably at the writing table in his pyjamas and slippers and set to study the stolen directory. It had hard brown covers with several lighter coloured letters of various sizes embossed on it in three lines of unequal length in the usual unfamiliar script. The title page displayed twenty to twenty-five densely set words and groups of words with numbers beside them, undoubtedly the numbers of various public utilities. Straight after this followed some seven pages of unbroken text with hardly any spaces between the words, presumably the regulations regarding use of the telephone and postal service, then some diagrams, most likely showing the tariff for various kinds of call. The list of names ran to somewhere between eight hundred and a thousand large-format pages, each with five columns, in letters so small Budai had to strain his eyes to read them. As far as he could tell without any clue as to what the words meant, by means of the typography alone, the list was not alphabetical but sorted under different sub-headings, possibly of a commercial kind, an endless set of numbers, headings, text and numbers. But the curious thing was that the numbers – not only the ones at the front but those in the body of the book – were not of equal length: two, three or four figures, five, six, seven, even eight-figure numbers appeared one after the other, jumbled up, without any apparent system. He tried dialling a few of the numbers set in bold type, those presumably of public utilities, but with little success: there was no connection, the line did not respond or was engaged, the buzzing broken, and even when there was distinctly the sound of ringing, few of them picked up the phone, or, if they did, gabbled in the usual incomprehensible way however many languages he tried.

There was no point in going on like this, he realised, so he turned his attention to the text. Although the history of writing was never his area of specialisation he did remember from his earlier studies how Champollion succeeded in deciphering Egyptian hieroglyphics, Grotefend the runes on Ancient Persian stones, and how someone recently managed to decrypt the inscriptions of the Maya and the wooden boards of the Easter Islanders. In all these cases the scholars were dealing with items in two or three languages or scripts like the Rosetta Stone or the trove at Persepolis, sometimes with the advantage of earlier, possibly somewhat puzzling, superscriptions that might, however, be deciphered, given enough patience, hard work and a bit of luck. The procedure was much the same in most cases: it was to assume that certain signs or group of signs approximated to certain words, names, or known combinations of sounds, then to look for clusters of such and substitute the assumed meanings until the meanings of others could be inferred to the point that the whole was rendered readable. And yet, even with the aid of the most up-to-date equipment, how many had failed and how often! Furthermore, those who did succeed might have shed decades of bitter tears in the effort. And nowadays of course there were fabulously powerful computers to facilitate the analysis of mountains of data.

What was he to do then, stuck without any help, all by himself, faced with the unfamiliar script of an unfamiliar language? What assumptions could he make, what range of data should he match up with another when he had nothing to go on, at least nothing so far, and was able to associate neither this or that group of characters with a particular word nor any particular word with any meaning? What set of characters could he try replacing with what? Despite all this he set about writing down all the different characters he could find in the telephone directory, the last page of which happened to be blank. Here he copied them one after the other, as many different ones as he could find in the text. This quiet activity, the rhythm of which resembled that of his normal scholarly process at research stage, had the effect of slowly calming him, restoring his temper, and, for a while, entirely reconciling him to his situation, so that once he had focused his attention on a restricted range of data and the nature of his problem was better defined, he had almost forgotten where he was and how he had got here. He had had such a full meal at the buffet that he never touched the remnant of food on the windowsill though he did uncork his second bottle of wine.

Once again he concentrated and began to speculate on what kind of alphabet it might be. The characters were extremely simple, consisting of two or three strokes at most, a little like Old Germanic runes or Ancient Sumerian cuneiform, though it seemed odd and rather ridiculous to compare what he was now looking at with those two long-dead scripts. He also noticed a conspicuous lack of diacritics, that there was no distinction between upper- and lower-case letters, at least none in this book, all letters here being of the same typeface and point size. He soon realised that he had noted over one hundred characters and that he was still discovering more. Sipping at the red wine he wondered what that meant and where the information would lead him? Could it be after all that each character was a word, each word a new character and that was why there were so many of them? Or maybe the characters stood for syllables as in ancient Crete and Cyprus? Or perhaps it was a complex system, like the Ancient Egyptian, comprising various elements: words, shorter phonetic clusters and individual phonetic signs in hieroglyphic form? It occurred to him that it might even be a series of combined phonetic symbols, the kind linguists worked with in order to differentiate between subtle levels of meaning and pronunciation. Or perhaps they simply employed a system that represented this particularly wide range of sounds? Questions, questions, nothing but questions! In the meantime, without noticing it, he had drunk the rest of the bottle. He couldn't remember the next morning when and how he fell asleep.

He woke to the same even, grey light as on the previous morning. His head was muzzy and confused: he felt claustrophobic, full of guilt for drinking too much. He was angry with himself for having set himself a difficult task and failed. He did not dare think back over the last two days since the whole period seemed to be one of muddle and guilt and the feeling that he couldn't go on like this. That, in fact, was the one thing he could see with absolute, blinding clarity. He turned on the cold tap in the shower and was soon shuddering and sniffling under the jet of water. This was all a nightmare, nothing but madness and bedlam and he had to wake from it because it couldn't go on, it simply couldn't go on!

He dressed, made a sandwich out of what remained from the day before and by the time he had eaten it had a plan of action: he was only amazed that he hadn't thought of something so simple, so stupid much earlier. If all the hotel employees were idiots with whom one couldn't exchange a solitary word, if there was no information desk or if it was located in such an obscure place that it couldn't be found, then he had to find somewhere where there were bound to be foreigners: a tourist or information bureau. A railway station, for example, a long-distance bus terminal, an airport, an airline office, or a harbour or dock if there happened to be one. All he had to do was to find a taxi and somehow explain to the driver where he wanted to go. The rest was up to the driver and once they had arrived, surely there would be someone who could advise him. This appeared so obvious now that he was on the point of packing his bags and never again returning to his room but decided against it since he not only had a bill to settle but they had his passport too and he couldn't go anywhere without that. He could always throw everything into his bag at short notice.

The blonde in the blue uniform was working the lift again and in his distraction Budai allowed his glance to linger on her. Once again he noticed how lithe and slim she was, how delicately boned and how refined was the structure of her long face. She wasn't reading this time but staring straight ahead of her with a tired, blank expression. How many times had she made this same up-and-down journey? It was only once they reached the ground floor and the door opened that he detected the merest flash of recognition in her eye. Budai gave her a faint nod and smiled as he stepped out: he was unlikely ever to meet her again. He couldn't help admitting to himself that he was a mite sorry about that: she was the only thing in the city he would be sorry to leave.

Somehow everything was different this morning, not only in the lift but down in the lobby too. He couldn't tell at first in what way, what made the difference and why, it was simply something he sensed. The place was just as crowded as before, or pretty well as crowded, but there was less aggression in the air, the movement in the great hall seemed lazier and slower somehow, not quite so frantic, more patient perhaps. Later he noticed that the souvenir shop was closed, its glass cases empty, its front locked away behind metal shutters. The newsagent was closed too, sealed behind a metal grille, and the long bank of exchange counters that used to be busy was now being attended by no more than two or three women, the rest closed. It occurred to him that he had left home on Friday and that he had spent two night here so this must be Sunday and that here too it must be a holiday. It was only at the reception desk that the queues were still the same length as before and he took new fright at their sheer extent, but he waited all the same and handed in his key. Box 921 was still empty but he had stopped expecting to find anything there and would have been surprised if there was something. The exchange counters being empty, he decided to seize the opportunity and try one of the three women who were clearly left to deal with whatever business might come their way on a Sunday. He went over and waited by one of them but she paid him no attention so he knocked on the desk. She ignored that too so he knocked louder until she finally came over. He tried talking to her in various languages but she stared him with such incomprehension and contempt she had clearly taken him for the village idiot. He took out his notebook, drew a train as best as he could, then, underneath it, an aeroplane, and even extended his arms to imitate an aircraft, trying every possible way to convey what he was looking for and where he wanted to get to. The woman was middle-aged, somewhat yellow in complexion and wore her hair in a bun. She answered in a surprisingly sharp manner, apparently angered and offended, with a stream of incomprehensible but clearly rude words that Budai took to mean: 'what a nuisance, what cheek, one can't get a bit of peace even on a Sunday', though it was possible she meant something completely different. He saw it was useless trying to explain so he took the bold step of pulling the largest denomination banknote from his pocket and putting it down on the counter in front of the woman. She carried on grumbling but took the note and went away with it so there was no harm in hoping that she might, after all, help. She quickly returned and subjected him to another annoyed tirade while giving him a few notes and a bit of change – exchanging the large denomination note for some smaller ones – then turned on her heel and left him there.

Even the crowds in the street seemed a little less pushy. The road traffic was no less dense but was moving in a more relaxed way. He worked his way over to the kerbside and waved energetically at passing taxis. But there weren't many of them and when they did appear they were already occupied, often full to overflowing, some by nine or ten people, men, women, children, old ladies all together. And those few that were empty were proceeding without the available sign showing or in a lane far away from the kerb so it was impossible for them to pull over against the dense traffic. Finally he saw a taxi approach slowly right in front of him, one that was empty and available, but however he shouted and waved, even putting a foot out into the road, the driver did not stop but looked right through him and might even have run him over had he not smartly jumped out of the way. By the time he recovered the taxi was almost lost in the distance ... So he fought his way back to the hotel entrance and addressed the fat, fur-collared doorman in various languages, using a range of gestures, attempting to convey the fact that he needed a taxi or a taxi rank, adding that surely there must be one in the vicinity, obstinately, determinedly repeating the word that meant the same everywhere:

'Taxi! Taxi ... taxi?'

The man blinked at him stupidly, continuing to salute him, tipping his gold-braided hat and looking at him with those tiny eyes in his fat face before politely opening the swing door for him. When Budai leaned closer and shouted what he wanted practically into his face, the doorman merely muttered:

'*Kiripudu labadaparatchara … patarashara …*'

Then he saluted once more and pushed the door open again as if he were no more than a robot able to choose between only two options. In the meantime others were pushing their way into the hotel, bumping into them as they jostled at the door. Budai didn't want to block the way any longer and was worried in case his temper got the better of him and he actually punched the idiot, so he returned to the kerbside. He had no better luck trying to wave down a taxi and had begun to wonder whether the red flash at the side of those grey cars actually meant that they were taxis. He had all but given up when one at which he had made only a vague, uncertain gesture, suddenly stopped right in front of him. The driver leaned out and asked him something with his mouth full, something to the effect as to where he would like to go, thought Budai. He quickly tried to explain, making flapping motions with his arm to indicate a plane, then imitating the pistons of a railway engine, even adding the characteristic choo-choo sound. The driver laughed and shook his head, though whether that was because he didn't understand or because he had no intention of taking him to those places was not clear. Meanwhile other vehicles were stuck behind him impatiently sounding horns, revving engines, creating ever more of a bottleneck. The next lane was so busy they could not get round the stationery vehicle. Frightened that he would lose this opportunity, Budai brought out a large banknote and waved it in front to him. The tone of the driver's reply was that he had been ordered elsewhere, or that he was at the end of his shift and was on his way to the garage. But all the while the never-ending traffic behind him was growing ever louder, ever more impatient, the horns of the jammed cars blaring furiously, so the taxi driver eventually turned the key and put his foot down on the gas. In his despair Budai drew out another note and pushed it through the window but the taxi was moving by now in the dense traffic so the money was swept from his hands into the cab where it remained and there was no way of getting it back.

For a minute or two Budai stood stock still, quite paralysed by his latest failure, though maybe it was not a failure, and what he took to be a whole chain of misfortunes was simply the rule here, for someone like him at least, someone who did not know the language. But eventually he pulled himself together and decided that one should be able to find a station even without a taxi. He was only sorry to have lost his money, those two notes of whose value he could not be certain though, on the basis of what he had learned so far, it would not be negligible.

Most of the shops were shut, even the groceries, but the metro was as busy as ever. By the time he got to the steps in the round little traffic island he had worked out how he might achieve his goal. He pushed his way over to the large map again, it being the only fixed point of certainty he had so far been able to cling to. Here he only had to identify his position and could then move forward. He looked for intersections between lines, those circled stations that appeared more important, since in every major city the metro service was directly connected to the main railway routes. He reasoned that the names of metro stations at the main terminals might comprise two or more words, and that one or other of the stations might be like the Paris terminals, Gare de l'Est, Gare du Nord, Gare de Lyon, and so forth. He was constantly jostled as he stood there, often being shoved right away from the map but time and again he steered his way back. With great difficulty he located a few of these two-and-more-word stations, the last word of which was the same, or pretty nearly the same in every case, the difference probably being merely grammatical. He made note of a number of them, copying the unfamiliar characters. The first and nearest of them was on the yellow line.

He had to stand in a queue at the ticket window – everyone was paying with the same kind of coin – and then at the down escalator since the crowd descending had swollen. Once down there he was carried along a confusion of corridors, the crowd swirling this way and that, past placards and posters, round bends, past crossings and adjoining tunnels, coming to yet more stairs that led down first, then up again. Coloured arrows pointed out different routes, electric signs with blue, green, red, black and yellow writing. Budai followed the last of these though he lost track of it at one point, the crowd possibly having swept him past an opening, and it was only after a good fifteen minutes of searching that he found another one. He was careful this time, paying absolute attention, and slowly the other colours disappeared, leaving only the yellow and there he was on the platform with the rumble of trains approaching and departing and the draught of busy tunnels. He was only concerned not to set off in the wrong direction, so he took out his notebook, looked up the name of the station he was seeking and had written down, and scanned the list of stations by the two arrows to see which of them contained it.

The train arrived and the crowd rushed to get on board, struggling through the equally dense crowd getting off, a chaos of swirling bodies at each door. Budai managed to squeeze his way on just in time before the black conductor blew his whistle. It was close and hot on the train: he had thought to ask someone for information, to explain or draw some image of where he wanted to get to, but the passengers were so tightly packed he could hardly raise his hands and in any case he was prevented by the constant lurching, shoving and fighting for position between those who meant to get out and those getting on. At least he didn't have to worry about missing his station since there were a number of maps on the walls showing where he was at any one time and the stations to come, so he easily found the three-word station whose name he had noted down, and correctly anticipated where he had to leave the very fast, sharply braking train whose jerky movement resulted in passengers constantly landing in each other's laps.

There was the same confusion of corridors here too so he scurried and stumbled about for a long time before realising that it was the bigger white arrows that led to the exit and followed them up another infinitely long set of escalators ... He arrived in a wide square. A fine, cold rain was quietly falling, the sky just as murky here, just as impenetrable. Nor was the crowd thinner. He set out without any sense of where he was going and soon wandered into a market or shopping centre. There were people selling things everywhere, on stalls, at tables, even directly from the pavement. Salesmen were shouting, music playing, loudspeakers blaring. It was mostly second-hand clothes for sale as far as he could see. The crowd carried him slowly along as they drifted round the square, past furniture stores, chandeliers, fabrics, threadbare fur coats, dinner services, carpets, junk, antiques, factory rejects, toys, balls, great piles of sponges and plastic goods, tubes of various colours and sizes rolled into rings, as well as tyres, hoses and sheets of plate glass. A loud record player was booming in a tent, the shelves inside groaning under the weight of countless records. Budai tried to worm his way through to it, pressing through groups of bystanders in the hope of hearing a familiar tune or discovering a label he could actually read. That might give him something to hang on to, a solution of some sort, one he might be able to use to solve further enigmas. But however he burrowed among the records, going through the whole stock – there were other potential customers exploring it – he found nothing familiar, and only the same incomprehensible writing on all the labels. The record player continued booming and someone right next to him was continually blowing a cracked, rasping trumpet, the same two notes all the time, a fat man in a stripy sailor-top, looking a little like a Chinese ship's cook. It was insufferable. He abandoned the search and moved on.

There was white fluffy candy-floss and little spicy sausages spluttering in fat but so many people were waiting to be served he thought he'd not get near enough to buy one. Stalls offered their wares of seeds, flowers and soil, then, a little further on, a range of animals: white rabbits, domestic pigeons, canaries, cockatoos, tortoises, and – something he had never seen before – a kind of scaly, crested, six-legged serpent-like creature sitting in a cage, motionless and glassy-eyed, stiff as death. A huge, red-faced man wearing a chequered jacket with a threadbare velvet collar – his enormous hands and feet reminiscent of Patagonians in travellers' tales – was demonstrating some cleaning fluid, pouring ink, oil and tomato juice over a pair of light-coloured trousers brought out for the purpose, then making the stains disappear while continually jabbering on in patois. A little further off a fishmonger in a blood-stained apron took Budai, who had just glanced at him, for a customer, grabbed hold of him and was pulling at his coat, trying to sell something that might have been a fair-sized sturgeon, waving his cleaver, explaining, persuading, drawing the blade across the fish's delicate skin to show how fresh it was, dangling it before his nose, gesticulating, demanding, practically throwing the fish at him ... But in most instances it was a case of Budai addressing others, trying first oriental, then Slavonic languages and then again English, Dutch, Spanish and Portuguese. The answers he received were once again incomprehensible: some people simply stared at him in a puzzled, faintly foolish fashion, while others paid him no attention at all, or shoved him out of the way, clearly regarding him as a nuisance, possibly even as a beggar. Unable to take any more of this Budai relapsed into awkwardness and confusion.

Nor could he see any sign of a railway station whichever way he looked. There was a big, grey building of glass and steel near the market but as he approached it turned out to be a covered market-hall that was temporarily closed. Only at the side entrances was there any sign of activity: packages were being stacked, empty crates and piles of sacks were being thrown onto waiting trucks while, behind them, incoming goods were arriving on conveyor belts with cranes to lift the heavier bales and hoppers while workers carried on heaving barrels, vats packed in straw, blocks of ice and lard and frozen meat. Then a new truck appeared loaded with vegetables – leeks or some such thing – and the stout, blue-overalled driver got out. Seeing Budai standing and staring at the ramp, he grabbed Budai's arm and pulled at him, indicating the loading area beyond, saying something that sounded like:

'Duhmuche bruedimruechuere! Kluett!'

The man had taken him for a tramp thinking that was why he was hanging about here. Had he been looking for amusement he would have found this amusing but as it was he made his way back to the underground station to continue his investigations in the queue as he made a note of the stations that might turn out to be railway terminals.

According to the map he should follow the purple line, then change to the green one. The carriages were no less full than before. He made a brief anthropological survey of his fellow travellers to see what was the most common skin colour, type and shape of face. There was a wide variety even in this narrow sample from coal black through brown to the extremely pale, though pure racial types were, as he noted, quite rare, few at least that might be considered pure European, African or Far Eastern. Not that any part of the world was likely to be ethnically homogenous, since larger cities, such as ports, for example, would expect to have mixed populations. Whatever the case, the majority of people here seemed to be of mixed race or at some transitional point between various races like that Japanese-looking, slant-eyed, young woman with light blonde hair and slightly Negroid lips who had just stepped from the carriage alongside him carrying a handbag and so many shopping bags that they got tangled up with each other. Budai seized the opportunity to turn to her and since speaking proved useless to imitate an engine with his arms in order to communicate his request. The woman smiled as if she understood him and even said something, then hurried on nodding to him to follow her. At last Budai felt he made contact with someone and kept close to her making quite sure they were not separated while she nodded to him from time to time indicating the way ahead. The exit was relatively near at this station – once again broad white arrows indicated the direction – and they must have been quite close to the surface, the corridor leading into a large star-shaped hall from which other corridors radiated, when out of one of the side passages a great wave of humanity suddenly broke over them and by the time he had recovered they had been swept apart by an irresistible force so that however he struggled, whatever he tried, he could not keep up with her. Her blonde hair flashed before him one last time a few metres ahead, then another seething mass bore her away and she disappeared without trace in the dense impenetrable swirl of anonymous others. Budai waited for her in the street a while but failed to spot her among those emerging from the station.

He set off to the left, the direction indicated by the woman. This part of town was not quite like the others, looking older, with a more intimate air, the streets narrower, though just as crowded. It must be the city centre, he thought, that is if the city had one. He walked past an old-looking wall that was part of a somewhat later house but deliberately revealed by the surrounding stucco, with a carved inscription above it, no doubt something to the effect that this was a historical monument, possibly part of the ancient city wall. The shops here were shut too. He turned down a winding lane where paint had peeled from the walls of crumbling houses, where rubbish, dirt, and fruit peelings littered the ground and cats wound between people's feet, slipping into foul-smelling gateways. A light drizzle started again: blank-faced firewalls rose damp and grey into the empty air.

He arrived at a square with a fountain at its centre, a stone elephant spraying water from its trunk. The traffic flowed around it in a ceaseless and forbidding stream as if it had been there for ever and would continue into eternity. Another similarly busy square opened from this one, the cars sweeping through a wide gate to a fort several floors high, its ramparts, complete with arrow slits, running around the walls and a dome on top. The whole thing seemed vaguely familiar but he couldn't place it. He examined it from various angles until suddenly he recognised it: miniature copies of the tower were being sold as souvenir key-rings back at the hotel! What age and what style the fort was built in was rather difficult to say. The lower part with its pointed windows might have been Gothic but the hemispherical dome seemed more oriental, possibly Moorish. The fort must have served as a military post at some time but architectural monuments of this type, to a tyro like Budai at least, tended to look pretty much alike, comprising heavy dense masses, raw unshaped stone, all amounting to a chilly utilitarianism such as may be found in Roman stockades, medieval watch-towers, even the Great Wall of China.

There was, however, no railway station here either though he reasoned that the various airline offices should be situated somewhere in the area and that he would recognise them even if they happened to be closed today for there would be model aeroplanes, maps and pictures of possible destinations in their windows. But all he saw were squares and streets, tenements large and small, closed shops, drawn blinds, cars, people, more streets and more squares. He began to wonder whether he was in the city centre after all since the old town, the historic centre, might not be the centre of the city as it now was, much as the City of London was no longer the centre of London. Or was there an even older quarter somewhere? Or maybe there were other inner cities? Whom would he ask? How would he find out?

He took the underground again, getting off at the stop where he had studied the map. He soon found himself wandering to and fro between various anonymous, unremarkable buildings; the rain had started again and even when it stopped clouds continued to hang darkly over the rooftops. Then he found himself in a park that was just as crowded as the streets with children in sandpits or scampering over lawns, setting tiny boats afloat on the pond, swinging on swings watched by mothers with prams along with dogs on leads, dogs without leads, every bench occupied, queues of people forming even there waiting to sit down. He bought a pretzel from a stall and saw they were frying sausages here of the kind he saw elsewhere so he ate one for lunch: it had a delicious aroma but the taste was slightly sweet and sickly. Could it be that the much repeated word on the map that he had taken to mean 'station' meant simply street or ring-road or square or gate or some such thing? Could it be a kind of epithet such as 'old' or 'new'? Might it be a famous figure, a general or poet after whom various places were named? Or might it, who knows, even be the name of the town?

Next time, he got off the train where most other people seemed to, where the carriage all but emptied. Everyone was heading towards a stadium, a huge, grey, concrete structure that seemed to float through the air above them like a vast ocean liner. Even from a distance he could hear the rumble of the crowd. The weather cleared up. Aeroplanes criss-crossed in the early afternoon sky. Budai bought a ticket like everyone else and followed the masses flowing up the steps at the back of the grandstand right to the top tier. The bowl of over several hundred metres diameter was packed and buzzing with countless numbers of spectators and ever more kept coming: the seats had long been filled and the crowds in the stands that ringed the upper tiers were growing denser, still more swollen with newcomers, so much so that the whole place looked likely to collapse. The pitch below was hardly distinguishable from the spectators, it too being utterly packed with at least two or three hundred players in tight groups or running here and there in ten or fifteen different sets of team colours. The crowd seethed and roared. A thin, unshaven, weasel-faced figure in a yellow cap was bellowing furiously right next to Budai, his voice cracked, shaking his fists. However attentively Budai watched the movements of the players below him, trying to work out the rules, he understood nothing. He couldn't even tell how many teams were on the field. The rectangular playing surface was marked with white and red lines that divided it into smaller areas and there were at least eight balls in use, the players kicking, throwing, punching, heading and rolling them hither and thither or just holding them under their arms as they argued. There seemed to be no goal, no net anywhere, though the pitch was surrounded by a wire fence that was some four or five metres in height in some places while scarcely shoulder-high in others.

The action at this point became more concentrated: the players were actually standing in ranks. Suddenly one of them sprang from the rank with the ball in his hands and scrambled up the wire fence, presumably with the intention of leaving the field. As soon as they spotted this the others threw themselves on him and, though he had his left leg over the fence already, they got hold of the right and started pulling him back. The crowd roared making a fearful noise. The fugitive fought in vain to free himself but there were too many below him unwilling to let him go and in the end they succeeded in dragging him back, so in the end he just lay on the grass, the ball having bounced away and the rest left him in peace, not bothering with him. Then a tall black player in striped kit broke away on the far side, right where the fence was at its highest and, being remarkably nimble, looked as though he was going to escape. Everyone rushed to tackle him, including the man who had just failed the lower fence, racing after the dark figure, and they only just managed to grab him so that however he kicked and hung there eventually he too was brought back down. The crowd was going wild, now encouraging, now threatening, though it was far from clear to Budai which of them was supporting whom. Whenever somebody tried to escape from the pitch there were shouts of support for him, though once the others were in pursuit, grabbing and tugging at him, the crowd seemed to transfer its sympathies to the pursuers, roaring them on with furious, bloodthirsty vehemence.

The most enthusiastic grabber and downer of fugitives was a brave, powerfully-built, little fellow who stole the ball from the tall black man. He sprang from the ruck with such vigour, so unexpectedly, that he was quickly up and on top of the fence and by the time the others got to it he had leapt over, scrambling down the other side. They made to snatch at him through the fence and got hold of his vest, trapping him tightly against the wire so he hung there as if transfixed. But the little guy was not giving up so easily. He kept thrusting and twitching, wriggling until suddenly he freed himself from the vest that continued to hang on the net and sprang to his feet, bare-chested, waved happily to the crowd and dashed off into the dressing room, patting and bouncing the ball as he went, disappearing just below the stand Budai happened to occupy. The others stared after him from beyond the fence as they might from a cage in the zoo. The crowd too took a deep breath, resolving the tension by clapping, laughing, drumming, and having formed a solid mass before, now dissolved and began to leave in a series of slowly pulsing, wave-like movements. Budai too drifted out, his heart light with a dizzy kind of joy, all confidence and delight.

After that he wandered here and there, all over town. It was evening again and the streetlamps came on while far off in the distance the red and blue neon letters on top of a skyscraper started their regular rapid blinking. He found himself in some kind of downtown area with bars, clubs and theatres from which music of both the live and mechanical kind poured into the street where lights flashed and sparkled and the window displays were filled with images of performers, dancing girls and strippers. This part of town was just as packed with heaving crowds; there were even people dancing on the pavement, the rhythm of constant movement faster here, an infinite rolling patchwork of yellow skins, black skins, creoles wearing flowers in their hair reminding him of gypsies, and a number of soldiers. There seemed to be a lot of uniforms about generally. Policemen with rubber truncheons patrolled the area, mingling with the crowd. He had noticed them earlier in the market and by the stadium too. And besides them there were bus and underground employees of both sexes, firemen in red helmets (if that is what they were), postmen – or were they railway workers? – in blue tunics, and a number of children, many schoolgirls in a uniform of green raincoat and similar coloured trousers or skirts. Most numerous, however, were the heavy, brown canvas dungaree-wearing manual workers whose uniforms carried no insignia, men and women dressed exactly the same, probably for practical reasons. Or were they perhaps members of some organisation?

It felt like the evening of a public holiday, a leisurely jostling in the streets, vendors selling things from trays, shouting their wares, and everywhere the press of the crowd. Budai was tempted to behave like them and spend the money in his pocket, so he went on a spree, buying and consuming whatever he could, for did he not owe himself this much at least? He bought a paper from a paper boy so he could examine it properly back at the hotel, then stood in queue for pancakes being fried at a stall by a young man in a white coat, a bowtie and straw hat, whose copper-coloured Native American skin was glistening with sweat. Having bought a pancake, he bought a drink first here, then there, sipping at a slightly sickening, sweet liquor they measured out at long counters. The drink did little to quench his thirst but he craved more and more of it. A man covered in sores stood on the corner in a torn pullover bellowing and jabbering, busily binding his companion – a miserable little hunchback – up in chains while regularly taking time off to accost bystanders for money. Having secured the chain, he wrapped him up in paper then wound a length of thick rope round him several times over, tying knots until the shape became quite unidentifiable, like a mummy or a parcel in a warehouse and he ended by pulling a sack over the lot and tightening a rope over the opening. He blew on a whistle and the bound man started squirming, gingerly at first, then, as he gained a little more freedom of movement in the depths of the package, thrusting with shoulders and feet. The act might have consisted of him freeing himself entirely through his own efforts though that looked impossible since he was well and truly trussed from head to toe. But the feeble little creature was struggling ever harder, every part of him wriggling, his knees and elbows vigorously thrusting against the fabric, aiming presumably to free one of his limbs inside, a finger at least, emitting a low growling sound while the man in the pullover offered a loud commentary on the proceedings, gesturing and demanding money. The sack tipped over and rolled and squirmed along the pavement: it seemed the hunchback was engaged in a painful struggle, working on the fabric that imprisoned him, expending all his strength and powers of invention, muttering and blowing furiously, tugging, thrashing, even throwing himself into the air. Suddenly the knots yielded and a thin little finger appeared in the opening, then a hand, and then an arm. From this point on it all happened quite quickly, his limbs emerging one by one, then his head, his shoulders and finally the hunched back. One more minute and he had shaken off the lot, sack and chains and all. He stepped clear and took a bow. His face was freckled and twisted as he looked about him blinking in confusion. The crowd applauded and threw money into the bowl.

Budai was feeling thirsty again so he took a drink. There must have been alcohol in the sweet syrupy concoction for it was slowly going to his head: he felt dizzy and his skin was prickly. He still saw everything clearly, perhaps more clearly than before, it was just that he saw it as if from a distance, not as part of the proceedings. He was detached from his situation, almost indifferent to it, that is if he considered it at all, or maybe it was rather that he was numbly, mechanically searching the back of his mind: after all, it wasn't his fault that things had turned out like this, he had never wanted to come here, it was up to others, those who had planned the conference to search for him and find him ... For the time being he was more interested in the evening traffic, those thousands of tiny incidents on the pavement and in the road: he allowed himself to become part of the noisy, colourful, celebrating crowd. There were a lot of drunks swaying and singing with paper hats on their heads, squirting water-pistols at each other, grabbing at things, lurching this way and that. Being slightly light-headed, he felt himself to be one of them and wanted to be in their company. He followed one loud, unruly gang of youths who were shouting, pointing, pulling faces, fooling about, jokingly pushing each other around, playing leapfrog, blowing water through glass tubes and splashing passing girls. He followed them as they turned down a side street, still crowing.

It was a funny little street with extremely narrow houses no wider than could be compassed by a pair of outstretched arms, their walls painted bright green, bright red and orange, some of them even in chequered patterns. The windows, on the other hand, particularly those on the ground floor, were relatively large, high and wide, some extending the whole width of the building. In every one of them there sat a woman wearing heavy make-up and an evening dress with deep décolletage or else some other item of clothing that revealed her shoulders and curves, drawing attention to her breasts. The women winked at the men and beckoned them in. Budai, of course, could tell what kind of quarter he had stumbled into even without the invitation. And though he had not frequented such places since his own student days – they tended to repel him now and he would avoid such streets at home – it occurred to him that here at last he might establish some contact, speak to someone, ask them a question that they might be able to answer, or that he could at least try to explain if only there was someone prepared to listen ... Suddenly he felt so excited the sweat soaked through his shirt. He stopped at the next bar and stood in a queue again for a drink to work up courage and overcome his shyness.

There were as many kinds of women on display as there were colours of houses: honey blondes, young girls, women with slant eyes and combs in their hair like Japanese geishas, even one coal-black beauty wearing a heavy silver necklace. There was a woman dressed in white tulle who had a heart-shaped face and long dark lashes and gave a lingering Madonna-like smile, who did not invite anyone but just sat there looking out on the street. She attracted Budai's attention. He walked to and fro in front of her window so she was bound to have noticed him but still she did not beckon him, only followed his movements with the same modest and happy half smile ... Making a sudden decision, with heart in mouth, he rang her bell like a guilty schoolboy. An answering buzz told him he could enter.

He found himself in a dim-lit hall with an old woman sitting at a table. As he passed her she gave him a tiny slip of paper with the number 174 on it. He didn't understand what this was for and handed it back to her enquiringly, but the old woman just muttered a complaint of some sort, and pointed upwards. He had to go up to the first floor where a bald, withered old man stood by the door, his face red and wrinkled as a baked apple. He asked for Budai's ticket, punched a hole in it, then tore a ticket from a book of tickets and handed it to him. Not being able to understand each other it took a while to establish that there was something to pay here, a note bearing the number 10. Budai felt this was expensive and didn't even know whether it was an entrance fee or whether it covered everything. He was already regretting having come in.

He was ushered into a circular room with four doors beside the one he had come in by opening off it. There were chairs and benches arranged around the wall, all of them occupied by some twenty to twenty-five men waiting as if at the dentist's so there was nowhere for him to sit down. A speaker was playing waltzes, guests were chattering and laughing. Budai felt no inclination to engage in the usual sign language, suspecting it would be pointless in any case: he doubted that he could explain his presence. Once we are face to face, he thought ... From time to time one of the doors opened and a lightly-clad woman turned around and flicked up her dress. This was what the guests had been waiting for – they had got to number 148 so far – and one of them would go off and disappear with her. But there were occasions when no one came forward, in which case the possessor of the next number accompanied the woman while the first man waited for one of the others. Eventually the whole range of women had made an appearance but the one with the Madonna face was not among them. Perhaps she was just for window-display?

Business was pretty brisk, doors opened and closed with great regularity: the women would spend between ten and fifteen minutes with each guest, sometimes less, while all the time new customers continued to arrive. The loud, constantly changing crowd had practically used up all the oxygen in the room. Several people were smoking though there was no sign of ventilation anywhere. The air was thick with a heavy male smell combined with smoke, sweat, cheap perfume and some insidious disinfectant or insect repellent. Eventually Budai found a seat though he felt no better for that since his head was swimming and his stomach heaving: he blamed the drink he had consumed. He wanted the whole thing to be over but was worried in case it looked like he was running away: he had missed any opportunity of leaving. He regretted spending the money too. In the end he decided not to be choosy but to go with whoever came for him, it didn't matter which woman it was. The sheer speed and volume of the traffic had put him off in any case.

It was a good long time before they got to 174: a big, stout, red-haired girl with brown skin or possibly a deep tan called the number out. Budai rose and followed her silently into the neighbouring booth. Though they closed the door behind them they could still hear the music as well as the chatter and laughter of the waiting room. The woman was wearing a lightweight white blouse, a wide green skirt, beneath which flashed her healthy stout thighs, and a pair of summer sandals. She immediately started to undress and had already pulled the blouse over her head when he raised his finger to stop her. He addressed her in several languages, pointing to himself, making sweeping movements with his arms, opening his palms in enquiry. What he wanted to know was the name of the town and the country, that kind of thing. But she can't have understood him though she raised her eyebrows and asked him something twice in a deep, harsh, nicotine-stained voice. He tried to respond by drawing the shape of Europe as best he could in his notebook, complete with its three major southern headlands and major rivers, marking his own birthplace beside the Danube and the city he had come from, repeating its name carefully, syllable by syllable, jabbing at his own breast. The girl gazed thoughtfully at the drawing while indicating that he should sit down and make himself comfortable. He was still fully dressed and unwilling to remove any of his clothing apart from his coat, which he laid on the chair. He hovered in the tiny room, preoccupied, so the girl signalled to him to sit down beside her on the leather couch. She did not hurry him, nor did she show any impatience, though there must have been new customers arriving all the time outside to judge by the rattling, scuffling and scrapings of chairs, as well as the music that continued to pulse. In all the noise, and despite the language problem, she must have been touched by the loneliness of the foreigner and guessed that he was after something different.

Budai tore the page out and gave it to her along with the pencil to indicate that she should draw her own map. The woman misunderstood him, folded the sheet and put it in a metal box that she drew out from beneath the bed. He tried to discover her name as a beginning, then held up his fingers as if to count, one, two, three ... But he could not be sure whether the overlong and slow answer she gave, giving an occasional bitter laugh, was in fact to his question. It was hard to know. She took her box out again, removing a number of miscellaneous items: buckles, brooches, ribbons, scraps of paper with writing on them, old letters, photographs, a pair of opera-glasses, a ring, some coloured marbles and a glass pearl. This must be where she kept her souvenirs and mementos. She closed then opened the box again and carried on talking in the deep hoarse voice:

'*Tevebevedre atchipachitapp! Atchipachitapp?.. Buttureu jebetch atchichitapp?*'

She kept repeating the sound *atchichitapp*, as she picked out a child's shoe from among her things, her eyes suddenly full of tears. Budai had no idea who the shoe belonged to, to the woman in her childhood? Or to a child of her own? And if she had a child where was it? ... But she hugged the little shoe so passionately one couldn't help but pity her: he stroked her hair, soft, red, electric, so it almost sparked as he touched it, caressing her brow and neck too. The woman caught his hand and put it to his face, to her mouth, smearing it with her tears: he felt awkward but he lost his coldness and was overcome by deep emotion. There was much annoyed shuffling and drumming in the waiting room, someone even knocked on the wall. Being hurried like that made Budai nervous and he would have disengaged himself but the girl wouldn't let him, clinging to him, pressing his head into her lap, practically kneeling before him. He wanted to pull her up but found himself sinking down beside her instead and that was how they remained, clumsy, between floor and couch, in a most unnatural position but in a tight embrace, almost of one body.

People were shouting and banging outside: they really had to hurry now. The woman kissed him on the lips as if in farewell but that only made him sink down again ... He turned away as he put on his coat, and after a moment of hesitation, awkwardly placed another ten-unit banknote on the chair. She wasn't looking at him but was silently adjusting her hair in the mirror. Budai left by the back door, down side stairs that stank of cats.

The narrow street opened onto a square where a giant ferris wheel was turning and streams of many-coloured lights flashed over booths offering games, target shooting, dodgems, boat-swings, carousels, all the fun of the fair. There was an enormous illuminated roller-coaster; people were shrieking, shouting and trumpeting, small explosions were being set off. Everywhere the unceasing swirl of the crowd, no less dense, no less packed than elsewhere. There were slides, ghost trains, stalls with hoopla and ring-the-bell, conjurers, acrobats, sword-swallowers and fire-eaters, an Indian Rubber Man who could wind his legs around his neck and a two-ton woman who simply stood on a platform immobilised by her own weight, helpless and vast as a Polynesian idol.

There were boats for hire too if you were prepared to wait long enough though he no longer cared about time. Time didn't matter any more: who cared what the clock said! He paid and was helped into a one-man punt. A slow current carried him down a barrel-vaulted, cave-like tunnel where music blared, some swaying barcarolle, and atmospheric coloured lanterns dangled either side, some even floating on the water. There were miniature castles and forts along the way, waterfalls, sluices, power stations, bridges and the rest; all the usual stuff, nothing special. For him though it was the greatest, most unexpected pleasure of the day, his first moment of pleasure since arriving.

Back home he used to canoe on the Danube. He'd start early in the morning and row a long way up the winding tree-and shrub-lined stream. The water never quite formed a smooth mirror as he proceeded between islands and sandbanks: it was constantly folding, trembling and sparkling, patches of dark billowing beneath the surface. Even on a windless day the river was alive and breathing. He usually tied the boat up on the same tiny unnamed island and took a rest: at high water it would be covered by the Danube, and later, once the water had retreated, the grass would remain exactly as it had been bent by the current, grass blades and the bases and branches of shrubs still tangled in wisps of water-weed but dry, as if the trees had grown beards. A narrow lagoon divided the islet into two, the water continuing to trickle through it. The little boat was easily maneouvrable and could be guided past bending branches and lianas that hid it from view. He never met anyone here, he disturbed a few birds at most. The current picked up where the lagoon ended, the river suddenly lurching into movement, clear and transparent right down to the pebbles at the bottom. This was where he best liked to bathe, the current carrying him, filling the pores of his skin, the water sweetish and soft on skin and tongue. One May morning he saw wild ducks by the sandy bank and observed them silently so they did not see him. The mother duck was teaching her brood to swim, dive and catch fish.

He set off back to the hotel in a light reverie full of happy memories. He had noted the name of the metro station he was aiming for, had even written it down, but just at the moment he didn't know where he should get on. He was a long way from the station where he had arrived and was unlikely to find his way back to it, nor did he have any success in discovering another entrance with those characteristic yellow rails. He started asking around again in the hope that there might just be someone who understood him, stopping passers-by and pointing down at the paving. Finally a Tataric-looking woman in brown overalls seemed to grasp what he required and encouraged him to come with her, even taking his arm, and indeed, a mere two blocks on, she had succeeded in conducting him to the entrance of an underground public convenience.

By this time he feared he was permanently lost, no longer able even to find the hotel. It was getting late, close on midnight when he realised what he should do: he should watch the crowd and see where it was densest, see what direction it was moving in and note the main current. He located that current and tried to follow it, careful never to be parted from it. There were ever more people around him. Then they turned a corner into an even wider stream that a few hundred metres further on poured into a flat-roofed round building with steps leading down into the metro. Once there it was easy enough to find his way around: he could locate the map, seek out the relevant line on the correct level and note where he had to change trains.

He arrived in the little square from which he had started out that morning. The skyscraper he had been gazing at was still in construction. He counted the floors again to check: there were sixty-five though he clearly remembered there having been sixty-four before. He counted them twice more but it was sixty-five both times with the framework for the sixty-sixth already in place. They must have managed to finish a whole floor since he last looked ... The fat doorman blinked, saluted and pushed open the swing door. Surely he was a robot, thought Budai, not human at all, a machine dressed in uniform programmed to perform two or three movements. He felt like tapping him to see what he was made of, though he immediately recoiled from the thought: he might get an electric shock ...

Waiting for his key, he faintly recalled having left a letter at the desk addressed to the management. What if there were an answer waiting for him in the pigeon hole? Might they have returned his passport? There was nothing there. It was a different clerk again and he couldn't be bothered with repeating the whole pointless charade. He took his key without a word and went to stand in the queue for the lift.

He hadn't expected the blonde woman operator to be on duty since she had been there in the morning: it surprised him to see her as the doors opened. She looked exhausted and broken, her face too red, her eyelids drooping as she played the keys with her long, carefully manicured fingers. Could she have been working all this time? Or was this a second shift after a break at home? Where did she live, in fact, in the hotel or with a family? Does she have a family, a husband? ... The air in the lift was more oppressive than usual and only later did he notice that the ventilator was out of commission. Entering he had positioned himself so as to be quite close to the girl. Under the light, tiny drops of perspiration twinkled on the faint down of her brow. Budai's inhibitions had been loosened by drink and he used his newspaper to fan the girl's neck and forehead. She slowly turned, more in amazement than protest, and said something too, giving a short laugh. It was the first time Budai had seen her smile. Suddenly he felt weak and tender: he wanted to stay with her, so that she could relax at his side ... Yes, whatever way he looked at it, thinking about her and about himself, that was all he wanted, to lie down with her in one bed and wait patiently as she nodded off, hearing her breathing, seeking out the pulse on the tight skin of her wrist: indeed, that would be the most satisfying thing he could possibly do. She had to remind him to get off when they reached the ninth floor. So she remembered. She had noticed him.

His room had been tidied again and the bed made but the telephone directory he had pinched yesterday had gone. They must have discovered it as they were making the room up and taken it away along with the notes he had made at the back of the book. He had the paper and could start again but really did not feel like it now. His muscles ached with tiredness, after all, he had been on his feet all day, coming and going, tramping here and there – thinking that, he realised he had wasted another day, or, rather, that he didn't know whether he had or had not made any progress at all and was seized by a mixture of terror and ironic self-recrimination. He removed his clothes in confusion: one moment he was shuddering and feverish, disgusted by the thought of failure, the next he was drowsy and faintly drunk, thinking '*who the hell gives a damn*'. He showered and lay down without turning off the bedside lamp. The fault must be in his character: he found any kind of aggression or self-promotion distasteful. The truth of this dawned on him slowly as he dozed. If he could not overcome his shyness and sensitivity, his instinctive reluctance to put people out, he would never get out of here, nor would anybody find out where he was or lift a finger to help him. He must fight this battle alone, there were no two ways about it: he must transform himself from top to toe, it was the only way to rediscover himself and assert his being.

Awake now, he felt so indignant that he smashed his fist on the bedside table and the glass on it cracked and cut his hand. He was bleeding quite badly. He bandaged the cut with his handkerchief then twisted a towel around it for good measure but the blood still seeped through: he hated, he utterly loathed this town that was nothing but cuts and blows, that was forcing him to act against his nature, that gripped him and would not let him go, that hung on to him and pulled him back.

He was having a recurring dream. He was in Helsinki, in that long familiar harbour town, walking its cool damp streets and wherever he set out from – whether it was from the cathedral, the opera, the fish-market or the Olympic Stadium – he always arrived at the sea. He liked this dream. He liked seeing the horizon slowly brightening to blue behind the rows of brown and white houses: he could almost conjure it up when awake, draw it forth from his distant memories in the period of shallow consciousness hovering between light and dark while waking or falling asleep. The conference would be pretty near over by now as it was only programmed to last, at most, some three or four days, depending on the number of speakers. He had hardly seen any water since arriving here, no river, no lake, none that he could remember, except perhaps at the fair where he took a boat, or in the park the pond where children played with model yachts.

The cut on his hand was slow to heal. It hurt and pulsed and he had to bandage it several times using clean handkerchiefs. He decided to keep off drink as he seemed to have become rather too accustomed to it here. He wanted his mind to be clear and sharp, not muddled, and he kept his resolution over the next few evenings. He developed an interim regime for himself. He ate twice, in the morning and the afternoon, usually in the same self-service buffet near the skyscraper, and spent the rest of the time exploring the streets and the metro system. Two or three times when he left the hotel he did not hand in his key so as to save queuing when he returned. But then he thought better of it: it would only lead to confusion if people were looking for him and were unable to determine when he was in his room or outside somewhere. Besides all this, his passport had failed to reappear and he never saw the grey-haired clerk with whom he had left it that first evening.

There were ever new schemes and plans to consider that served to conceal the nature of his situation for there were days when he simply could not face it. One of his schemes was to make several copies of a notice in six languages that he posted at various places in the hotel – along the corridors, in the lift and in the entrance lobby – asking whoever might read and understand it to seek him out in Room 921, or, if he wasn't there, to leave a message for him at the desk in return for a handsome reward. Having put those up he knocked at a few neighbouring doors but mostly he received no answer: it might not have been the best time, the guests might not have been in their rooms, or it may be that he knocked too quietly. When he did find someone in it seemed he had disturbed them. At one door an aggressive female voice demanded to know something, at another when, having received an incomprehensible answer, he opened the door he stumbled in on two young olive-brown men in pyjamas who sprang apart, one of whom – a short, bespectacled, skinny chap – ran past him out into the corridor and disappeared round a corner. The door next to it was already open and he peered through the crack before warily stepping inside but an overwhelming smell, worse than a pigsty, stopped him in his tracks. There was no one there, only cages containing fat, overgrown angora rabbits. The room was full of rabbits: on the floor, on the chairs, on the luggage rack, on top of the cupboards, even under the bed, in the bathroom, in the shower cubicle, in the toilet bowl, all nibbling, all snuffling in their cages, all stupidly mizzling and stinking with urine.

Then he came up with a new idea. At dawn he would go down

to the hotel entrance and wait there for the bus that had brought him from the airport. But he was no longer able to remember either what time the bus had arrived or what colour it was for he hadn't seen it from the outside, and though he had been the last to get off it was by no means certain that this was the bus's last stop, it might have been pure chance, the bus stopping only for a moment. That was why he started hanging about outside in the constantly seething crowd among all those elbows and knees. He stood firm, careful not to be swept away, but was unable to identify the right bus in the traffic. It might have been that the flight on which he had arrived was not a daily service.

The excursions were not wholly useless though because, seeing a passing policeman with his rubber truncheon, he suddenly had an idea, his best and most important yet, something so brilliantly simple and sure to succeed that he actually gave a whoop when it occurred to him. If he were to be taken away by the police, for whatever reason, he was bound to be questioned and listened to, and if they did not understand him they would be obliged to supply an interpreter to whom he could finally tell his story ... He hurried back to his room to rest, to think the scheme through and settle on a course of action that would be certain to end in his arrest. He could start a fight, he could assault a passer-by, put a brick through a shop window or the pane of a telephone booth. He could puncture the tyres of cars stuck at traffic lights, possibly even smash their headlights. He could light a fire in a square or a park using newspapers and scraps of waste paper. He had, however, always felt nervous about committing any common breaches of the law and was concerned in case angry local people hurt him before the police arrived. He had seen a fountain in the shape of a stone elephant in the old town: what would happen if he decided to bathe in it? It might be enough to undress in the street but his natural reticence shrank from the idea. And what if he pretended to be ill, to simulate an epileptic fit, to throw himself on the ground with some soap in his mouth to make it froth, the way some conmen did?

He made no final decision but went down again and stood in front of the hotel, trusting to a moment of inspiration. He didn't have to wait long for soon enough a policeman appeared pressing his way through the crowd at the edge of the pavement. Budai took a deep breath and hesitated three times to gather courage before worming his way over and choosing the most effective method of attracting the policeman's attention. He gave the policeman a sharp jab in the ribs with his elbow. The policeman must have thought it was merely the normal bustle of traffic for he drew aside to let him pass, but Budai could not leave it at that. He was egging himself on by now and with one bold movement he knocked the policeman's peaked cap right off his head. It exposed his low brow, shiny and red, lightly covered by a tight crop of hair. Once he realised what had happened the policeman blew angrily on his whistle then gave his assailant such a rap on the head with his rubber truncheon that Budai's eyes misted over. A second thwack and he lost consciousness.

He woke in a small crowded place with faint light filtering through a small barred window. It must have been a police van. His head was ringing and his fingers felt two very painful bumps the size of nuts on his brow, but apart from that he felt a deep sense of satisfaction that he had achieved his aim, or in any case was well on the way to doing so. They were travelling for quite a long time, half an hour perhaps. He squatted on the low wooden seat still dizzy from the beating. It had begun to rain outside. He could hear it pattering on the roof of the van and this made him doze off again.

He woke suddenly to find they had stopped and the back doors being opened. Two policemen appeared, neither of them the one he had assaulted, and indicated that he should get off. They were in a large yard with high grey walls on all four sides where lots of uniformed and non-uniformed figures were moving to and fro. He was escorted from the van into the building and a long crowded corridor. He moved unresistingly between the two policemen, following wherever they led him but unwilling to engage in conversation with them since it would be hopeless anyway and soon there would certainly be far better opportunity to talk. It was very warm, the air heavy as in a greenhouse, stuffy and humid, not an open window in sight.

He was ushered into an office where a fat officer with a purple face and drooping moustache sat at a table covered with an ink-blotched green broadcloth. The officer's tiny eyes were sunken and kept blinking. He was eating, cutting up a piece of gently dissolving, rank-smelling bacon that lay on a ragged sheet of paper soaked through with grease. It was unbearably hot here too and Budai couldn't think why the place had to be kept at such a temperature and how the people who worked here could bear it. The officer gave him a sleepy look, wiped his mouth and his perspiration-covered face with a chequered handkerchief while the constables gave him a lazy salute and the one on the left babbled something, probably giving the reason for the arrest. The officer nodded slowly, audibly breathing, and without asking Budai anything, fixed his narrow, whey-coloured eyes on him, dried his greasy finger on the tablecloth then grunted something in an enquiring tone.

Now was the time, Budai judged, and took a small step forward – but stopped in his tracks. This was when he most needed his passport: it would have served as proof, as excuse and statement all at once and obviated the necessity for long explanations. He could have set it down before him and they'd know what to do ... As things were, he was forced to try all the various languages and gestures he had already tried countless times before, such as pointing to himself, repeating his name, his nationality, his place of residence and requesting an interpreter. There was not the slightest glimmer of understanding in the officer's eyes. The stuffy atmosphere was sapping Budai's energy too. He was losing his earlier determination and the dressing on his hand, as he noticed in the heat, was soaked through with blood again, though that might have been a result of the tussle with the first policeman. The officer in the meantime had finished his bacon and had taken out a crumbling piece of rancid cheese that had already begun to sweat and melt. He set it down before him, gazed at it for a while then slowly began to consume that too. The telephone beside him was ringing but he waited before he reluctantly picked it up. His conversation consisted of a series of incomprehensible answers employing the minimum effort. Every so often he belched into the receiver while wiping his face and neck with his hankie. Once he was done with the call Budai had another go, this time a touch more insistently, beating the desk with his fist, demanding to be interrogated, to be allowed to give proof of his identity, to defend himself and explain his behaviour, and so forth ... The officer simply stood up, strolled over in a leisurely fashion and with the same careless movement smacked him across the face as hard as he could, then returned to his chair, breathing hard. He slumped indifferently down again while continuing to eat. His palm was plump and soft but it must have been used to slapping people about since Budai could feel all five fingers complete with a broad signet ring. He was shocked and humiliated by this unexpected insult – the rubber truncheon had at least been expected – and fell completely silent, struck dumb by incomprehension. Nor did he put up any resistance when they handcuffed him and passed him on to another uniformed man who took away his tie, belt and shoe-laces then escorted him out of the presence of the cheese-and-perspiration-smelling officer who was presumably not only a policeman but a kind of magistrate too.

Down he went, down more endless corridors, just as crowded as the others had been to be met at a cage door near the crossing of two corridors by a tall black warder or guard. The man was dressed in the uniform he had seen about the streets: a brown jerkin, this time with a belt bearing a large ring full of keys. The policeman who passed Budai on to him must have told him he was drunk because the warder gave a laugh, showing his healthy white teeth and red gums, slapped Budai on the back in a friendly manner, removed his handcuffs and half-shoved, half-ushered him down a side passage. There was a whole row of cells here, all with the same steel doors, going a long way down. The black guard stopped at one of them, laughed again then bawled at him, indicating he should get in, helping him on his way with a push. He slammed the heavy door so hard the whole corridor was set echoing.

The cell was for two and was lit by a single bare bulb hanging from the high ceiling. One of the bunks was already occupied by a sleeping figure turned to the wall who didn't bother to look up when Budai entered. This place too was overheated, the air damp and suffocating, the radiator constantly crackling with no means of turning it down. Budai had had a headache ever since they brought him in. It was the only thing he could think about now. Why it was so unbearably hot in here, why was there no ventilation, nor indeed any window? He lay down full length on the spare bunk, closed his eyes and waited for the shooting pains in his skull to stop.

He had probably dropped off for a while – he was feeling rather numb after the beatings – and woke to see his cellmate sitting up, watching him. He must have been another drunk; that must have been how he got here, having disturbed the peace one way or another. He was bearded, disreputable looking, middle-aged, his clothes dirty and torn, his face scarred and bruised with violet patches. He looked confused. When he noticed that Budai had opened his eyes he jabbed at him with his finger and addressed him in a deep, throaty voice, his breath stinking of alcohol.

'*Tschlom brattyibratty?*'

He was probably asking something like, Who are you? Budai

felt less resolved than he had done, nor had his headache greatly improved but his instinct told him that instead of trying to explain or introduce himself it might be better to ask the same thing of the other man. That is, if he had heard him properly.

'*Tschlom brattyibratty?*'

The bearded man snorted, gave a wave and started searching in his pockets. He spent a long time looking and muttering, turning the pockets inside out – there were holes in them – feeling around the lining before emerging with a mass of miscellaneous items: a dirty handkerchief, the dry end of a loaf, matchsticks, a worn-down pencil, nails, rusty screws and, finally, a miserable looking cigarette from which most of the tobacco had fallen out but of which he offered half to Budai. Budai spread his palms to indicate that he did not smoke. Could the original question have been: Have you got a cigarette? Or: Would you like a cigarette? Who knows? Budai tried the usual languages, German, Dutch, Polish, Portuguese, not to mention Turkish and Persian, even Ancient Greek, but in vain. The other man took little notice, interrupting him.

'Sherederebe, tódzsig hodové guehruehguehleu pratchch ... Anta pratchch, vara ledebedime karitcharaprattye ...'

'What? What do you want?' Budai bellowed in his own tongue, breaking the words up into syllables so the other man should better understand him. 'Tell-me-what-it-is-you-want!?'

The bearded man looked at him a while with empty, clouded eyes, lit the cigarette, drew deeply on it, blew out the smoke and carried on talking exactly as he did before. Budai tried hand gestures and facial expressions to convey the fact that he was a stranger here and did not know the language but there was no way of cutting across him. The man just carried on jabbering, apparently indifferent as to whether he was understood or not. He had launched out on some longer story, his powerful, hoarse voice becoming more sweeping, more epic, pausing only to puff at the cigarette which had burned down practically to the end almost to his fingernails, at which point he chucked it away and trod on it. He continued talking, going on and on, growing ever more passionate, sometimes employing vehement gestures, occasionally croaking, bringing up phlegm, snorting, clicking his tongue, raising his voice at moments of high emotion, giving Budai the odd comical, conspiratorial wink as if to say: I'm right, aren't I? Budai was dying to get a word in but the other cut him off with a decisive gesture:

'Durunj! ...'

And so he carried on telling his story, droning on without a break, making Budai quite giddy. His headache was coming back too. On the other hand, being locked up like this with one man was really his best opportunity yet to establish communication with someone, to discover at last where he was, to glean from his cellmate – surely there must be a way of doing this – a few key words that he might build on later. Again and again he tried to interrupt the bearded man, drawing figures in his notebook, pointing out numbers with his fingers, jabbing at himself, then at the other man in an enquiring manner, finally losing his temper and shouting at him. But nothing he did could make him shut up, he just kept talking and talking and talking.

Another thing: whenever he reached a particularly important part of his oration, he raised his left hand, closed his eyes and, for a few seconds, fell silent as if in a reverie, overcome by his own passion, breaking it with a burst of theatrical laughter. He beckoned Budai closer, bidding him just listen to *this*, his voice shifting, singing. It was a rich bass voice singing an unfamiliar air, an aria from an opera perhaps, in any case a more solemn, serious kind of music. You could tell from the steadiness, modulation and intonation of the voice that he was gifted, indeed trained, and that it was only his low quality of life, his itinerancy, the alcohol and nicotine that had ruined the voice, blurred it, distorted it and made it croaky. The performance seemed to take up every ounce of his being. He was completely lost in his singing, his voice recognising ever fewer barriers as it soared. The aria culminated in a grand passage in which he first climbed the scale then descended it slowly, note by note, step by step, ever lower until it seemed impossible that there should be anything lower, but then lower again, reaching his finale at the deepest point of experience, on a long-extended, dark closure.

Budai didn't know whether to applaud or not. After the undoubted effort exerted in delivering his aria the bearded man was clearly exhausted and had started looking for another cigarette but continued to ignore Budai's questions, staring straight ahead instead, his face grey and waxen. He blew out some more smoke, then stretched out full length on his bunk and turned to the wall. It was hotter than ever. They seemed to have turned the heat up but there was no draught anywhere. Budai's shirt was soaked through. He took off his coat and jacket, laying them down beside him. The whole thing was so impossibly stupid, the heat so unbearable even though he was in shirtsleeves, the radiator noise so intensely disturbing that he suddenly felt so angry he started banging at the steel door, demanding that they take him away and give him a proper hearing with an interpreter present, repeating that they could not keep him in this airless cell locked up with a mad opera singer.

He made so much noise that eventually the little observation flap opened. The black warder's face appeared, laughing again, all his teeth showing, amused by these two idiotic drunks. But when Budai shouted at him, demanding to know what right they had to treat him like this, he angrily closed the tiny flap and no amount of noise could summon him again.

The bearded man was either sleeping or talking – he talked so much in the end he must have told his entire life story. It clearly did not matter to him whether anyone was listening or what the other person said. Budai had started to think the man was deaf and that

that was the reason he paid no attention to the questions he asked. To test his hypothesis he tapped the radiator with his ballpoint pen in the middle of one of the man's tirades but the man stopped for a second and took notice – in other words he could hear – then continued as though nothing had happened, blathering on.

It had been evening when they brought him in here and he hadn't eaten since the morning. But it seemed to be past dinner time here, at least there was no sign that they'd be receiving food soon. His cellmate seemed to be preparing for the night, squatting astride the slop pail, his trousers shamelessly round his ankles, though that did not stop him talking. He must have been cursing someone, because he was stamping his feet, threatening the unknown man with his fists, his face full of hatred and bitterness. It took the man some time to calm down, though his fury soon got the better of him again and he quickly slapped at the air twice more before turning away as if he had finished with his adversary. He wiped his hands on his trousers and spat.

Budai found it difficult to sleep on the hard prison bed, being kept awake by heat, hunger and helplessness. And when, after a long while, he did eventually succeed in dropping off with his whole body covered in perspiration, he had a vague feeling that the man had sat down beside him and was still talking, waving his hands about in front of his face, breathing cheap brandy at him. It might have been no more than a dream. It was very hot and now it was not only his head but his hand that ached.

In the morning the black warder handed them two pieces of dark brown bread and a mess-tin with some coffee-coloured liquid in it. The bearded man took a swig of it, then handed the tin to Budai who didn't fancy it. The warder reappeared after a short interval and beckoned Budai to go with him. He was led along the same corridors as he had been the previous evening, back to the same officer with the fat pock-marked face. The policeman was still eating – a soft, over-ripe watermelon, this time, spitting the pips here and there. The room was just as hot and foul-smelling as it had been before. No one can have opened a window in the meantime. They returned Budai's belongings to him and after finishing his melon, the policeman picked his teeth, wiped his moustache with his chequered handkerchief and barked at him:

'Goroge tutun epetetye! Wiripij.'

Budai stood before the ink-stained desk. What else was he to do? The officer was still breathing heavily, staring at him, his small slant eyes as sleepy and as bored as before, his eyelids closing now and then. He raised both hands to Budai, spread out his fingers, took them down then raised them again. Budai was unable to guess what he wanted but then the telephone started ringing so the officer picked up the receiver and replied slowly and deliberately, searching out some papers while scratching the back of his thick, veiny neck. He took some time to work his way through them, then looked up at Budai as if to say, Good heavens, what's going on, are you still here? Nevertheless he continued sitting there for some time, sluggish and obese before reaching for a scrap of paper and writing down the number 20. He gave the sheet to Budai. Budai did not appear to understand so the man drew out his own wallet and produced two ten-unit notes of currency, pushing them in front of him. It seemed unlikely that he was being offered money. Budai suddenly guessed what was expected of him. He was being given a fine: that must have been what those two lots of hands and fingers meant.

Pleased to have finally understood, he had no wish to argue, fearing that if he complained too much it might end not just in a fine but in more time in the cell and he didn't want that. So he fished in his pockets for two tens and put them down on the green tablecloth: he didn't have much money left. The officer did not give him a receipt, instead he was forced to write his name in a large book, the officer pointing out where with his fingers. The man's nails were dirty.

And with that the matter was more or less over. Budai had one or two more goes trying to explain why he had had himself brought in but hardly anyone was listening now. The black warder had disappeared and the fat officer was on the phone again, having taken a blue saucepan with some cold stew in it from one of the drawers. He sniffed at it, then set about rapidly consuming it. He made a horrible slurping sound and the sauce kept dribbling from the spoon so his moustache was completely covered and he had to wipe it again with his handkerchief. Budai was afraid that if he spoke up too loudly he'd get another box on the ear. In any case, the stale, muggy heat seemed to fill every corner of the enormous building and he was finding it ever harder to bear. All in all he was quite relieved when they led him out and he could breathe easily for the first time, free at last.

He found the nearest metro entrance the same way he had done before, that is by following the main drift of the crowd. Once underground he consulted the map and located the station he was currently at, it being marked with a red circle at the top right hand corner, and quickly found his way back to the station nearest the hotel ... Arriving, he saw the same skyscraper under construction with a lot of men at work on it and great loads on pulleys being conveyed up and down. Out of sheer curiosity he counted the number of floors. There were two more now, making sixty-seven in all.

He took some tea in the self-service buffet and was already sipping at his oversweet drink when he realised that he had picked up his breakfast without noticing he had had to queue for everything. His heart started thumping in his chest. He had been convinced it was the last thing he should get used to, for once he accepted, however unconsciously, the necessity of these queues it meant he had given up, surrendered the one hope that remained, the hope that he was different from the natives, a visitor, someone who did not belong here, someone who, by the same token, could not be detained.

He hurried back into the hotel. This time he no longer thought or expected but knew for certain that there would be something waiting for him. He was almost happy to see the fur-collared, blinking automaton at the door, to have him salute and push the door open, though the little multilingual notice he had put up before his adventure with the police seemed to have disappeared.

When he took his place in the queue for his key at the desk – once again there was a new clerk on duty, a smooth-faced, blond-haired young man, practically a child – he could see even at a distance that there was a roll of paper in box 921 though whether it was a letter or a folded note such as those on which hotels use to write messages was not clear. He was seized by such excitement that his fingers began to dance on the counter as the queue slowly moved forward. Never before had he found the wait for the desk-clerk so unbearably long. Could it be a reply to the message he had sent the management? To his multilingual notice? Or had someone rung him, the airline perhaps looking to find him, someone seeking him from home or possibly Helsinki, though he hadn't managed to arouse anyone's interest in town and not even the police could be bothered to find out his name? Suddenly his eyes filled with tears and he was unable to contain them. His chest and Adam's apple started to heave so violently he feared drawing attention to himself as he struggled to control his emotion. Meanwhile the queue moved on one place.

At last he got to the young clerk and showed him his room number that he kept safely in his pocket. The clerk bowed politely, took down both the key to 921 and the note or whatever it was from the pigeon-hole. The sheet was folded into four. Budai spread it out on the counter as the clerk mumbled a few incomprehensible words:

it looked like a kind of form with printed text and some numbers in ink. With quick, practised movements the clerk set up and entered information on his hand-held computer, presumably checking the figures, then wrote down the sum with his ball-point pen, twice underlining the total, scrawled something beneath it in large letters, and slickly rattling off some well-learned text, handed it over to Budai. It was clear by now that this was a bill. He calculated that he had been at the hotel precisely a week since arriving last Friday. Guests, it seemed, were required to pay by the week.

It was the amount that was the most frightening: the bottom line read 35.80. If he subtracted that from what money remained in his pocket he would have practically nothing left. It was true that since he had cashed his cheque he had been spending rather freely as if it were toy money and it had never occurred to him that he might run out ... The clerk pointed to a neighbouring window, presumably where he had to pay, at the very counter where Budai had collected eighteen freshly minted ten-unit notes. With heavy heart he now returned four of these – that's after a good half-hour of queuing, of course – and realised with bitter irony that he had gone through much of the value of the cheque without even learning the name of the currency.

He stuffed the bill in his pocket and waited for the lift while counting up again how much he had left. There were three tens and a few smaller notes, ones and twos as far as he could make out from the faint screwed-up bits of paper, plus some small change. It was dangerously, horrifyingly little: he hardly dared think what might happen once he had spent it. He just had to stay here. What other choice had he? He counted feverishly, adding and multiplying, calculating how long he could make it last if he carried on spending at the current rate, or rather what was the best way of rationing it – he had to eat, after all. Or should he give up travelling? Should he just sit in his room and wait for relief to arrive?

His mind worked overtime but he was running on empty: then, suddenly, just as the lift was arriving at the ninth, he was full of ideas, each better than the last, however late. This one should work! Here was another he could try! That was if he did not have to watch every last penny ... He could, for example, show someone a ten-piece note in one hand and a notebook sketch of an aeroplane in the other, and that would make it clear that he was seeking the latter, that is to say either the airport or the airline office. The trick was to show the money but to withdraw it while brandishing the drawing so the other person understood that he would only pay if he was actually conducted to the place. Or he might tempt one of the poorer-dressed people on the metro, the way one might entice an animal with food, by rattling his change while making train noises to imply that he wished to be taken to a railway station. He could try it on one of the hotel employees, using much the same ruse, persuading them to get him a taxi or some other car that would be certain to carry him wherever he wanted, for a fee of course, he being pretty certain he could settle with the driver. All these and other schemes flashed before him, but behind them all remained the sense of chill horror: what would happen if none of these worked and his money ran out; whom should he turn to, whose help could he count on? Going by his experience of local people so far he could die of starvation as far as they were concerned.

Nothing had changed in his room since he left it except he had fresh sheets, new towels, a new bedspread and a different oilcloth on the table. They must do these things weekly. Budai looked down on the street at the inexhaustible flow of traffic. The conference in Helsinki would have been long over by now, the delegates departed each to his or her own home: even the most distant of them would have arrived ... He took off his clothes, drew the curtains and lay down on the bed, drawing the covers over him. Within a minute he felt his body stiffen, his torso and limbs grow numb as if he had been hypnotised. He was incapable of getting up again or even turning over. He could not move at all. Nor did he want to: all he wanted was to lie absolutely still, his eyes closed for as long as possible, not to rise even to get a drink of water; he simply wanted to lie there without moving a muscle, not thinking, for hours or even days, for ever.

If he counted from the day he left home it would have been the fourth, fifth, or at the latest, sixth day and they would have expected him back by now; in any case he should have been there a good while ago. What might they have been thinking when he hadn't written, phoned, sent a telegram or given any sign of his being alive? At what point would they have started to look for him, and where? In Helsinki? There they would quickly have been informed by the committee of his absence from the conference, that they had waited in vain for him to turn up. At the airline, at the transit points, working their way through the various possible airports he might inadvertently have found himself at? Where would they have turned, how would they have gone about it? In an increasing panic? Where in the world might he have disappeared to in such mysterious fashion? What would they put it down to, his relatives, his friends, his colleagues, and, above all, his wife? How would she explain it, what must she be feeling? And his small son? And his dog? ... By now all this was causing him actual physical pain, imagining their astonishment, their anxiety, their puzzlement, their ever more despairing attempts to locate him, their horrible suspicions that he might have met with an accident, imagining his helplessness: it was intolerable, their situation was a hundred times worse than his. He had to dismiss these thought or chase them away whenever they assailed him.

He couldn't tell how long he lay in bed: two or three nights might have passed like this. In all that time no one appeared, called or knocked on his door, at least he did not hear anyone. They didn't even come to clean the room. He woke suddenly to find it was morning again, the dirty grey light filtering in through the window, as overcast, as leaden and melancholy as before. Since he had arrived here there had been only an hour or two of sunshine. He roused himself, went into the bathroom, took a shower and shaved. He took another brief glance at the bill he had stuffed into his pocket: as far as he could make out the details, they consisted entirely of numbers, not letters. If only he could only work out which group of signs corresponded to which numbers! Once he knew that much he could try to learn – provided he got the right kind of question and could actually ask it – the sounds of the various numbers, and so, step by step, he might eventually be able to decipher the writing too, and then the language, though all this would of course take some time. And that was only provided he had a text in which the numbers, one way or another, were actually written down in letter form. The trouble was these forms had nothing like that ... Recognising this he put the bill away for now along with the various related questions to deal with later.

He had more important, more serious matters on his mind now and he decided to do most of his thinking in the room, leaving it only to eat in the familiar buffet, or, to save money, to buy food of the possibly cheaper sort in the shops; some bread, ham, cucumbers and so forth. He didn't actually have much of an appetite, not even after days of doing nothing physical, all his energy being absorbed by intense mental activity. He hadn't yet lost all confidence in logical thought: if he could only force his mind to review everything that had happened to him from the first minute of stepping off the plane when the bus brought him into town, something would reveal itself. A total would appear at the bottom of the column of figures. He sat at the writing desk, drawing and scribbling as he used to do back home when faced with a difficult and complex question in linguistics, shuffling tiny slips of paper bearing the various phonemes he had jotted down here and there, grouping and regrouping them, playing with them until, sooner or later, they suddenly appeared in a clear and logical order. That was if they fitted in the first place ... He had a certain trust in his ingenuity, in his quick and nimble mind, in the way he could delve into the heart of complex matters, in the vital role of inspiration even in scientific enquiry and maybe in luck too which, so far in his career, had always seemed to be on his side, so that when he began something he generally finished it. He was accustomed to thinking systematically: that was his craft, his vocation, his living. He felt exhilarated as he drew various diagrams and scribbled bits of shorthand in his notebook. Even now he was enjoying this instinctive mark making – it was almost a pleasure working on a logical problem that meant pitting his solitary wits against the city's million and more secrets. He just needed to make an inventory of all his experiences, to feed the accumulated data into his mind as he might into a computer, and he would simply have to wait for it to come up with an answer.

The most important conclusion he came to was that, however painful, however bitter the process, there was nothing for it but to discover precisely where he was, for until he did so there would be no going home. There was no getting round this order of events or trying to change the relationship between them, since one followed from the other. He could wait for ever for chance to intervene on his side: all ad hoc attempts to escape had proved unsuccessful so far and there was no guarantee that they would prove more successful in the future. He was persuaded that whatever shore fate had abandoned him on he would not easily get away.

It was not that his leaving was not a matter of urgency, but perhaps the very fact that he was in too great a hurry was a problem: he had been in such a rush to escape that he had quite neglected to discover whether this place was on the map at all or if he was the first of his kind to arrive here. Because if he was the first he should not be in quite such a hurry: the explorer in him should commit himself to make basic notes and observations. He should determine the location of the city, the name of the country and continent, find out who lived here and what language they spoke, so that he might return home fully informed about everything.

Was he on planet earth at all or in some other part of the cosmos? In an age of space exploration and science fiction the question did not seem utterly ridiculous. But no, let us keep a cool head about this, it must be earth really. Many signs pointed to the fact: the plants he had noted in the parks and public spaces were certainly terrestrial trees, grass, flowers, as was the limited range of animals he had so far encountered, dogs, cats, doves, sparrows, insects and those angora rabbits in the hotel room he had walked into. Then there were the fish on the market stalls, the canaries, the parrots, and the tortoises in the livestock market, though there was a six-footed lizard too of a kind he hadn't seen before. The air tasted and felt much the same as it did at home. And above all, most obviously, there were the people, people in unprecedented numbers, in buildings, in streets, in the hotel, in traffic, in vehicles, on the metro, as dense a throng of people, or pretty near as dense, as you would find in any other great city. And apart from this there was an entire recognisable way of life, the whole rhythm of it, the shops, the cafés, the food, the circulation of money, the way they cashed his cheque, the Arabic numerals and the use of the decimal system. Not to mention the week being divided into seven days, the Sunday holiday. And, and ...

He hadn't seen any stars yet, the sky generally having been overcast, but fortunately it cleared for an hour the next evening. Budai had no great knowledge of astronomy and could identify only one or two constellations, the Pleiades, Orion and the Plough, from which last he had learned as a child to calculate the position of the pole star. After a brief survey he succeeded in finding them, which suggested that he was in the northern hemisphere, for he was pretty sure the Plough could not be seen in the southern one. But if he was on earth, at what longitude and latitude? He had never taken much interest in these matters and could remember only what he had read in children's books and travelogues. He struggled to recall the proper method of calculating such data and tried to work it out through sheer intelligence. He got so far as to take midday here, that is the point at which the sun was at its height, and compare it with the time at home, that is if he had had his watch with him and had not adjusted it, and to calculate the distance from the difference, dividing twenty-four hours by 360 degrees, meaning that every difference of four minutes would signify one degree. He might, in other words, have worked out whether he was east or west of his starting point, but he had forgotten his watch. Without it the method of divining distance would be a matter of speculation, at best a matter of strenuous mental gymnastics. The most promising way would be to measure the angle of the pole star relative to the horizon, but in order to do that he would need specialist instruments – a sextant or a theodolite – and where would he find one of those? With his naked eye he could only guess the rough height of the pole star – if that indeed was the pole star – and compare it to its height at home. The two being roughly the same, he was left to conclude he was on roughly the same latitude. But where? In Europe? Asia? America? Or in some hitherto unknown part of the globe?

He had already considered the unpleasant climate and the ethnic diversity of the populace but it was hopeless trying to work anything out from that. There was nothing particular about the forms of dress here either, it was what you would find in most large European cities, just a little greyer and dingier on the whole, with a preponderance of uniforms. This reminded him that the black warder at the police station had been wearing the same kind of one-piece canvas boiler suit he had seen in many other places. Could it be that all those wearing similar uniforms, regardless of gender, were also guards and warders?

In the meantime there was the blonde lift operator going up and down. He tried to work out what shift she was working but was confused each time because sometimes she was there when he calculated she should be, at other times not and, conversely, just when he felt sure she would be off duty there she was again by the noisy opening door. They had got round to greeting each other by now and there were occasional signs that she was showing some interest in him too. Twice she addressed Budai as he was about to get out and he smiled and shrugged his shoulder by way of an answer to show he had not understood. The crowd in that narrow space gave no time for explanations and he was quickly swept away by the others getting off.

The next time they reached the ninth floor she put her hand on his arm to detain him and Budai finally understood that she wanted to take him somewhere. He remained in the cabin as it climbed floor by floor, slowly emptying, the numbers lighting up one after the other until they were on a much higher level. It was the top floor, the eighteenth, and by that time there were just the two of them. The girl opened the door and signalled for him to get out with her.

The layout was quite different here. There can't have been too many rooms, not for guests at least. There were large white containers and tubes of various sizes and thicknesses, probably part of the building's heating system or related to the lift mechanism along with cogwheels and steel hawsers. And there was a kind of cafeteria or bar, closed just now, probably only deployed in the summer when it was hotter, a kind of top floor tower restaurant with a vista surrounded by an open terrace, as far as he could tell through the locked glass doors.

The girl lit a cigarette and offered him one. Budai didn't smoke and politely turned it down. She on the other hand was clearly a heavy smoker. She drew the smoke down hungrily and blew it out again as though she was well used to it. Smoking cannot have been permitted in the lift. She smiled at him somewhat apologetically as she smoked. Now that she was rested and relaxed, her face clear of exhaustion, her manner was easy, bright and careless. Her hair and make-up looked perfect. She did not try to force conversation, knowing it would be hopeless but did address a word or two to him.

'Yeye tlehuatlan ... Muula alalálli?'

She gave a soft, slow, melodic laugh, puffing out more smoke, her back propped on one of the containers. There was a buzz in the open lift, someone downstairs was calling it but neither of them moved. Budai pointed to himself and repeated his name a few times then pointed at her questioningly. She gave another laugh and answered with a two-syllable word. He didn't quite catch it, and asked again.

'Pepe? Tchetche?'

Her pronunciation was so odd it might have been *Bebe*, *Veve*, *Gege*, *Dede* or anything else: each time she said it, it sounded different, sometimes it even sounded as if it had three syllables – *Edede* or *Bebébé*, though this might have been merely a pet name or an inflected version of her proper name. There was constant buzzing by this time, hordes of people must have been waiting on the floors below. Her brief break over, she stubbed out her cigarette and Budai entered the lift with her. As they descended it filled up with passengers again wedging themselves between him and her so they could not see each other at all. Only once they had reached the ninth floor could their eyes meet and exchange a complicit glance of farewell.

It was light in the darkness: a thread, however narrow, that constituted a relationship, a connection, the first in fact since he had arrived here and, if he was careful not to lose it, that he might be able to follow out of this monstrous swarming labyrinth. Perhaps he would make a discovery that would startle the world and the time would come when, all things being equal, he might think himself fortunate to have found his way here, to have stumbled on it like an explorer. On the other hand he might simply have been fooling himself.

Whether he was or not, the fact remained that he had to carry through the tasks he had set himself now, the first of those being to make some estimate of the city's extent. So next morning he set out early, got into the first metro that passed that way and rode to the end of the line where the whole train emptied. By that time he was wondering which way to go once he was above ground so that he would be moving away from the centre rather than back towards it. It seemed logical to note the direction of the track he had travelled on to make sure he would go the same way, though the exit routes from the platform were so complex and winding with corridors, stairs, bends and intersections that he was lost by the time he arrived outside and had to make a snap decision as to which unknown direction to walk down. In order not to get lost on the way back he drew little pictures in his notebook of the salient corners, crossroads and buildings as he passed them.

It was like all outer suburbs with endless stone walls, fences, chimneys, gasometers, wide and muddy streets, row on row of dull brick houses, a large factory in the distance, its roof jagged like a saw, its vast bulk silhouetted against the grey sky, the air smoky and sooty, bitter-tasting. Here and there he spotted a few grocery shops, some rag-and-bone tradesmen, and one or two general stores whose window displays were packed with dubious items. And wherever he went there were exactly the same dense crowds, no less dense than in the city centre. Could he have got on the wrong train? Did the rail network not extend to the city limits? Had the town outgrown itself? He wondered how it felt to have been born and spent all one's life here. Perhaps they no longer noticed the overcrowding of every street, no longer cared about the eternal queuing and the terrible and degrading effect it was bound to have on their lives. Or could they no longer imagine anything else? Did they think it natural? Were they simply used to it? Is it possible to get used to something like this?

Nor was the motor traffic any lighter here. Budai tried to read the number plates but couldn't make much sense of them: the letters remained indecipherable, accompanied by a number composed of three or four or five figures, with not an international number-plate to be seen, nothing from which he might deduce the country he was in. Were he able to drive he could try to get hold of a car – to steal one in other words – and then consider at leisure what he might do with it. But he couldn't drive and he didn't want, didn't dare, had no inclination to steal one, and in any case he was by no means sure he would be better off navigating the labyrinth of all these streets and squares without a map in a never-ending rush hour. It occurred to him that he had seen a bicycle in a shop window somewhere but he didn't think he had enough money left to buy it and was not altogether sure whether it would help having one. It might make it just that much easier to get lost.

Once again there was no sign of a railway station, not even of a railway bridge or railway cutting where he might at least begin to follow tracks. It was equally impossible finding an airport though every so often he would hear an aeroplane droning high above him. But it was useless speculating where it was going to land or where he might board one. If the city was on the coast it would be a good idea to find the way to the harbour or to trace the line of the sea until he discovered ships at dock, then proceed from there, sailing away, free as the wind. Any direction would do. But he could find no river nor canal, nor any kind of moving water that might lead him to the sea if only he walked long enough, since sooner or later all moving water had to arrive there. All he found were a few artificial pools between houses on a vacant site, their waters dirty, turning black and stagnant, like reservoirs constructed during the war. And an ornamental pond in a neglected park that he crossed but there was no waterway leading from it. It was full of wastepaper and empty bottles. Pools of oil floated on it.

And so he set to asking passers-by again, trying the word *sea* in various languages, using his hands, palm down, to indicate the motion of the waves, and making swimming movements with his arms. He repeated the word time and time again, in this language and that language, in all the languages he knew, even in Greek:

'Thalassa! Thalassa!'

It was soon clear that no-one understood him, everyone hurrying about his or her business, some of them too preoccupied to attend to his tedious private affairs. After a while Budais' lack of success started to inhibit him. His tongue grew stiff in his mouth. He lost heart and stopped asking. Nevertheless he kept pressing forwards through the constant crowd, driven on by an instinct stronger than any conscious notion. Having determined not to give up, he had to see something through to the end, utterly committed, whatever the result.

Fog, cold and sharp, was settling on the streets, so dense in places he could hardly see six feet in front of him. Cars had put on their lights and were moving at walking pace, locked together to the music of horns, cries and revving engines. Budai paid particular attention to landmarks now since he would have to find his way back. In a clear patch between wads of fog there rose a circus tent, a huge, peaked, white canvas structure, then it disappeared again. It was of no interest to him. What was it to do with him? He strode on swathed in grey-and-lilac mist. Now there was an illuminated gateway. What might it be?

Eventually he noticed that there were far fewer cars and that he was surrounded by a ring of tiny swaying lights. They blinked mysteriously, flickering here and there through the milky vapour that had suddenly descended. Were they stars? Nightmares? He couldn't tell how far away they were, all perspective lost in the soft-thick air. It was only later, having stumbled over mounds of freshly dug earth and into some blocks of stone and marble that he realised he had wandered into a cemetery and that the little lights were candles and tapers, some on graves, some in the hands of visitors. There were so many of them proceeding down the narrow cinder paths between the tombs and the mausoleums that there seemed to be no space left. Budai wondered if it was All Souls Night? But who knows whether they kept such feasts here? Or had he got himself mixed up in a particular funeral procession, that of a well-known figure perhaps, whose burial would attract a great crowd? Or was it simply that in this city everything was crowded? There was music coming from somewhere, impossible to say from where, the sound of an organ or some other heavy, dense sound and human voices too perhaps, a slow, attenuated wail that might have its origins far above or far below him. The monuments seemed to be of various shapes and sizes as far as he could tell in the fog, some with statues, some with pictures of the deceased, some with flowers or vases for holding flowers, but the differences between them were, as ever, minor with only the cross missing or perhaps it was just that he couldn't make it out on the ones he was close enough to see. The inscriptions were in the usual cuneiform lettering. There was not much opportunity of examining them at leisure since he was continually being pushed forwards, nudged this way and that, so it seemed likely that the flood of people was actually heading in a specific direction. Then he found himself outside the cemetery as suddenly as he had found himself in it.

The fog was slightly less thick now. He was on a workers' estate, in a row of uniform small houses with plaster falling off the walls and tiles missing from roofs, their yards serving as minimal kitchen gardens. He came to a high stone wall with a large stone gate. A great mass of people was gathered here, many hundreds, not standing in queues but in loose knots as elsewhere, jostling, loud masses of them, all pressing inwards, swarming through the entrance. Budai's attention was drawn to them and their noisy mysterious endeavour but all the time the size of the curious horde behind him was increasing. He couldn't turn back now even if he wanted to. They continued slowly to press forward though the gates were too narrow to accommodate them all. New people kept arriving, ever more of them, pushing and shoving. At one point they were so jammed together he feared being crushed to death or being trampled down. When he finally got in he felt he had been through a grinder.

He seemed to have arrived in a zoo or at least an ape and monkey enclosure because there were no other animals here. Of apes, however, there was no lack: cage after cage were full of them. But there were just as many visitors staring at the cages, shouldering and elbowing their way through in the effort to get ever closer to the bars, mainly children of course but a good number of adults too. There was a very wide range of anthropoids, at least in so far as he, with his limited knowledge of zoology, could establish: chimpanzees, macaques, baboons, huge gorillas and tiny silk-monkeys, gibbons, mandrills, marmosets. The odd thing was that however many there were they were all individual, each clearly different from the other as one could see if one looked at them long enough, and, furthermore, each was of a wholly unique character, some running, some dangling, some stalking impatiently to and fro, some nibbling with careworn expressions, some peeling fruit, some playing, some scratching or absentmindedly hunting fleas, some proud, some uncouth, some charming, some terrifying, pulling faces that were now pious, now meditative, some screaming, some muttering, some chattering, some croaking, some crowing, some excited, some bored, some loathing each other, some devoted to each other, fighting, mating, or simply squatting in a corner, resigned to a kind of world weariness, dreaming of forests and freedom.

There were notices everywhere on the cages carrying longer or shorter texts. Budai preferred the short ones of course. They were the ones most likely to give no more confusing information than the species of monkey on display together with its Latin equivalent as was the general custom in zoos. It wouldn't even be a problem if the latter were written in the so far indecipherable local characters, in fact that might help in offering a key to understanding them. For example, if he knew what the Latin for baboon was – and he happened to remember it was *papio* – it would be easy enough to work out what character represented what sound, or group of sounds, and that information could then be carried forward to the next word and so on until the whole alphabet was solved ... This was all very well but there were so many notices, some of which might be warnings or instructions regarding the feeding of the animals or information about the extent of the animal's natural habitat, its lifecycle or other such matter, or simply directives not to smoke or leave litter and so forth. Given such a profusion of notices it seemed an impossible task to work out which of them referred to the specific species of monkey behind the bars, particularly in Latin, that is if the Latin name was provided at all.

There were very long queues for the green-painted lavatories with separate ones for men and women, and since there was no way of avoiding them he had to wait for as long as it took ... Later, standing on a bridge, having chosen for no particular reason to go one way rather than another, he saw an open-air lido in the distance. There were many pools, both bigger and smaller, and despite the cool wintry weather, all of them were crowded, the various bathers hardly having any space in which to move and yet everywhere one or other figure was leaping into the water, splashing about and making a general noise. People were hanging like grapes off the diving boards. He looked to find the place where the used water might drain away but it was hard to see through the mist and steam and there seemed to be nothing on the surface, no ostensible way of conducting the water. There had to be underground pipes.

It seemed much more like an outer suburb now with fewer houses and those broken up by vacant sites, lawns and play areas, though the traffic on the main roads was no less busy. The fog had lifted: it felt cold and dry and soon the soot-red disc of the sun appeared, its edges sharply defined in the dirty sky. Here and there a few improvised dwellings stood, made out of cardboard or the carcasses of old buses, while in the distance a rust-coloured slag heap closed off the horizon.

He came to a place where both pedestrians and road traffic seemed stuck in a bottleneck so there was no forward motion at all except by thrusting his way through the crush, using his shoulders and hips: there must have been some kind of obstacle stopping them. Budai felt his mission was more urgent than theirs and, knowing there was no alternative, he set about shoving people aside. After some ten to fifteen minutes of struggle and a good few kicks and blows received in retaliation he reached the point at which they were being held up.

Cattle were being driven across the street, a lot of them, an entire herd, proceeding slowly, their lowing mingled with the sound of whips cracking, dogs barking and a general sound of lamentation. The herdsmen wore rubber boots and leather or cord jackets, as well as wide brimmed hats or berets. They looked a cross between cowboys and drifters ... Budai thought it might be a good idea to follow them so he left the road and made his way over the grass to walk beside the cattle though he was dressed quite differently from the herdsmen. He couldn't have explained quite why he was doing this but it hardly mattered which way he went now as long as it was out of town. No one asked him what he was doing there and his presence hardly registered in the constant confusion, in the clouds of dust and the universal movement, from which, occasionally, one of the wilder young bulls would break ranks, causing a great to-do as excited dogs barked and determined herdsmen whooped as, together, they drove it back into the herd.

Now they were on sandy ground, moving past a lumberyard where circular saws whined cutting tree trunks into smaller sections, then past another built-up estate where the herd clattered and beat on the paving with a noise like dull thunder that took a while to die away. Eventually they drove their mobile market into a fenced-off area like a sheep-pen and from there directly into a high-vaulted building. Budai forged ahead of the others here, partly out of curiosity, partly carried along by his own momentum, but once inside noticed that while most of the cattle had already ambled a long way into the great hall he could no longer see the head of the herd which must have been accommodated in spaces further off. Men and cattle completely filled the hall. Beside the drovers there were men in canvas overalls too, bustling about while the mooing and bellowing noise grew ever more baleful, each sound echoing off the bare walls, the air thick with warm, living-sickly smells. This must, no doubt, be the slaughterhouse.

The whole noisy melée was goaded into one vast hall lit by a great skylight. The floor here was running with slippery scarlet blood. The animals must have scented the danger because the smell of blood, if nothing else, made them halt and resist though there was no way back, nowhere to run, because ever more cattle were being driven in behind them. When it came to their turn each was suddenly surrounded by a group of strapping men, one holding its horns, another tying it down with a rope, until it was forced to stand astraddle. Then, whoever had the cleaver brought it down on the nape of its neck. Its poor legs gave way and collapsed. At the moment of collapse another man delivered a blow to its brow, cutting it open. But the beast must have lived on a good while yet for it fell sideways and carried on kicking on the stones, throwing its head back now and then, even when they buried a knife in its throat and drained its life blood, at which point the sad martyred look on its face very gradually glazed over.

Budai could not bear to look. He wanted to turn away but whichever way he gazed there were dying animals sprawling on the ground, ten, twenty, maybe thirty at a time, who would then immediately be dragged further along, cut into pieces, skinned and sliced, while all the while fresh ones took their places under the cleaver so that they too might be cut down in turn, the process lasting, it seemed for ever, blows raining down again and again. It was if every cow in the world were being driven to slaughter. There was no end to it. Budai could not go back for fear of being crushed by the incoming herd so had to move forward right through the thick of the killing, treading over skin and guts and viscera and sections of flesh, wading through blood and the steam of blood, between butchers and youths covered in blood, past blood-stained walls, past bloody pillars. He'd faint if he did not get out soon.

When finally he emerged from the hall he found himself in a corner of the courtyard. A variety of processing chambers opened on to it, rooms for sausage and salami production. There were machines for mincing the meat and turning it to slop. The further he got from the cleavers, from the indifferent industry of slaughter for the meat trade, the harder he found it to forget what he had seen. His knees were trembling and he felt so weak he had to grasp a nearby metal bar to avoid collapsing. Frail and lonely, seeking a comforting thought to help him recover from the shock, he brought to mind the lift girl puffing away at her cigarette on the top floor of the hotel. He felt very close to her now, as close as to a life-support machine. He wanted to hold her tightly, even if only in imagination. Unable to speak her language, he would never be capable of sharing his nightmare experience with her. He didn't even know how to address her in his thoughts: *Bébé*? *Tetéte*? *Epepe*?

He found the back door out of the abattoir and followed the line of a long ditch. He saw that the water in it was moving but the fallen leaves on its surface did not even tremble, simply sat there, muddied, in a mush of fermentation. Further along, rather surprisingly, the terrain became more urban once more: there were more buildings of a greater variety with a modern round-tower rising into the sky at one street corner. Could he have turned in the wrong direction after the metro station after all, or had he turned off at some stage and found himself back in one of the central districts from where the train had set out? Or was this an altogether different town? But would one be built so close to the first?

In front of him was a shoe shop where a young man, paralysed from the waist down, was sitting in a wheelchair and playing the violin – though he was losing track of events so fast he could not be sure later whether he had actually seen him or if he was a memory from some other, earlier occasion. The empty violin case was next to the wheelchair on the pavement. It was open and there was a note of some sort fixed to it whose meaning Budai tried to work out by considering the context. It must be an effective cry for pity since passers-by, as many here as elsewhere, were busily dropping coins into the case with even more coins lying on the ground. A considerable crowd had formed a circle round the young man, obstructing the traffic. The boy played reasonably well, handling the instrument with confidence and was probably a music student as the text might possibly have indicated. It was a strange melody he was playing, simple enough to be catchy, the phrases clear and packed, suggesting an aching desire for something, or at any rate that was how Budai interpreted it. Feeling in no particular hurry to move on he joined the ring of listeners. The young man in the meantime continued playing the same melody over and over again, his useless withered legs and shod feet dangling from the wheelchair. His face a trifle puffy, he bent his locks over the instrument and kept bowing away, ever the same tune, never looking up, ignoring everyone, his gaze empty above the violin. Might he have been blind?

Going by the audience response and the steady accumulation of offerings, he guessed the text on the case might have suggested something to the effect that the crippled young man was enrolled at a school for music and required support to help him continue his studies, studies he had had to abandon on account of a financial crisis. And whether this was merely what he imagined to be the situation or whether that was what the writing actually suggested – even though the whole thing might have been a confidence trick, one of many such played on the naïve susceptibilities of a credulous urban public – Budai still found it touching and was moved. True, he was feeling bereft himself with no idea how long he was doomed to tread the pavements of these endless streets with their acres of brick dwellings and countless inhabitants, but despite having decided to strictly limit his spending henceforth and to buy only what was absolutely necessary, he too threw a coin to the violinist.

Then he went on his way, forging on. Now he seemed to have arrived in an area that felt more central: the roads narrowed, there were traffic policemen on certain street corners, one or two older grand houses appeared and another tall fortress or ruined bastion of the kind he had seen before. He was tired with all the walking he had done by now but there was no park or bench on which he might sit and take a rest.

Seeking a resting place he entered a glazed and vaulted building complete with tower and dome, with four great clocks telling the same time on its dignified façade. Behind it stretched a vast long hall whose front and side doors were continually packed with people entering and leaving. The form of it was so familiar there must be one of these everywhere in the world. Might this be a railway station? Budai's heart beat faster. But there were no carriages, no engines and no platforms inside that hangar-like, enormous space, roofed with a vast cloak of glass rimmed in steel. In fact, something about the sweep and movement of the crowd suggested something quite different. And yet the whole building, at least from outside, in its main features, and, examining it more closely, even in its floor plan, resembled a station to the degree that he felt obliged to consider the possibility that it might have been planned as such, and that only later was it adapted to some other purpose. What purpose that was he could not immediately tell; the wide hall full of people must have served as a general waiting room for something. To either side, right and left, opened a series of colonnaded passages full of groups of people, some standing silently, others engaged in vigorous discussion, mostly gathered near the exit doors. There was, however, nowhere to sit down.

The glazed doors led to other, smaller areas. He forced his way into one and took a peek, A dark-suited man at a table on a raised stage sat facing an audience ranged on a row of benches. Further off in a corner of this first room stood a structure that might have been a kind of pulpit where a crop-headed black woman in a blue outfit was making a speech. There were the same arrangements in the next room where the pulpit was occupied by a tall man wearing a canvas tunic uniform. At first he thought he had wandered into a school or college, that those in the pulpit were lecturers and the rest students – but if that was the case why were they sitting there in overcoats and, anyway, how could they tolerate the constant coming and going? But he was too tired by now to think about it: he opened the door to one of the rooms at random and there being an empty place at the end of the last row, he sat down.

An insignificant-looking little man in the pulpit was explaining something in a somewhat laboured manner, his eyes rapidly blinking, having to stop now and then, getting lost, clearly unused to public speaking. From time to time another dark-suited man in the front row asked him a question, as did the man sitting on the raised platform. Budai finally guessed where he was: it was obviously a court of law, one where in all likelihood, judging by circumstances, tone and atmosphere, civil cases were being tried. The man he had first taken to be a lecturer must of course be the judge and the man asking the questions some kind of barrister, while the figure in the pulpit was the plaintiff or the accused or a witness. Beyond this there was not much he could understand, the garbled language of the place being an insuperable obstacle. It was true that he was not paying much attention; the long excursion that had begun in the early morning and the endless walking had quite exhausted him. He closed his eyes for a while. He might even have fallen asleep.

He woke with a start to hear the woman next to him standing up and loudly addressing the chair. She seemed to be making some comment on the proceedings. The woman must have been there before but he had not noticed her. She was wearing thick glasses and the eyes behind them were red and swollen as if she had been crying a lot. Despite that, she was rather handsome, not above thirty or so, with a green hat perched on her blonde bun of hair, her lips finely arched, her figure, as might be expected in her state of agitation, full, tense and desirable. She had clearly been upset by something the little blinking man had stuttered, her entire face red with excitement, her mouth partly open, ready, if necessary, to intervene again. Might he have been her husband? Could these be divorce proceedings?

The barrister asked another question and the man answered unusually firmly and immediately in a single word. That was when all hell broke loose. There was muttering in court and an elderly woman in the front row sprang to her feet waving her umbrella.

Soon everyone was shouting. The judge started ringing his bell but it was not enough to staunch the flood of passion. Budai's neighbour began to sob and an old grey man with a Kaiser Wilhelm moustache turned pathetically to the chair pointing to the woman. Uniformed guards and clerks appeared and tried to calm the situation, ushering people back to their seats, the judge continuing to ring his bell. At this point the woman in the green hat – no doubt one of those most touched by the case – pushed her way past him to the pulpit and threw herself at the man currently testifying. He clumsily tried to free himself from her. The woman staggered and cried out in pain. Now it was all fury. It was the insignificant-looking little man who looked most frightened, blinking in panic, making a grab for the woman, the expression on his face so anxious and tender it seemed quite out of character.

This time Budai made an exception and did not try to work out what was happening. Even if he had known the language he would probably have made little sense of it: it was a private matter, hopeless and infinitely complex, completely alien as far as he was concerned. It was nothing to do with him and he felt no desire to know more. Thinking this, he picked himself up, broke through the people crowding at the entrance and left.

Once out in the street he looked back at the remarkable elevation of the building and it occurred to him that if it was really intended to be railway station then it was possible that various other city stations, some of them at any rate, might be located in the same quarter, maybe on the ring road as in Moscow – and if that were the case might there not be one that had not been redeveloped for some other purpose? It was, admittedly, a long shot but a possibility nonetheless and he couldn't think of anything better. In any case he set off down the street in the direction he thought most promising, but the street soon led to a T-junction with a narrower street and he looked uncertainly right and left wondering which way to go. Or was it pointless hoping to discover a system? Might the railway stations be scattered randomly only to appear in the most unexpected places the way they did in Berlin, Paris and London? Was there perhaps one single major terminus through which most traffic was obliged to pass as in Amsterdam, Frankfurt and Rome? Or perhaps two, like Grand Central and Pennsylvania Station in New York?

He came to a square where a tall, wide church was crammed between ordinary houses, overlooking them. It looked like an ancient cathedral, an architectural monument with many towers and an enormous dome, complete with arches, buttresses, columns, balconies, friezes, statues, piers, ornamental masonry and other forms of decoration in such an eclectic welter of styles it was hard to tell when it was built, though it was likely to have been centuries ago as were most other cathedrals. There was a long queue comprised of people in pairs, at the main door, winding right round one of the aisles and disappearing. Having come so far, he felt, he should devote some time to this so he found the very back of the queue and joined it.

Pigeons strutted and spurted in dense flocks, impertinently pushing their way into the queue. Whenever they spotted anyone with breadcrumbs they did not wait for the crumbs to drop but grabbed them from people's hands, settling on their shoulders and on the top of their heads, their wings beating the air, purring, rising in clouds and settling, dropping feathers and mess everywhere. Budai tried to start a conversation with an old lady wearing a fur collar just in front of him as she was feeding the birds but he must have been speaking too quietly or else she misheard him for she simply did not react but carried on dropping crumbs, cooing to the doves until they covered her completely. And he couldn't even tell whether this great crowd was entering the church on a wave of religious enthusiasm or out of architectural curiosity.

When, after a long time – he no longer took note of how long anything took, his sense of time having been blunted – he finally reached the doors he hoped he might find a simple leaflet of the kind you'd normally find in places like this. But once through, the momentum of the thus far disciplined crowd suddenly swept him on, everyone dementedly rushing on to the various commercial stalls and salesmen stationed inside. There were oils, creams, and some suspicious-looking paste or plasticine for sale, mostly items connected with religion as far as he could make out, stuff required for local rituals as well as candles and incense, but no sign of a booklet or guide. People were pushing each other aside. Those who could grabbed a jar or little bottle and were immediately on their way back again, all knees and elbows. The sweet old woman who had been feeding the pigeons was now furiously kicking anyone who got in her way. Her worn fur collar had slipped off in the hand-to-hand struggle and was streaming behind her like a flag.

It was hard to make sense of this complex, heavily-decorated inner space so packed with believers and priests. Services were being conducted in various places, or that at least is what seemed to be indicated by the thicker knots of humanity gathered around gowned and capped figures who were busily intoning or singing. There were paintings, images, frescoes and mosaics covering the entire wall, as well as statues, stuccos, reliefs, baldachins, pulpits, booths, side chapels, arches, vaults, floors inlaid with marble, deep-piled carpets and heavy wrought-iron chandeliers everywhere, the lot in such rich profusion that he found it impossible to isolate any details. He tried to work out the dominant style in all the brilliant jumble but he didn't entirely recognise any of them, no Romanesque, no Renaissance, no Baroque as such, though he couldn't entirely rule out their influence. Not that he was any kind of expert. He couldn't even identify the specific religion or myth that the various pictures, statues and ornaments represented: there were images of men and women, young and old, mostly in ancient monkish hoods, people in groups huddling together, hunting scenes, deer, fawn, dogs, a lion, standard bearers and archers, and a knight-in-armour tussling with a serpent. The images seemed to rush at him like a sudden assault on the eyes. Though the iconography was mysterious, one thing was certain: this was neither a Christian nor a Jewish place of worship for it lacked altars, crosses and Stars of David, nor could it have been an Islamic shrine since the Koran forbids images. But if he had wandered into some other kind of Eastern temple he would have expected to find seated Buddhas or a Shiva with its various arms ... But now he was thinking of what wasn't there, not what was. For all he knew there might have been other temples elsewhere just like this. The inscriptions on the wall and elsewhere were the usual runic, perhaps with more curlicues, a more archaic form of the script he saw everywhere. The language of liturgy might relate to living speech much as Church Latin did to Italian, or Old Slavonic to modern Russian.

The ritual itself was strange, rather barbaric. Budai joined one of the biggest groups near the entrance and saw that not far away a very large fat woman was lying on a sort of table covered with a roll of dark cloth. She was dressed in her best clothes and surrounded with flowers. She did not move. She was dead. Her large pink face might have been painted for the occasion; her neck and chin were as fat as the hand resting beside her body, a well-cushioned hand, plump and puffy, the gold rings on her fingers seeming to have grown into the flesh. The crowd who had come presumably to mourn the woman had, curiously enough, turned their backs on her and were listening to the priest who at that very moment was raising a large, rattling metal dish complete with chains – it looked rather like a teapot – his voice, as he did so, taking up a mournful chant. At this sign the faithful joined in wailing, lamenting, many of them throwing themselves against the stone floor with such power Budai thought they might break their heads open. They continued moaning and weeping like this, their lamentations rising into the vaults, echoing through the whole arena, blending with waves of litany from elsewhere. Some people were in tears. A thin woman in a black headscarf collapsed in a fit of sickness and had to be helped out through the crowd.

Boys in red surplices were fixing candles around the body of the dead woman though even now the crowd paid her no attention. They were staring at the priest who spread his arms wide so the sleeves of his gown rode up to his elbows. He shut his eyes and, his face transformed in ecstasy so that he looked almost lewd, cried out the same thing twice in a harsh, loud voice. Or maybe it wasn't the same thing but two things that sounded similar, the two chiming like halves of a rhyming couplet, like this:

Zöhömö, pröhödö
Türidümi mödölnö

This drove the crowd to a point of mad excitement and even those who were standing quietly started sobbing and screaming and all but collapsed, remaining upright only because there was not enough room to fall. A gaunt old man, ripped his clothes off and threw them away, everything including his waistcoat, his shirt, his trousers and his boots, leaving himself clad only in a single chequered pair of knee-length underpants. His chest was covered in dense grey hair. His eyes were swivelling crazily this way and that.

Others were stripping off too despite the cold, even women and young girls, all apparently possessed as if offering up their nakedness ... Strangely enough Budai felt neither outraged nor even surprised by the sight: he too was feeling the trance-like urge to throw himself on the marble floor, to kick off his shoes, undo his collar and loosen his tie. A heady joy seized him at being here, at being able to take part, to melt into the great communion of the faithful.

A censer had been lit ahead of him. The priest raised it and swung it high in the air. And now, as if they had been waiting for just this signal, everyone started to press towards him though even at the peak of their religious ecstasy they approached him in pairs. Some people did try to sneak into the queue from the side aisles in order to reach their goal all the sooner but the rest wouldn't let them and pushed them back: there was real hand-to-hand combat between them for the privilege of being there first. One bowler-hatted, fat gentleman with a walking stick was cruelly trampled down in the process despite waving his arms and giving out thin little piglet-like squeals.

The point of all this pushing and shoving was to force a way through to the priest, cower at his feet and kiss the shoes that peeked out from under his robe. They were little black-lacquered shoes that must have been perfectly polished but their toecaps were quickly smeared by all the mouths that touched them. Having arrived at the front, Budai bowed down and made some pretence of putting his lips to the lacquer, shrinking back in disgust. Under his breath he gabbled a short sentence to the priest, first in Latin then in Greek, trying to use the brief moment allotted to him; then, for good measure, in Hebrew and Old Slavonic too, in fact in any language that might be employed in church ritual, anything that might be recognised by a man conversant with theology. The priest was utterly immobile, rooted to the spot, no sign on his heavy, bronze, finely-carved face that he had understood any of it. He swung the censer he was still holding above his head but Budai was being pushed from behind by a little walrus-moustached, bald, Chinese-looking man, all chest and shoulders, and had to give way so that the man might cover the priest's black-lacquered shoes with kisses.

The service seemed to be over, the congregation drifting away, so he allowed himself to be carried along. He was tired and had no energy left to ask anyone anything. He was content to go where everyone else seemed to be going. The great mass of people started to ascend a spiral staircase that led gently upwards. He chose to follow them, climbing higher and higher, round and round with them. He was gasping for air by now and his legs felt numb but everyone was moving so fast he could not help but pick up their pace, driven on in any case by curiosity to see where they would end up.

Having climbed for some time so he could no longer recall how many spirals he had described, the steps changed direction. They had emerged into a circular passageway covered by a great bell-like dome. They were actually within the cupola. The corridor rails were set sufficiently wide apart to allow him to look into the dizzy depths some eighty or hundred metres down where the jostling crowds appeared to be no more than a dark grey mass of indifferent, undifferentiated heaving matter. But it was still more dizzying to look upwards, into the narrowing eye of the dome, the curved ribs rising to the apparently infinite height of a focal point far enough away to make the heart beat faster: it was at least as high again as the point he was looking at it from.

He had to go round the whole dome following the direction indicated by innumerable arrows. The tour then took him through another door, to another set of stairs that were much narrower and steeper than the ones before, people following each other in zig-zags through the shell structure. Then the stairs came to an end and one could only progress by ladders. Then the ladders too vanished leaving only narrow planks and precarious breakneck rope-ladders, ever more exhausting, requiring ever more stamina to climb until one might as well have been a circus acrobat to master them. But there was no turning back because there were people behind him, following him in an endless single file as far as he could see.

He must be close to the top now, he calculated, and indeed he found himself clambering up a last set of vertical steps into a round space surrounded by windows. This would have been the small cylindrical room intended to illuminate the area below: its technical name, he remembered now, was the lantern. Above it, at the highest point of the temple, was the eye of the dome, a little cap or hood of glass. A solitary rope ladder led up to it. The eye could accommodate only one person's head and shoulders as he stood at the top rung. The discomfort was worth it, however, for the view. It offered a complete panorama.

The sun was going down. Budai could almost feel the sky turning an inky-blue-black though it was impossible to tell whether that was because of the smoke-and-soot-polluted air or because of a large rain cloud louring over the rooftops. The city spread over a plain into distances further than the eye could see. Whichever way he turned there was no end to it, nothing but houses and apartment blocks, streets, squares, towers, old and new quarters of town, mildewy storm-battered rented barracks and skyscrapers faced with modern marble, main roads and alleys, factories, workshops, gasometers and the clumsy-looking great hall that he recognised even from here as the slaughterhouse. And chimneys, chimneys everywhere he looked; chimneys like so many long-necked dragons stretching towards the sky, spouting white, black, yellow and purple smoke. The wind carried the smoke, churned it, thrust it into dirty bundles and shreds, chasing it here and there even around his look-out point. The wind battering at the dome was cold and fierce, making its ribs creak and groan beneath him, the lantern visibly swaying. Wind swept through the little cage where Budai was stationed. He shivered and trembled but remained, unable to drag himself away from the view.

He looked in vain though for any sign of railway tracks or terminals. It was dark of course and getting darker so it was hard to make out detail. Nor could he see a river or a bridge, let alone a shore, however he peered. There were, perhaps, only a few reservoirs of the kind he had passed twinkling for a few seconds in a late stray sunbeam before sinking back into the obscure depths. He thought of looking for the vacant plots he had crossed earlier, believing them to be the edges of town. He caught sight of one in the very last moment before it finally vanished, a narrow strip or band of derelict greeny-brown among heavily built-up areas. But what it divided from what, whether it was in fact a division of some sort or had any geographical significance at all remained a puzzle he could not begin to solve ... He was no wiser for the panoramic view. Could he have found his way into another town or was it the same place?

Whatever the answer, he decided he would go no further that day. Not primarily because of his exhaustion: as far as that was concerned he could continue; he had, after all, plenty of stamina and determination, having kept fit at home by engaging in various sports and developing the discipline to stick to a chosen target without sparing himself or indulging in feelings of self-pity. But he knew that he could find his way back to the hotel from the temple and was less likely to do so from further off, especially in darkness. He would find it impossible to keep all the various landmarks in mind. And if he had really wandered into another town, what hope or assurance had he that he would find his way round this one more easily? The language, the alphabet and other such details would be just as incomprehensible and it was exactly the same indifferently jostling crowd here as there. Ideally he would start again at the very beginning, take proper bearings, gather the right information, get used to the traffic system and give up the lifestyle he had so carefully and painstakingly constructed for himself at home. He hadn't anything to his name here, no back up. Where could he spend the night but at the hotel and, if he were forced to ask for accommodation elsewhere, how would he frame his request?

The lights started coming on in blocks, each estate or major road in one go, all the tiny pieces slowly fitting together as an entire lit area rose out of the grey-blue. There was no end of it as far as he could see. In the far distance the rows and clusters of illumination melted into a single mass, its edges lost in glimmering fogs and milky galaxies like the stars in the Milky Way whose light comes to us from a distance of thousands or millions of light years ... Budai had been a city dweller all his life, the city, for him, being the only possible place of work, routine and entertainment. He was constantly drawn to the great cities of the world: the metropolis! And while the proportions of this one horrified and imprisoned him, he could not deny its sheer enormous urban beauty. Looking down on it from such a height he was almost in love with it.

Budai had accumulated a number of texts since he first arrived, texts that he thought might prove useful in studying the local written language. First were the notices he had ample opportunity to observe on the hotel walls that probably referred to house rules. He also had a newspaper that he had bought on his first Sunday evening in one of the downtown areas but hadn't yet looked at. For now, however, he was concentrating on the receipt the hotel had given him on his payment of the first bill, that being the only piece of writing to hand that offered some clue as to what it might say. He had already noticed that the totals were indicated in numerals only, not in letters, but he still thought it worth closer study.

The printed form had the figure 921 at the very top among a group of unintelligible notes. Presumably the figure referred to the payer since he was the occupier of the room referred to but whether the rest of it was his name – that is to say if they knew him by name at all – was beyond proof or falsification, at least on the basis of his examination so far. He tried to figure out what each column might stand for and how they had arrived at the total of 35.80. The biggest figure would no doubt be the cost of the room and the rest would probably relate to it, including telephone charges or perhaps the heating or some kind of tax. But he couldn't find a particularly significant amount: 5.40 was the biggest, the others including 2.70, 3.80 and so forth. There would have to have been some multiplication too, the per-night figure times seven for the week since he had received the bill precisely a week after he had arrived. But despite going through it untold times he was unable to find evidence of any such operation, neither multiplication nor addition.

And so he started looking for the date, checking the top and bottom of the sheet: nothing of the kind there. It was impossible that there should be no date – could it be part of the text, written out in letters? But why? Or was this the custom here? ... Then he thought again and concentrated only on the printed columns but no one had filled them in by hand. He supposed that the reason these columns were empty was that they were for services he hadn't required, such as breakfast, laundry, ironing and so forth. Stuck for ideas, he tried to isolate individual groups of letters hoping blindly to guess what each was, but that was no good of course because he would first have to know how they sounded in the local language. That's when it struck him how short the words were, most of them consisting of one or two characters and not much more. Might they be abbreviations? In so far as they were, they would have been common enough for him to notice in other texts he had seen about the place, such as electricity or telephone bills, though if that was the kind of thing they were, his task would be extraordinarily difficult, not to say impossible.

So he studied the newspaper instead, examining it, turning the pages over and over wondering what he could learn by studying them. But as he was doing this he had a peculiar and nasty surprise. Up to this moment he had worked on the assumption that the characters here would read from left to right, the lines from top to bottom as in Latin and other European scripts. That is what the bill, the house rules and the phone book he had pinched from the desk-clerk, the one that later disappeared from his room, told him. But now that he examined the paper more closely all kinds of doubts assailed him. For the name of the paper – in much bigger and bolder type – was not only at the top of the front page but also on the back page, precisely as it was on the front. So where to start reading? From the front? From the back? From the top or vice versa? Or maybe it could be read in mixed order, like Ancient Greek, in *boustrophedon* or 'ox-turning' manner where the direction of writing changes in every line, now left to right, now right to left?

Or might it be that this newspaper was produced in a different language using a different script from the others? He tried a random test, picking out a letter here, a letter there and right from the beginning he found correspondences. He understood it less and less ... But there was no date here either, not in figures at least, and however he looked there was no way of telling whether this or that group of letters referred to the name of the city or the place where the newspaper was printed. Should he look for it in the title? Below it? Above? It seemed logical that such information should be displayed somewhere near the title, but which title, the one at the front or the one at the back?

Then he thought of something else. He took out his remaining cash and sorted it by denomination. The notes showed portraits of unknown people, some landscapes with unfamiliar buildings seen from a distance, a few allegorical figures and some decorative motifs as most banknotes tended to do. Nor did the coins differ much from coins elsewhere: female heads, sheaves of corn, flowers, birds. He tried to work out the names of numbers by examining the text under the numerals for that is where they should have been on the notes. But there was a lot of writing there of various sorts, the entire banknote crowded with letters, words and phrases of various sizes, including reproductions of scrawled signatures. These might have referred to almost anything: the issuing bank or institution or the state itself, possibly the legislature by whose order the notes appeared. Perhaps he could find the usual formula to the effect that on presentation of this banknote the possessor was entitled to receive such and such amount, that forgery was a punishable offence and a good many other statements that are at times included – but whatever the case there was too much here to be certain of anything.

It looked more promising to study the inscriptions on coins: coins, as far as he could remember – and indeed according to his experience of other countries – usually contained only the numeral, the unit of currency and the name of the state that had minted them. He jingled his change: there were 50s, 20s and 10s. The writing on all of them however was circular, on the perimeter, without any gaps, the end, wherever it was, leading back to the beginning. Given this, he not only failed to discover the name of the currency but even where he should start reading the various characters.

He wasn't going to get anywhere like this: it was like going around blindfolded, seeing nothing ... Should he set about writing down such individual letters as he could discern in the various inscriptions? And what good would that do? It was pointless, he hadn't enough material to work on, not a single solid piece of information on which he could build a case or develop a view, nothing to go on at all. He needed a dictionary, or some bilingual piece of text, some brochure or other.

He should look for a bookshop then, which is what he did, searching the town until he found one. True, he had a feeling that he had seen one in the course of his earlier explorations, in the quarter behind the building site with the skyscraper – which he found had reached the sixty-ninth floor. The streets were narrow there and the traffic was dense even by local standards, people packed together, the crush before certain shops almost life-threatening. He might have stumbled into the end-of-season sales. He had left home in mid-February and sales were generally held at the end of winter there too. All round him salesmen were crying their wares even out on the pavement, offering suits, knitwear and underwear at a clearly reduced price: shoppers rushed them, surrounded them in tight impermeable groups, the merchandise passing from hand to hand, in and out of boxes and cases as people bargained for them, everything mixed up and confused. The shops too were full to bursting point. Some had pulled down their shutters so as to keep more from entering but there was a scramble even in front of these, people shouting at those inside, clinging to the ironwork, some managing to push the shutters up and forcing their way in, ever more waves of them, pressing through, ever denser, ever more crushed. Here were vast numbers of shoes, carpet slippers and stockings on offer along with many other items. A blind sweet-vendor was repeating his trade cry in a high, falsetto, sing-song.

Things were no different at the bookshop. Hordes were picking over towers of books, some searching the piles on the floor, some at the tables, some taking books off stands and discarding them just anywhere, throwing up great clouds of dust while others clambered up steps to examine the top shelves. It was such a chaotic state of affairs that Budai couldn't work out which among them was the vendor. Jammed as he was in the crowd he tried in vain to address various customers, even bellowing in their ears but there was so much extraneous noise no one took any notice of him. People were either reading or browsing. It was only after he had spent a considerable time casting his eye about that he spotted a fat, liverish-looking man with a fleshy nose in the depths of the shop. The man wore a soft leather coat and drew attention to himself by being particularly loud and aggressive: he was busily putting books out, wrapping them and tying them up with string while at the same time vigorously bargaining, now taking books from the pile, now adding to it. He might just as easily have been selling potatoes or tomatoes. There was certainly no great opportunity here to explain anything or make a request, not even to point to something for however he tried to get close to the liverish man and make him understand what he wanted there were always others swarming around him, all talking at once. Whatever Budai had to say was lost in the hubbub.

So he too started searching the stands hoping to come across a dictionary or at least a bilingual publication such as a travel guide, anything in a language he might recognise so that he could hold it open and explain to the owner that it was in fact a dictionary he wanted. But however many books he took down they were all in the same runic writing. Most of them were old antiquarian copies in various shapes with various bindings, often ragged and squashed, but there were also some almost new books with uncut pages. He tried to determine the direction of the text in these, left to right or vice versa, as he suspected had been the case with the newspaper. Simply leafing through the books like this offered no clue either way though there were some that seemed to have two title pages, one at the front and one at the back, or perhaps it was the main title page at one end and the half-title at the other.

Here too there were reductions in price, the numbers written on the inside of the back cover being ruled out with ink and smaller figures inserted. But even so the prices looked frighteningly high compared to the cash he had in his pocket. The lowest were priced 3 or 4, the rest at 10, 15 and 25, which was more than he had altogether. He carried on browsing for over an hour flicking through a great variety of books. There were volumes of verse, things that looked like novels, small press publications, popular books in cloth and paper bound editions, technical and scientific material printed on shiny paper about what was likely to be an extraordinary range of fields, not to mention diploma works on chemistry and mathematics complete with diagrams and footnotes, the textual parts of which might have been worth studying in greater detail were he not so abysmally ignorant of their subjects. There were also periodicals of uncertain content, complete runs of them, bound catalogues with serial numbers and endless notes and figures indicating who knows what; folios of drawings and caricatures of people he did not recognise, some with indecipherable signatures and even a few lines of verse; theatre and concert programmes; magazines about this or that wholly unfamiliar actress photographed in various costumes; then children's books, story books – if that is what they were – and maybe a few school text-books too, and much else ... But he did not come across a single book written in another language, not even in part. For want of anything more helpful he would have taken a handbook of grammar but he found not one among the many thousands on thousands of books on sale.

All this was depressing enough and exhausting too with all the pushing, shoving and noise, though everything would immediately have been all right if he could have explained his need for a dictionary. The crush was such that he failed to make any sort of contact with the dealer who was surrounded by an impatient crowd of customers. He tried communicating with him but simply could not get his attention. Having had enough of this farce and judging any further attempt to be pointless he finally chose a book for himself. He had just enough time to catch the dealer's eye, show him the book and pay him the money.

The book seemed to be a collection of short stories, that at least was what the typography suggested, that and the amount of dialogue in the text. Here, however, unlike in the other books, the writing ran unambiguously from left to right and top to bottom as he could tell by the titles of the stories and the way the beginnings and ends were presented. The book was not particularly thick and the price was relatively low too, a mere 3.50. The cover showed an exotic landscape in green and blue pastel colours: a bay, palm trees, a hillside with a crowd of white villas, roof rising above roof in the background. It might have been the deep blue water and the wide horizon that first attracted him. The flap carried a photograph, presumably of the author, a man of about forty or so in a polo-neck jumper, his face round, his hair cut short, his body relaxed, apparently unposed. He was standing in front of a slatted fence, his eyes narrowing, his expression tired or slightly bored, with a slightly mocking smile playing about his lips as if he were in the act of suppressing a yawn. Everything about the image looked familiar but he couldn't remember where he had seen it. In any case, his look, his pose, his general appearance was clearly that of a contemporary writer, Budai felt, which might have been another reason he had noticed the book. He wouldn't, after all, get far with an old work using archaic language or with one written in high poetic manner, nor with anything technical, scientific, jargon-laden, specialist, didactic or abstract. What he needed was something written in contemporary colloquial language, the sort of language spoken on the street, which he would have to learn word by word. The most likely books, in fact the only books properly fit for the purpose, would be short stories or something like them.

Once back home he stopped in the hotel lobby and studied the maps displayed in the gift shops. There were various kinds for sale, almost all different, and he was suddenly confused as to which he should choose. He picked up one at random and opened it out, assuming it would show the city. But he found it hard to orientate himself in it: the streets and squares looked tiny in the densely scrawled plan that entirely filled the sheet and there was no sign of the outskirts of town where estates should thin out, or was this perhaps a map of the inner city only, or of a single postal district? He saw no railway lines, at least none of the thin black lines that normally represented them. Nor was there a river, not at least in the area covered by the map, only a few tiny dots of blue that might have been municipal ponds or the water reservoirs he had seen here and there. In the bottom right-hand corner of the map he found a long narrow light blue band that would clearly have continued on another sheet, the other end of which, however, snaked on until it simply stopped, thereby dashing Budai's hopes that it might represent flowing water. It must have been at most a minor tributary of some distant river though there was no way of being certain of that. More likely it was a ditch of the kind he walked past near the slaughterhouse.

He would like to have discovered the hotel on it and to work out its relationship to the maps he saw in the underground. But how could he begin to do so when he didn't even know which way up to hold it? He couldn't remember which end was the top when he picked it up. He had noted down the name of the metro station nearest the hotel; it was just that he couldn't find it on the map. He couldn't even see metro lines, neither the continuous line nor the dotted one normally used to indicate networks that ran underground. There were no single or double circles, empty or full, with or without a single line through them that stood for stations on other maps. Most cities, he recalled, represented metro stops with a capital M. Yes, but what letter was the equivalent of M here? Or could it be that the quarter of town represented had never historically possessed an underground system? Might it be that this wasn't a local map at all? But then what town was it?

He turned one of the folds over to see what lay there. It contained a dense body of text in various colours and sizes but it was not immediately apparent which of them was the most important, that is to say, the town or district. For even the words in the biggest font might have meant a range of things such as New, or Latest, or Map, or perhaps Cartographic Office. This or that word might be the name of the company, the street, the number of the building, or simply Welcome! or Greetings! or Be Our Guest! or maybe even, Happy New Year, or whatever else could or might be printed on such a document. They could have been advertisements for beer or vermouth or chocolate or perhaps for a restaurant or a hotel ... The letters, legends and numbers on the map itself were tiny and covered every millimetre of every street: he'd have needed a magnifying glass to see them clearly. The thought was so daunting he didn't even want to begin.

He turned to the saleswoman instead and tried, by miming, to get her to point out the name of the city on the map or where the hotel was or, if they did not appear on the map, to direct him to one where they did. But the woman was already looking at him rather crossly, no doubt thinking him picky, intrusive or attention-seeking while others were requiring her attention at the desk. However he tried she was unwilling to engage with him but simply grumbled something and waved him away. Even when Budai rattled his change at her and asked the price of the map she took some persuading to write down the figure 12 on a scrap of paper. Budai paid up and quickly left, mumbling and cursing at the cost.

Having cooled down, he started to wonder whether a map would really be useful. He couldn't even be certain that the map was of this town, and if it was, of which district. Were the effort and expense worth it? Would they help him achieve his aims? Would they, in any case, be the most direct way of achieving them? Wasn't there a quicker, more effective, more productive way? Nevertheless he returned to his room to begin a proper, thorough examination, making best use of modern scientific method and his own expertise. He was determined to employ the tools he had to hand, combining them to maximum effect to decode the local language and whatever variants of it existed.

Since arriving Budai had often regretted that he had paid such little attention to the history of writing and even less to cryptography. He had specialised in etymology, the study of the origin of words. However, he now recalled that, as a child, he had read Jules Verne and that Verne gave various accounts of the deciphering of secret messages. In *Mathias Sandor* it is a grid that helps solve the case, in *Journey to the Centre of the World* it is the principle underlying a certain rearrangement of a set of letters. More recently, in reading of the two world wars, he had learned that the secret services had developed mathematical and statistical models to produce perfect decoding systems capable of deciphering any given enemy message. Any code, even the most convoluted, was breakable by such methods. The code-breakers were working with languages they knew, of course, languages that had been merely disguised and reordered; that was why they could come up with the keys required to unlock the text. Budai, on the other hand, was faced with a language utterly unknown to him so that even if he succeeded in reading it he would not be able to make sense of it.

It was true that the ingenuity and patience of historical researchers had managed to solve even puzzles of this sort, and not only in the cases already mentioned when they were dealing with a range of languages. There were, for example, two great pieces of scientific bravura this century, the decoding of Hittite script and of the Cretan so-called Linear B, both from the all-but-unknown scripts of hitherto unknown ancient people. Nevertheless the qualifier all-but had offered a starting point, the slightest of nudges enabling scholars to take a first step. The clay tablets of the Hittites contained a good number of ideograms that could be identified with those in the earlier-deciphered Babylonian script. And the solver of Cretan Linear B, the English scholar Ventris, was able to employ these correspondences – clearly verifiable after some examination – by checking them against the long-solved runic of Cyprus. So one thing led to another and, after various speculations and combinations, this first selection of sound-equivalent syllable-characters made possible the working out of the rest. In other cases scholars had good reason to assume the recurrence of certain proper nouns in the various texts, such as the names of ancient Knossos and

Amnisos on the Cretan tablets: that was a decisive element in their success.

Budai's task was made still more difficult by the lack of any single recognisable character or any related script on which he might base a working theory. Not that he could actually conjure up memories of the various, mostly long-disused runes he had never properly studied. He had no hypothesis, nothing tangible, not a word or a name that could serve as a faint guiding light. But shouldn't there have been one somewhere?

In determining the nature of a text the first consideration must be the number of characters used. Systems where a single word represents a concept tend to have a great many: Chinese, for example, supposedly employs 50,000 of them. Systems using syllables would, naturally, need fewer. The previously mentioned Ancient Cretan uses eighty-nine, Cypriot script forty-four, modern Japanese 140. Systems that rely on individual letters, like modern European ones, require even fewer; English has twenty-six, Russian thirty-two, French twenty-two, and so forth.

So he set about scribbling down as many characters as he could find in the book. These quickly exceeded a hundred without showing any sign of running out. Did that mean the script employed syllables? Individual groups of characters seemed too long for that. Was each character a word? He carried on working but his collection of signs seemed ever more difficult to sort into groups and examine. He started to wonder whether he had written out the same thing several times.

Having got to number 237 he lost hope of ever coming to an end and gave up. Now he tried another way, picking out characters at random and making quick improvised calculations to work out what characters occurred most or least frequently. Assuming that there tended to be fewer vowels than consonants, there should be more of the former. In Hungarian, for example, the commonest letters were e and a, followed by t, s, n, and l, the least common being x, q, and w. It would be different for different languages of course. The only problem was that if it turned out to be syllabic script each character was bound to comprise at least one consonant and one vowel and then all his efforts would be in vain.

Another question occurred to him. Did this language contain articles as Ancient Greek, Arabic, Hebrew, English, German, Italian, Spanish – and a variety of other languages – did? Because, if it did, he could use that as a starting point. Better still, it would be easier to detect such things in written text than in speech where the sound of the article might merge with the sound of the noun. The way the blue-uniformed lift girl pronounced her name on the eighteenth floor might have been a clue: it sounded longer the second time, *Etyetye*, *Pepepe* or whatever. Might there have been an article there? That *e, pe* or *tye*? And how might it be written? If he could discover that, he would have one or two letters that he might be able to read, even if only as ancillaries.

That was what he looked for now: short, identical or similar words that might be assumed to appear at the head of longer rows of words, at the beginnings of sentences or paragraphs, for example. But however he leafed through the newspaper and the newly acquired book, he found few such characters and even when he did discover some that seemed to resemble each other, they comprised five or six characters at least, which seemed to suggest that they were not articles. There was a group that might perhaps have served as such, a little word that did recur and consisted of two characters only but invariably it turned up at the end of paragraphs and at the end of certain chapters or short stories. He remembered that in Romanian, Bulgarian, Albanian and Mordvine an end-sign took the place of the article – could that be the case here? Or might there be no articles at all, as in Latin, Finnish, Chinese or the Slavonic languages? This little closing word might be the equivalent of a phrase or utterance such as the Latin *dixi*, or the *uff,* familiar from Indian novels.

If the words for yes and no exist in a language then it may be assumed that *no* should turn up relatively often. It is the same for how and but and and although they might be combined with other words, such as the Latin – *que*. He had once read that in Hungarian the most common agglutinating substantives are people, house, flat, country and so forth. But would that be the same here? And if so, how should he fish these out or sift them from the ocean of text before him? How would he be able to tell which was which?

What if he could hack his way into this jungle of language by studying the syntax? In order to do this he would have to look out for groups of characters that were similar but not identical. If, for example, the first few were similar but the latter part different, then one might assume that these were various inflexions or agglutinations.

He spent a whole day looking into this kind of thing, neatly noting down everything in columns for easier scrutiny. He found mostly those where only the first two or three elements were the same. Of course he couldn't exclude the possibility that these were individual words, their resemblance merely coincidental, such as *batter* and *battle*, or like the English *six* and *sister*. But if they were root-words or syllables, exactly as he hoped they were, then what did the various agglutinations mean? Were they substantives, verbal inflections, formative syllables, notations, postpositions? Might they represent differences of gender as in the case of the French *directeur* and *directrice*? It might be that what he took to be root was verbal prefix, or the first term of an agglutination comprising several parts. Or indeed much else.

If, however, the last syllable matched – for he did come across some in his enquiries that did – it was possible to image that these were different words with one kind of inflection. In Hungarian, for example, there were *szobában* (in the room), *házban* (in the house), *városban* (in the town), or *szobának* (for the room), *háznak* (for the house) and *városnak* (for the town) and many others that worked in similar ways depending on how many inflections there were available in the language. But there was no way of establishing what suffix corresponded with what inflection or how they were to be sounded. It all lacked foundation. And what if it was not a case of inflection but simply a coincidental rhyme, such as paper and caper in English, and what about damper and hamper, not to mention pamper and the like? It might have been a verb that took a prefix, such as undergoing, thoroughgoing, partygoing and masses of other such, to judge by the thirty-odd languages he could more or less read. But then back to the basic problem: how to establish what was what?

It was no use: the whole thing was sterile, a series of guesses with practically nothing guaranteed. He'd not get far with vague theories, logic, hopeful chance substitutions and games of patience, or if he did get anywhere it would be at a snail's pace. And even if he was capable of the titanic effort of performing correct calculations based on notions of statistical probability, calculations that required endless supplies of energy, even if he did somehow succeed not only in assembling an alphabet but in solving all the associated phonetic problems without utterly exhausting himself – an achievement that was nowhere in sight for he had not yet identified a single letter – that would still not mean he understood any of the language. Scholars can, for example, read the ancient Etruscan script without difficulty, but not even the finest minds employing the most up-to-date means have yet succeeded in making sense of the language, bar a few dozen words and two or three grammatical features. Furthermore, the very origins of the language, its place in the family of languages, remained mysterious and controversial – and this local *epepe* might be an idiomatic expression just as isolated and unrelated to other idioms and languages as did the Etruscan to the Basque or some of the African to Caucasian tongues.

On the other hand he was certainly in a far better position than someone having to reconstruct a dead language. Such a scholar would have only remnant texts to work with and would therefore be forced to rely on indirect, circuitous, speculative and fruitless experimental methods. Budai was confronted with a living language, that symphony of a million voices available in street, square, hotel and metro: he simply had to pay close enough attention and distinguish between specific strains and tones and score them later. Thinking this, he put the newspaper and other printed matter aside, for the moment at least, and decided to keep his ears open.

He could after all learn the language from any of the city's inhabitants, slowly picking out words, absorbing the rules of grammar and so on, if only someone were willing to spend enough time with him. But courtesy and helpfulness seemed to be in short supply in a population that was constantly rushing and jostling: he needed someone to whom he could explain what he wanted, someone who just once paid attention to his attempts at deaf-and-dumb mime. That was what no one had time for. No one seemed capable of such human contact. Although there was one, just possibly, one ...

He began by writing down the first ten numbers, hurrying out to the lift, finding Pepé, having her take him up to the top floor, then holding out the sheet of paper while pointing to the 1. It wasn't clear what the girl replied and he was sure she hadn't understood him or what he wanted, because she laughed, lit a cigarette and shrugged her shoulder saying something like:

'Tuulli ulumúlu alaulp tleplé ...'

That couldn't be the name of a number. Budai did not let it rest there. He raised his thumb then showed her a one-unit banknote and waited. Bébé gave a shorter answer this time, a one-syllable answer.

'Dütt!'

He went on to 2, 3, 4 and so on, noting down each answer phonetically. He had got as far as ten when the lift buzzer sounded. There must have been a lot of people down there. Just to be certain he pointed to the 1 again but this time the girl gave quite a different answer.

'Shümülükada.'

This confused him. Did this word mean 1 or was it the word she gave before? The buzzer sounded ever more impatiently. The girl stubbed out her cigarette and gestured to show she was sorry but had to go. He tried to persuade her by means of gestures that it was a matter of urgency. Please come back if you can, I will wait here for you, he meant to say. She hesitated a moment. Budai must have looked so desperate it must have communicated itself to her across the chasm between their languages. Edede nodded solemnly and gave a flick of her blonde eyelashes to signal that it was all right, she understood.

It was half an hour before the lift door hummed open again and the girl reappeared. Budai went over the same numbers but was not satisfied with the answers. Only two or three of them sounded as they did before. True, it was hard to pinpoint the names of the numbers in Tete's speech because she usually answered not with one word but with others that might mean something like good, that's fine, yes, so there you are, I understand, just a moment, I've already said that or any other sentence-filling phrasal gesture of the conversational kind. Maybe there were several words for the same number, just as in certain languages the figure 0 can be indicated by nil, zero, nought or even love?

After this he kept going out to the lift waiting for Gyegyegye to turn up – even after repeated enquiries he had not managed to work out her precise name – so that they might continue their language classes. The girl had to work, of course, conveying a never-ending stream of passengers up or down, and someone no doubt would be keeping eyes on her to make sure she was doing it properly. Because of this they could only spend brief periods of time on the top floor and even then the lift was constantly being called in a way that got on Budai's nerves. Sometimes he got back on the lift with her, having no alternative but to ride up and down in the eternally emptying and filling compartment as if he too were an arriving or departing guest. She would be fully occupied operating the lift, even having the odd telephone conversation with someone, possibly receiving instructions, so it was only occasionally that she could let him know with a flick of her eyes that she knew he was there and hadn't forgotten him ... The single fan in the lift did little to solve the problem of ventilation. It was one of the reasons he could hardly wait to get back to the eighteenth floor again, desperate to get a breath of fresh air and discover this or that snippet of information from the girl.

Strangely enough, not for a moment did she question the role Budai had allotted her. Indeed she was clearly ready and willing to act as his language tutor as though this were her responsibility, something she was positively aching to do. As soon as they got to the top floor she lit a cigarette, blew out the smoke and stood ready to help, prepared to answer any question he might have, though it would not have been a simple task for her either, trying to make sense of his scribbles and gestures. Surely she must be wondering what this guest was wanting with his impenetrable foreign words and phrases, what it was he was really after. Maybe she felt it was up to her to look after him, that she alone was capable of helping – or was it some other instinct that drove her?

However he tried Budai could not work out the precise terms of her employment or whether she had a fixed routine. There were times he could not find her when his life seemed empty, barren and pointless: it frightened him to think how vague his own place in the world was. He made no effort to experiment with other people, thinking it would only confuse him now and cast into doubt the tiny amount he thought he might have learned. And after all Dédé's kindness and patience it would have felt a little like infidelity.

He didn't flatter himself that he could stop the first person in the street and simply ask them to teach him the language: he already knew that was out of the question. There were a lot of drunks out there, especially after dark, not only in the street but in the metro, as well as in the hotel lobby: men and women, reeling about, singing, shouting, arguing, swearing and fighting – not much point asking them. It was chiefly the evenings he feared when his hotel room felt like a prison. If only he had something to read in whatever language as long as he understood it!

He couldn't really spend all his time trying to solve the obscure wherewithal of texts of which he did not recognise a single letter. He lacked the determination, he lacked the detachment: he feared going mad. In any case, to go out was to risk missing the girl: there were times when she worked both mornings and nights. But he couldn't just sit around in his room doing nothing: he was constantly restless, anxious to carry on researching and sniffing out the truth, to come and go, fearing that if he simply stood still no one would look for him.

So he spent most of his time in the lobby keeping track of the movements of the lift. The vast hall was always full, even at night, people sitting in armchairs, dozing or teetering sleepily to and fro. The queue at reception was always long with ever more guests carrying ever more luggage. What was strange was that he had only seen luggage enter the hotel: nothing seemed to leave it. Guests must be departing all the time, their luggage must be somewhere. Perhaps if he were to investigate that ... Might the luggage be carried out through another door? And where would that door be? Surely it could not be that people arrived here never to leave?

He glanced up and spotted the delegation of exotic hierarchs he had seen that first morning, that motley crew of bearded, brilliantly dark-skinned, caftan-and-chain-wearing elders in high fur caps, who were once more proceeding in silent and dignified manner past respectful crowds that opened before them. Nothing they wore hinted at what part of the world they came from or indeed which religion they represented.

He took a short walk in the street, passing the fat doorman who always greeted him by raising his hand to his cap. He only went as far as the skyscraper in construction to see how far they had got. They were still working away at great pace, armies of builders swarming over the structure, welders sparkling, mobile platforms rising and sinking under floodlights. It was odd that the building had only grown by an extra floor since he had last seen it and counted the floors – they had got to seventy – though he had been here longer.

There was just as much bustle at night as at any other time. People were constantly pouring in and out of the metro, great ranks of exhausted workers, their faces puffy with sleep, heading towards industrial estates on the outskirts to their dawn occupations. Others were merely dawdling, drifting along aimlessly, bumping into each other on corners or in squares, getting involved in arguments, discussing sporting events or waiting for the morning papers. There were syrupy alcoholic drinks on sale, the kind that had made him drunk before. He would have welcomed a little alcohol, the tipsy light-headedness it offered, the lack of responsibility it conferred, but he stood by his resolution and was thrifty with his money, what remained of it.

Far in the distance he noticed the same neon lights alternating between red and blue. What might they be advertising? From a basement room nearby there rose something he had thus far missed: the sound of drums and music, waves of general noise. Out of curiosity he looked in. It was a large room, a kind of dance hall packed to the rafters, though owing to the smoke, the racket and the crowds that filled every nook and cranny, he couldn't make out where the floor was. People were dancing between the tables, at the bar, by the wall and on the steps leading down. Of course it was mainly the young wearing the brightly fashionable or ostentatiously ragged universal uniform of youth. It wasn't just boys dancing with girls, but girls with girls and boys with boys too. They weren't really in pairs: it was more everyone with everyone, all higgledy-piggledy yet each alone, each an island unto himself or herself in the general movement. The sexes were hard to distinguish in any case, many of the boys sporting long feminine hairstyles, a lot of the girls in trousers. Apart from that, it seemed the whole world was there, each part of it, every human race represented by someone, all mixed up topsy-turvy, tugging and shrugging, kicking up heels, waving arms to the rhythm of the music.

There was no trace of musicians though: it must have been a record-player or some similar equipment. It was unbearably loud, non-stop, one piece exactly like another, consisting entirely of beat with practically no trace of melody, the whole thing broken, syncopated, aggressive, shameless, rhythmic. But it was the volume above all that hurt Budai, his head almost exploding with it: he couldn't understand how people could bear the constant pounding.

He was about to leave when there was a kind of disturbance or panic by the far wall. At first he couldn't tell what precisely it was, it was just that the movement was different, no longer to the rhythm of the music. After a few seconds he realised the cause of it: a fight had broken out, and, as the space cleared, he could see it was between blacks and whites. He had no idea what it was about and could only guess, for no very good reason, that the slim, straw-blonde girl who appeared for a moment between the groups of brawlers, the one with the indifferent, mocking expression on her face, had something to do with it.

By the time Budai noticed it it was practically over, the groups having been separated from each other. Officials appeared as if from nowhere, uniformed men wearing those ubiquitous brown boiler suits. They blew whistles and formed a line that served as a living barrier between the two camps. Despite this, the groups continued threatening each other with unchecked fury, trying to break the line, pulling faces and screaming. Budai was curious as to what they were saying, it might well help him in his quest for understanding. As far as he could make out under the music – for that had gone on uninterrupted – the imprecations and challenges consisted of raising one's fists and shouting something like:

'Gyurumba!... Ugyurumbungya!'

This could mean any number of things, like: Filth! Dickhead! Bastard! You just wait! Come on then! I'll smash your face in! Oh yeh?! All the same, Budai noted them down in his book phonetically along with the range of possible meanings.

At that point one of the white youths, a thickset young man in a pullover, reached across the line of boiler-suited figures and before anyone could stop him smashed a bottle in the face of a lanky black boy. There was a shattering sound – was it the bottle breaking or bones? The man who had been hit swayed about with dark red blood running down his dark face. The security men – or whatever they were – blew their whistles excitedly and tried to press forward to separate the combatants. But now, on the other side of the barrier, one of the other black boys snapped his flick-knife open, ducked under the linked hands of the guards and, lightning-quick, stabbed the man in the pullover. The man who had been stabbed looked around with a foolish, startled expression, wondering what had happened. He pressed his palm to his waist where the blade had penetrated and slowly, very slowly, fell forward and doubled up with the same blank stare of incredulity that this should have happened to him of all people. His body soon grew still in his companions' arms, the look on his face unchanged.

A siren started outside: it would have been police or the ambulance. The girl's blonde hair floated briefly through the mêlée, then the police burst in, their feet drumming on the stairs, using rubber truncheons to clear the way. Budai had no desire to resume his acquaintance with them. He sneaked away as best he could. However disturbing the scene had been he had not forgotten that his chief business was with Epépé. He didn't want to be away too long since she might be back on the lifts by now. He headed back to the hotel.

She was not there so he tried the telephone in his room again. He had a few numbers now that generally answered at night and he could even recognise one or two of the voices. It was a strange, dreamlike experience conversing with someone without being able to understand a word of the language. He rang them time and again. He was nourishing a hope that the voice at the end of the line might eventually give his own number as people often did when they had been misdialled. In actual fact, of course, it was impossible to sort the mumble and jabber from the information he was seeking and yet, despite the pointlessness of the exercise, he enjoyed saying hello, asking questions, listening to the person at the other end, knowing that he too was being listened to and imagining what kind of person it was ... Interestingly enough there were some people who didn't put the phone down for a while, who, despite knowing there was no sense in carrying on the conversation, nevertheless entered the spirit of this absurd game – perverts of some sort possibly. Or maybe they were simply bored with nothing better to do.

One time though, just as he was preparing to call someone, the telephone rang. This surprised him so much he suddenly felt terrified and did not dare lift up the receiver. And once he did pick it up he was at a loss as to what language to use and was able to do no more than mutter a faint hello. It was a female voice, fast, garbled, like someone in a hurry, wanting to get a brief message through, the tone of the last-but-one syllable pitched higher than the rest, suggesting a possible question? Having recovered a little, Budai tried to explain in English, French, Russian and Chinese that he did not understand her. Her response was to repeat what she had said more slowly, accentuating each syllable, but that of course made no difference. He tried various other languages as and when they occurred to him, but the woman did not hear him through and, giving a curt laugh, cut the connection.

Who was it? What did it mean? Had someone discovered his whereabouts? Was someone at home looking for him? Might it have been the airline realising there had been a mistake? Or was it someone answering one of the notices he had put up? Could the management have received the letter he had sent them? But they would know from that that he did not speak their language, for that after all was precisely what his letter had explained. And would they be calling him this way, by telephone? Or could it be a wrong number?

Suddenly he had an idea. It must have been Bébé! Why didn't he think of that before?! In all those trips up and down she was bound to have noticed his key with the number on it, why shouldn't she have rung him? And if it was her she would have been wanting to tell him that she had arrived and was back on duty, waiting for him.

And indeed there she was in one of the opening lift doors, smiling and winking at him. He could hardly wait till they could be alone together. Once he was inside the lift with her he tried to mime a telephone call, dialling with his fingers, putting an imaginary receiver to his ear to show that he had received her message and had come in response to it ... She smiled at him a few times while operating the lift but with a certain guardedness now. This made him wonder whether he was misinterpreting Veve's behaviour, thinking it was intimacy when it was no more than her normal kindness.

Once they had arrived on the eighteenth Budai tried to discover her telephone number by handing her his notebook and encouraging her to write it down, air-dialling, imitating the sound of the telephone bell and so forth. But she just shrugged, smoked her cigarette and seemed to understand nothing – or maybe just pretended not to understand, not wanting to give him her number. Might it be that she did not have a telephone? And in any case, where did she live, and with whom? Did she have a husband or was she still unmarried? Did she live with her family or alone? He knew nothing about her but if he was honest with himself such facts did not interest him too much anyway. What he required from her had nothing to do with her circumstances, or if her circumstances came into it at all it was only in so far as they allowed her enough time to be occupied with him. The circumstances might be of even less importance than that since what he assumed was that the minutes they spent on the top floor were stolen by Ete from her work. He couldn't afford the luxury of having his attention diverted, could not allow the one straw that chance had offered him to slip from his grasp. There was only one thing Budai wanted from the girl for the time being and everything else was secondary. He wanted her to be his language tutor.

They were still on numbers. He thought they might sound different because in her answers she was confusing cardinals with ordinals though these could sound very different indeed, as in one, two and first, second in English or egy, kettö and elsö, második in Hungarian ... But after long, exhausting, patient and sometimes nerve-jangling questioning he did succeed in establishing – albeit uncertainly and sometimes downright dubiously – the first ten numbers. So 1 is *dütch*, 2 is *klóz* or *gróz,* 3 is *tösh*, or possibly *bár*, 4is *dzsedirim*, 5i s *bár* or *tösh* (the numbers 3 and 5 seemed to be curiously interchangeable, or it might have been that he simply couldn't distinguish), 6 is *kusz*, 7 is *rodj* or *dodj*, 8 is *hododj*, 9 is *dohododj*, 10 is *etsrets*.

These names did not remind him of any language living or dead. True, there was some slight, if imagined, similarity between *dzsedirim* (4) with the Russian *chitiri* for the same number. *Kusz* (6) did sound somewhat like the Finnish *kuus*, and *etsrets* (10) recalled the Arabic *asr*. But these were mere coincidences. It was surprising to find the 7, 8 and 9 so clearly related to each other, though that too might owe something to misunderstanding or mishearing.

What made his life generally more difficult was that he could never be quite sure what sound he was hearing. At home he had developed a sure-fire ability to make fine phonetic distinctions as part of his work. It was just that in this city the locals employed strange articulations he had not met elsewhere. They seemed to voice words differently somehow, less clearly, not according to the normal rules – in civilised countries anyway – of enunciation. They spoke gutturally, from the throat, but not like the Chinese, Japanese or Arabs: the vowels were more murmured, their tones inconsistent; the consonants croakier, more chewed over, full of rattling, clicking noises. That seemed to point to an African language, that of the Bushmen/Hottentots, but the frequent use of *tl* suggested Central American Aztec. The preponderance of *ö* and *ü* sounds reminded him of Turkish. But this was all no more than impression, far short of certainty. Scholars had calculated that there were close to 3000 languages in the world. How could he relate this one to the others on the basis of such poor evidence?

His next recourse was to identify modes of address, hoping to catch some of them in Tyetye's speech. He listened intently to everything but however he tried there was only one sound he could pick out: *klött* or *klütt*, that was if he had heard it properly, recalling that on his first major excursion, at the market hall, the driver, who had taken him for an unemployed lout and had called him over to stack packages, had addressed him using the same word, as if to say, Oy! You! It was just that here it seemed to be the only form of address, a simple universal instead of the various alternatives on offer elsewhere, such as *tu, vous,* you, mister, darling, ducky, sir, madam, miss, comrade, mate, buddy and so forth. This was of little or no help. If the same form was directed to men, women, children and old people on every social level, with no hint whether the relationship was superior or inferior, the information, from a linguist's point of view, was not worth much. There was nothing he could do with it, no conclusion he could draw, little he could learn: it was a blind alley.

It was a similar problem with the form of greeting – *parasara* or *patarechera.* This was another term he recalled from earlier, at the hotel entrance, for example, where the fat man in the gold braid would mutter it while holding open the swing door: he said it morning, noon and night, when he left and when he returned. He kept saying it. It was another piece of information, useless from the linguistic point of view, a verbal unit incapable of being split into constituent parts.

Then he looked for common idioms, such as please, excuse me, *danke, bitt,* etc. It occurred to him that he himself could elicit some of these. If, for example, he bumped into someone in the street, or he invited someone to step on the metro escalator before him, the other person would be likely to reply with the equivalent of sorry, or thank you ... He got nowhere at all with personal pronouns though he spent long enough on them trying to isolate the appropriate words and work out how I or you or he or she might sound. He certainly tried hard enough, gesturing and asking the same question time and time again but however he quizzed Dededé the girl seemed not to understand at all. She simply shook her head and blew out smoke with an expression that said there was no point in continuing. Why was she being so negative now when she had been so kind and prepared to help before? It might be, thought Budai, that there were no personal pronouns here. It was theoretically possible that they addressed each other in a kind of nursery fashion, using only the third person singular that stood in for all else. That was the way children talked about themselves: Johnny eating, baby walking, walkies. There were some primitive peoples where such rules operated. But how did a city with skyscrapers square with stone-age inflections?

He hadn't really given the matter a thought but he soon realised through bitter experience how hard it was to settle on specific meanings and how difficult it was to set up a situation in which only one kind of reaction was possible. He either received answers that were too long and impenetrable or heard something completely different every time he asked the same question, words or mime. Take simple gestures: you wouldn't imagine the range of meanings they seemed to convey! Western Europeans moved their heads horizontally when wishing to indicate a negative, Greeks threw their heads back. Bulgarians nodded and called you by spreading their arms wide. Eskimos supposedly rubbed noses instead of kissing. There was a lot of this kind of thing – but who could explain the meaning of gestures to him here?

But his mind was tireless and never stopped working on ever newer schemes. The best of them was that he should concentrate on and collect public texts and notices where the meaning was clear and unambiguous or could be rationally worked out. For example, there was the word that appeared on the fronts of taxis to which there could be no obvious alternative. Or the notice that appeared on the yellow barriers of metro entrances. However it might be pronounced it seemed unarguable that the word should mean 'underground railway'. It was the same with out-of-order public telephone booths, from which he had tried to steal the directory before the policeman appeared. Or the sign on closed shops, the short single word that should mean closed. Besides these he noted down words he guessed might mean restaurant (or inn or grill or diner) or buffet (canteen, café, bistro) as well as working out the letters involved in laundry (or possibly cleaner, dry-cleaning, launderette).

Shops promised to be a productive hunting ground, displays and stalls all showing names of goods along with their prices. In this way he collected words that should signify establishments such as florist, ironmonger, wood and coal merchant (unless the word simply said domestic heating or some such thing), carpets, furniture, crockery, glassware, chandelier, musical instruments, fabrics, off-the-peg (or ready-to-wear), haberdashery, toys, sports equipment and so on. These too involved a margin of error of course. A shop sign would after all probably also contain the name of the owner and an address, or some generic trade name, such as Weave (a carpet or a fabric shop), Kristal (glass wear, crockery, light fittings), Houseproud (items to do with home cleaning and maintenance) or Textile (clothes, materials, etc) as elsewhere.

It was the grocery shop displays that were most useful. If an item was accompanied by a label and that label showed something other than the price, it followed that the other thing must be the name of the product. He was particularly interested in goods such as oranges, lemons, bananas, sugar, coffee, tea, cocoa and chocolate whose names tended to be the same, or pretty similar, wherever one went, that is to say, international words with a local variation. Later he had to admit that even this method was not foolproof, since the labels might say things like cheap, fresh, sale, offer, top quality, delicious, buy now, special, must go or any other choice phrase by which shopkeepers recommended their wares to customers. He put a question mark next to them in his notebook.

Doing his rounds he noted down the following more-or-less identifiable words on signs: cloakroom, till, drinking water (or possibly not drinking water), no entry, bus stop, take care, freshly painted, do not walk on the grass, road works, pedestrians other side (that would have been a pretty good guess if it was right), high-tension, or danger do not touch, that kind of thing.

Once he had collected enough of these he planned to ask Ebébé to read each of them out loud to him. But the first time he tried the girl happened to be in a bad mood, thoroughly tetchy, not even wanting to go up to the eighteenth floor with him. Something must have offended her: she ignored him in the lift, turned her head away and kept pressing the buttons in an apathetic manner. Budai would not be deterred though and patiently stayed in the lift as it went up and down, waiting for her to take her brief smoking break upstairs. But she had hardly taken a puff or two of the cigarette and he had only said a couple of words when tears sprang to her eyes, eyes that were anyway red, and she took out a handkerchief and wept.

Budai looked at her in confusion. How to console her when he had no idea what troubled her or hurt her? He had no time to occupy himself with such matters, he couldn't allow himself the liberty, he felt. He had no time, he had to be cold and matter-of-fact, selfish indeed, ruthless, for this was his only chance. He could only devote as much attention to the girl as would maintain their relationship, the rest was a waste of energy. And if she was labouring under some misapprehension about their relationship, well, it was up to him, he simply had to exploit it.

And so he stubbornly stood guard and would not let his victim go, eventually triumphing by sheer will: she put aside her mysterious frustrations and, ready to help again, started reading the list he placed in front of her, one item after another in a loud clear voice ... For the first time perhaps since arriving in the city Budai felt he had achieved something by the power of logic. There were various signs of this, such as Tete's facial expression and her gestures. He began to work out the meanings of individual words and groups of words. He was on the right track. In tiny ways he began to feel that the situation was not entirely hopeless. He redoubled his efforts, grasping every opportunity, almost enjoying the way the girl rolled off the list, repeating each word after her so that his ears and lips might retain the sound.

The trouble with the internationally-used words, he was disappointed to note, was that none of them was in, or even resembled, the forms he expected. Everything from taxi, bus, metro, hotel, buffet, orange, banana through to cocoa had a different name. What this suggested was that the people here – meaning particularly the linguists, the scholars and the press – must have been pretty fierce in their defence of the purity of the language against foreign influence. Or could it be that they were so isolated from the other peoples of the earth that there could be no question of influence at all?

He now had a store of some thirty to forty words and phrases, each with its pronunciation clearly noted along with its meaning and some possible options in cases of doubt. Even he was surprised how nicely all this rounded up. He whistled cheerfully as he rearranged his bits of paper, every so often with a glass of that sweet alcoholic drink. He decided not to seek out further material for now, preferring to make a thorough study of what he already had.

All the same, next morning he tried to persuade the girl to break his words down into signs and sounds, or at least to divide the most common phrases into individual words but this, to his surprise, proved a failure: they stumbled, started again and stumbled once more. The individual letters sounded different each time, now longer, now shorter, sometimes lacking any resemblance. Despite repeated questioning he got no better, no more coherent answers, quite the converse, in fact, for the longer he went on the more confusing it became. Maybe each sign was capable of being pronounced in a variety of ways depending on context, on the surrounding letters, syllables or words. Didn't this happen in English and French? Or, to reverse the argument, might it be possible that a single sound was represented by a variety of signs?

Of course all these analogies only worked if their characters actually represented letters, not syllables – which thought led him to consider the further problematic possibility that they represented entire words, as in Chinese, where characters stood for concepts. He didn't think that was very likely since Chinese characters tended to look more like pictures and involved more calligraphic marks than this script did and, more importantly, tended to express their contents more concisely. But in so far as they represented syllables they demanded a different approach since syllables tended to consist of a consonant and a vowel and if he happened to discover, say, the syllable, pe, he still wouldn't be able to work out which was p and which was e. That was because in such a system there would be one character for pe and another for, say, pi, pa, po, as much as for me, re, j, etc., in other words, the two sounds he was looking for would be hidden inside other syllabic characters. And should there be three-, four- or five-letter syllables what would be the connecting thread that might help identify them?

But if he made little progress with assigning sound or meaning to letters he did at least recognise the characters and the rough appearance of a range of phrases. It was a shame that these were, by and large, of peripheral importance, of no great value in everyday conversation and conduct. More to the point there were still too few to help him achieve the object of getting home. It was therefore necessary to continue collecting from an ever wider area.

He went on to street names. Strange he hadn't thought of this earlier. It looked like a well-planned city with street names clearly displayed on every corner, the format uniform on brick-shaped yellow boards with uniform black letters. Budai looked for common elements between them, words or clusters that would mean road, street, avenue, boulevard, alley, passage, ring, terrace and so forth. But however he looked he found no common terms. Could it be that they did not bother to provide such terms because they thought them redundant? Or maybe they employed the kind of name that did not need a qualifier, such as the Strand and Piccadilly in London, Broadway and the Bowery in New York, Rond-Point in Paris, the Graben in Vienna, and the Körönd or the old Oktogon in Budapest. These were exceptions in their cities but could this kind of name be the norm here?

He fared somewhat better with the advertisements, those on the steps of the metro, along its corridors, in the underground halls and on posters everywhere in the street, some of them enormous, filling entire walls. There were many he was sick to death of seeing: the blond pink-skinned man and the fat black cook who winked and bared her brilliant white teeth while lifting a serving spoon high in the air, the knight-in-armour with an umbrella raised above his head, the big family group sitting in a circle soaking their feet in a large common bowl and all the rest, though he didn't see any advertisements for goods and services generally available in Europe. The problem with the wall-mounted posters was that it was very difficult to tell the brand-name from the actual product. For example if he read Ship Soda he wouldn't know which was Ship and which was Soda. Nevertheless, he did manage to identify a few new terms such as washing-powder, tyres, laxative, cigarette-holder, lawnmower, stock-cube. Not that these were of any practical use to him.

There were a great many visual signs or icons intended to take the place of written instructions – pointing fingers, various diagrammatic figures, a number of silhouettes. The washrooms in the hotel displayed a bath or shower icon, the toilets a male or female head or alternatively men's or women's shoes. Telephone booths carried no text, only a simplified drawing of a telephone. If smoking was forbidden a smoking pipe was displayed with a red line through it, the red line being a feature of all notices forbidding something. Traffic signs too, he discovered, were of much the same kind as anywhere else and the directional signs in the metro were similarly reduced to their essence through colours and arrows. All these signs were of help in coping with everyday circumstances but it did not mean Budai was able to read the language. They simply enabled him to orientate himself and to conduct a fairly limited range of activities. At the same time, standing in as they did for written notices, such signs were merely a barrier to fuller understanding.

And then it occurred to him that when he was seeking the edges of town there had been an illuminated doorway glimmering through the fog but that he had hurried on and hadn't taken a closer look at it. Might it have been a cinema? And even before that, on that first Sunday when he was walking through the downtown area that he had happened to wander into, were there variety theatres or cinemas among them? ... He couldn't recall. He hadn't cared then but now it bothered him. He wondered whether to go back, whether it would be worth the effort and expense. His stock of cash was so low he resented spending it even on the metro. He didn't dare think what would happen if it ran out. Should he try locating the building? He had had so many disappointments since arriving here was it worth risking another? It might be better to wipe the thing from his memory, to let it go hang and pretend he hadn't noticed anything.

But he couldn't dismiss the thought of it. It continued to worry at him: what if he should miss one vital clue? He had become convinced that if he didn't do everything he possibly could, if he did not pursue every trail that seemed to hold out the faintest hope of success, if he once relaxed or tired, his instinct would be simply to give up and accept the situation. It would mean that he had lost the battle and was trapped here forever. In the end perhaps it wasn't so much the cinema and the potential experience it offered that drove him as the desire not to have to reproach himself with anything.

He dedicated a whole day to it, from early morning to late night. First he took the metro to the same terminus as he had last time, then walked on from there exactly as before in exactly the same direction. He passed the long stone wall and the gasometers. There was the factory with the saw-tooth roof, there were the water reservoirs – he never thought he'd take this road again! The white circus tent appeared: it was here he should find the entrance he had taken to be a cinema. Fortunately it was not too far from the station. There was no fog this time which meant no illumination either but he hadn't forgotten where it was and soon enough he found it on the other side of a busy overcrowded square.

It was, however, not a cinema but a department store, a pretty big department store when it came to it, some eighteen to twenty storeys high with people streaming in and out of its various doors. The range of available goods didn't seem – not on the ground floor at least – to be any greater than elsewhere: fancy, slightly out-of-fashion clothes, household objects, mass-produced items, modest stuff generally of inferior, market-stall quality, or crudely functional articles sold by the dozen. But he didn't want to buy anything in any case – what was there to buy? – so he didn't go in but turned and hurried towards home. There was still the downtown area to explore and with some effort he remembered which metro station he should aim for. Once he had been somewhere he was generally pretty good at finding his way back.

It was a weekday but the streets were almost as crowded as they had been before. As the sky darkened so neon lights began to sparkle and mechanical music to rise from bars and cafés. Drunks were teetering across the pavement, bellowing, blowing paper trumpets. He discovered the narrow side street where he had previously entered one of the houses: the woman with the white tulle, dark lashes and the pearl-bright face was smiling in the window again with a modest Madonna-like gaze. Budai thought a little nostalgically of the days when he had money for such things, to enter such a house, to take a boat out, to have a few drinks and enjoy a pancake.

There was no sign of a cinema but he was glad to pass this way again. He had been so lonely – the longer he spent in the city and the more populated he recognised it to be the more neglected he felt – that the simple fact of returning somewhere he had been before established a kind of relationship, a tenuous foothold in a sea of unknowns. The ferris wheel, the swing-boat, the target-shooting, the Fat Lady. He still couldn't work out whether there really were no cinemas or if he had somehow missed them. But he did not feel this was so important now, or maybe he just knew a little less than he thought he did.

It was his own fluctuating state of mind that preoccupied him for the time being. Briefly he found himself enjoying the heaving crowd of which he was a part, finding it bearable, quite pleasant in fact. Above all it was a sense of irresponsibility, the one not-entirely-to-be-dismissed pleasure that lightened his mood. It was good not to have anyone else be dependent on him, no one to question what he was doing why. He might eventually get used to the manner of life here, to the eternal waiting, to the queues, to the rough crowd; he might stop noticing it altogether: it might become as natural to him as to everyone else. All this of course was just a passing mood, or possibly the result of a creeping emotional anaesthesia, a brief break from its direct opposite. And somewhere at the core of the tiny spark of happiness there was Epepep too, that tingle of certainty that today or tomorrow he would see her again.

The next moment he was besieged by doubt and bitterness once more. No, no, no – he could never get used to it, however long he remained here, not to the food, the drinks or even the taste of the air, that sooty-sweet, granular concoction that was so heavy and cloying it seemed there was less oxygen in it; nor to the eternal jostling, shoving, elbowing and kicking: the saturation, the whole impatient, mad rhythm of life. Budai preferred sunny, wide-open spaces like Italian piazzas with their fresh breezes. What was he to do in this constantly crowded, apparently endless brick and concrete mass that looked like one enormous suburb? And he missed his wife, his family, his work, his home and the ordered circumstances of his life more each day. Furthermore, he had to fight to dismiss the constant agony of imagining what they might make of his disappearance, his vanishing without trace.

The wildest ideas occurred to him as his mind chugged along on empty, throwing out endless questions with not a single answer. Was it possible, for instance, that his arrival in the city was not the result of a misunderstanding? That it wasn't that he had blundered onto the wrong flight but that someone had deliberately misdirected him, in other words abducted him? They could have slipped a sleeping draught into his food so he shouldn't be able to tell how long they had been in the air. Might they be deliberately keeping him here, preventing his return home? But who might they be and why? What possible purpose could it have? And why him? Was he somehow in somebody's way? What had he done wrong? Whom had he harmed?

That actually would have been his preferred option. Anger, malice, hatred ... they cut both ways. Passion can be resisted with passion: one could work oneself up into the appropriate state, search out the enemy, take him on, do battle with him and, in this way, defeat him. If, on the other hand, it was only blank stares and mere indifference that were detaining him – which looked more likely – there was only negative energy to draw on, an immobility that would prevent him attracting anyone's attention or interest. And how, in that case, was he to extricate himself from this tepid slough of feeling when there was nothing to cling to, no firm ground on which to set his feet?

It was vital not to go mad! He must not to allow himself to

be overcome by confusion, by pandemonium, by isolation. Time and again it swept through him, the fear that he would give up the hopeless struggle and sink into the surrounding chaos, or alternatively become indifferent and surrender to melancholy and torpor. He had no weapon but his consciousness: it was the one beam of light he could aim at the waking nightmare.

He considered the cumulative effect of his various meditations and enquiries, weighing up how far he had got with the tools available to him. He recognised a few phrases he had picked up from everyday speech and knew roughly what they meant; he knew the numbers one to ten and how to greet and address someone. Beyond this he knew the approximate meaning of certain groups of written characters and could more or less pronounce them if Deded's pronunciation was anything to go by. These were chiefly the names of articles for purchase and two or three longer terms. On the other hand, he could only read complete words and had failed every time to break them down into their constituent elements. So far he had had no success at all in assigning any specific sound to any character, nor, conversely, point to characters appropriate to this or that sound or group of sounds: worse still, he had not the least idea what form of writing they employed.

His achievements thus far were sickeningly insignificant. He hadn't enough information to deduce a system: he could not even put a sentence together. And when he tried using the words he knew, or the words he supposed he knew, to enquire, for example, where he might find a café or a metro station he was surprised to find that he was either misunderstood or not understood at all. Could he be mispronouncing the words? That would not be unlikely, having heard the curious, alien-sounding articulations of the locals. Later though, in one of the underground tunnels of the metro, some kind of altercation broke out, and Budai noticed that everyone else was merely shouting and rambling, with no-one paying any attention to anyone else. Could it be that they themselves could not understand each other, that the people who lived here employed various provincial dialects, possibly even quite different languages? In a particularly feverish moment it even occurred to him that each one of them might be speaking his own language, that there were as many languages as there were people.

Next Friday on top of all this he found a new bill in box 921. The desk-clerk – another new face, how many were there? – calculated the total as 33.10, only a little less than last time. Budai accepted the bill with a silent nod but did not take it to the cashier to pay this time. There was nothing left to pay with. He couldn't scrape that much together despite having spent less this time round.

What would happen now? When would they act and what would they do? Maybe some good might come of it, if they invited him into the manager's office, for example, to seek an explanation. At least they'd be speaking to him and he could say something, ask for an interpreter ... But maybe nothing would happen, no one would say anything. How long could they put up with him staying here without paying? They were bound to find out. One way or the other the fact was he would soon run out of money. He counted up what he had left again: his entire wealth came to 9.75. That was what remained out of the two-hundred-plus he received when he presented his cheque.

He made some wild, panic-stricken calculations: if, in the first week, putting aside the rent for the room, he had spent some 130, and in the second, even after reducing his expenses to a bare minimum, his outlay was 26, the amount remaining would hardly be enough to see him through the next few days. What would happen to him if his luck did not turn? He had to get some money. But how?

To make matters still worse he now had a toothache. It was one of the back teeth on the top row that was causing the trouble. At first it was only a dull murmuring sort of pain that came and went and might have been merely his imagination, something he could ignore. But then it erupted, became acute, ever more furious, ever more intolerable. His jaw was inflamed, his face swelled up. He couldn't delude himself that it would simply go away if he waited: the pain was well-nigh unbearable now and he had no drugs, no analgesic. The small box of miscellaneous pills his wife had packed for him was in his lost luggage.

It was pointless trying to explain this or to show anyone at the hotel what was wrong with him for no one would pay any attention or, if they did, they would just jabber on as they usually did. He was so desperate with the pain he ran out into the street just as an empty taxi was drawing up at the traffic lights. Budai yanked its door open without a word and leapt in. The driver, having turned round, Budai held the side of his face and mimed the pulling of a tooth to indicate where he wanted to go. The driver appeared to understand. He did not argue but put his foot down. He was a young, impassive man in a peaked cap and looked faintly Chinese.

Hardly had they started and turned down the first side-street when the traffic came to a standstill. There was no way ahead or back: every available space was filled with vehicles nosing forward or stuck. They spent long minutes in the same spot, then the lines of cars moved slowly forward until coming to a stop again within a few yards. Their progress was unbearably, infuriatingly slow: far in front of them there must have been a crossroads or traffic-light holding things up, allowing just a few people through at a time. The meter on the taxi kept ticking even when they were not moving but there was not the faintest hope of early escape from this endless traffic jam.

Budai could bear it no longer and tried talking to the driver. The man did not want to turn round so he tapped him on the shoulder, pointing once again to his swollen face. But the driver was not to be disturbed. He retained his traditional oriental imperturbability, paying him no attention at all, showing no sign of understanding either him or the need for a dentist.

The next time he glanced at the meter he was horrified to see that it had just leapt past the figure of 8 and would soon be at 8.40, then 8.80 and so on though the car had made hardly any progress. The engine was merely ticking over. Within a few minutes the meter had crept up to 10 which was more money than he had in his pocket, and who knows how many extras there would be to add. His anxiety and fury were so intense now and his toothache so agonising that he had begun to regard the cab as his prison, a cell jammed between legions of cars, and regretted ever having got in. Things had come to such a pass that he would have beaten his way out with his fists if he could. He would happily have instructed the driver to smash at full speed into the truck in front of them: let there be wrecks and explosions, let there be anything, but let things change.

The more sober part of his judgement was in favour of escape. What would happen if he could not pay the fare? Would there be an outcry? Would the police be called? In his current condition both these options seemed perfectly dreadful, but what else was there? ... What else? The next moment, just as the driver put the car in gear again and they were rolling gradually forwards, Budai pushed the door open and leapt out. He stumbled over the kerb but was otherwise unhurt. He turned back for a split second to see the driver's Chinese eyes but the next time he looked the taxi had disappeared in the traffic. He too was looking to vanish into the crowd.

He hadn't been in this area before though they can't have got far from the hotel. The first man he stopped to show he had a toothache immediately grasped the problem and pointed to a nearby multi-storey yellow building. It looked to be a hospital, a clinic or some other medical institution, stately with wings and extensions and a crowd of people streaming both ways through its arched portal. There was an ambulance-like vehicle, a closed white car with siren blaring, turning out of the gateway ... Might it be that his Chinese-looking driver had brought him to the right place after all? And now the poor chap – the only man willing to help him – had to pay the fare out of his own pocket ...

Everyone here understood his gestures and he was quickly directed to the dentistry department. As he expected, there were vast numbers waiting in the surgery corridors, not just standing and sitting on benches, but squatting on the stone floor, some even lying down on it, many with bandages or sticking plaster on their faces and cotton wool dangling from their mouths. It was slow progress, mind-numbingly slow, people probably being called in the order in which they had arrived. Nevertheless, the order of their going was constantly subject to dispute with squabbles breaking out here and there. There were at least thirty people before Budai at the door he had decided to wait at. But he had no choice and was lucky he had found his way here at all.

It was a long long wait. He was perspiring with pain and time had lost all meaning when at last it came to his turn. Suddenly everything speeded up. As soon as he stepped into the surgery he was surrounded by men and women in white coats and he no sooner pointed to the bad tooth before he was pressed into a chair. One man held his head back, another sprinkled some cold sweet-flavoured liquid onto his gums and a fourth man, a large bulky figure wearing white gym shoes like a wrestler, was already applying a pair of glittering pliers to his mouth. There followed one skull-shattering arrow of pain, one loud crack and the man held up the bloody tooth before dumping it into a dish beside the chair. Someone handed Budai half a glass of water with which he rinsed his mouth then spat out what was left.

They went on to ask him something that might have been his name and he gave it to them together with his home address, though whether they understood this when he wrote it down he could not tell. He had no idea what they were going to do with the information. Nor did he have to pay, or at least no one indicated that he should. The next patient was already there behind him and as soon as he rose from the chair the other occupied it, the new man's place being immediately taken up by someone else. On the way out he decided to take a different route but was so relieved to be rid of his pain that he got lost. He wandered along criss-crossing corridors, down stairs, meeting dense crowds everywhere, the air thick with hospital smells. There were ever new corridors, twisting and turning erratically, now cutting across an open courtyard under glass. The building seemed to be comprised of various parts of different periods, one added after another. Eventually he arrived in a spacious circular hall.

It must have been the maternity department. There were hundreds and hundreds of little cots in rows with babies wrapped in white swaddling bands. The newly born, like the rest of the city's inhabitants, represented the whole gamut of races with every type of physiognomy, from the palest white to the darkest black. They filled not only this hall but the next and the one after that too, baby after baby, white, black, brown, yellow, all the way down the corridor as well, in cots that did not fit into the main halls. There were a few multiple cots, two or three in some wards, designed for twins perhaps or simply babies for whom there was no room elsewhere. And there were more extensions just as packed with infants, and still more after those as if there could be no end of them, and all the while nurses in white gowns were pushing trolleys with yet more babies, those who presumably had just been delivered in surgery, in groups of ten or twenty, all red and furiously bawling after their entry into the world

... Budai liked children and was generally touched by them but he had never seen so many all together and the sight confused and terrified him. He looked to escape, seeking an exit from the clinic. He was losing patience, wanting to see no more babies, worrying what would happen when the present batch grew up and joined the already teeming hordes in the streets.

Arriving back at the hotel, he found Bebébe in the lift. She immediately noticed his swollen face and looked at him as if to say he should not get out but continue up to the eighteenth floor. Once up there Budai tried to convey to her that he had had a tooth pulled and even opened his mouth to show her where. In examining it Vevede had to come so close that her blonde hair tickled his chin and he could feel the girl's skin and breath; later he tried to recall whether it mattered who started stroking whose face first, who kissed who, and whether it was she who first offered up her face and lips. Budai's mouth was still swollen and numb with the anaesthetic or perhaps it was his cut gum that was in the way. In any case he felt awkward and lumpen, hardly capable of sensation, and he might have been a little dizzy too since all this passed in a kind of fog. Meanwhile the lift buzzer started ringing so they had to go down and once it started to crowd up everything that had passed upstairs seemed distant and unreal.

But this did nothing to solve his financial problem. He had to find work, anything, to earn some money. But how and where would he find work? Who could direct him to an employer? After all, he had failed to elicit much simpler information from local people. Ironically, the longer he stayed here the less he found himself able to ask people things. There was nothing he could do about that, however often he had vowed to change: reticence and withdrawal were necessary forms of self-preservation in the face of so many failures and disappointments. He was becoming ever more confused and detached in his dealings with others, ever less willing to accost people in the street or anywhere else and when he did try to make contact he became almost speechless. It was as if he was frozen. Maybe that is how it had to be. Maybe that was the only way his personality, his constitution could deal with the situation.

Then he remembered that first Sunday when he passed the market and somebody shouted at him as if inviting him to work. It was the driver of the truck who wanted help unloading vegetables, so he found the cheapest items among his clothes, the more worn of his two pairs of shoes, those that had been practically walked to pieces on his various excursions, and the pullover that he had carried in his briefcase. He put them on and set out.

It took him some time to find the open market. He got out at the same underground station as before but had twice crossed the enormous square before realising that, this being a weekday, there were no stalls or booths, no folding tables set out with goods, that the square had in fact been swept clean and that in the centre stood a statue of a wounded soldier wielding a rifle. Might it have been a war memorial? The outdoor market, it seemed, was only here on Sundays or other public holidays. On the other hand, the covered market-hall at the far end with its glazed and barred stalls was busier than ever. A great army of customers poured in through the front while the big ramp at the side was busy with cranes, conveyor belts and people loading and unloading goods. There were casual labourers everywhere swarming around trucks that were parked nose to tail, ragged figures carrying bales, ice and boxes into the building.

It was easy mingling with them. They seemed to be working in improvised gangs on this or that load. All you had to do was to watch where the next laden truck arrived, get over there, offer your back and someone would immediately give you a sack to carry. His sack seemed likely to contain potatoes or onions, nothing particularly heavy. He followed the others inside with it and threw it onto a great pile of sacks like the rest, then returned for another sack. No-one asked him for any ID or other paperwork and, having addressed one or two questions to him that he couldn't answer, they assumed he couldn't speak the language and took hardly any more notice of him. There was not much for them to say in any case: his task was obvious and needed no explaining. Nor did the other temporary porters bother with him, being busy with their own affairs. Quite possibly they were strangers to each other too.

Budai was not scared of physical work. When he was a student on a grant he would occasionally take such jobs when short of money, doing all-night stints at Les Halles in Paris or at Covent Garden in London. His constitution was still strong and healthy and he found himself enjoying the effort and exercise. The only thing he didn't like was the sacks making his hands and pullover dirty. It took roughly an hour and a half to finish unloading the consignment at which point the driver paid them by pressing a single piece of lowest denomination paper money into their palms. Later he was set to carrying sides of pork, frozen goods, icy and damp to the touch, his back cold, his palms greasy and sweaty. Then it was passing the load from a truck, handing down cages of fat angora rabbits, the kind he had seen in the hotel room whose door he had opened. He earned altogether eight notes in the day plus a little change. He felt a pleasant tiredness and a certain pride too that here he was, making a living with his two bare hands. But at the same time he could hardly wait to get back to the hotel bathroom and a nice hot shower.

From then on each time he went to the market, whatever time of day, he almost always found some work of this kind. No-one ever asked him who he was. When he worked in the evening or at night he noticed that those who had packed up did not go far but entered the liquor store next door. Others simply lay down where they were among the bales, sleeping on empty sacks or in one of the larger crates in some quiet corner. They must have been tramps and homeless people, their clothes filthy and neglected, their whole appearance uncared for. This was the company he was now reduced to.

One time, heading home on the metro, he was just descending the long escalators with the host of those arriving streaming past him on the way up when he suddenly spotted a man holding a Hungarian magazine. It was no mistake! There he was holding a copy of *Szinházi Élet*, an old theatre and stage weekly, its title clearly legible. Even the actress on the front looked faintly familiar: she was in a striped swimsuit standing on the steps of the *Hullámfürdő*, the pool with the artificial wave machine; the actress blonde, slender, raising her free left hand high into the air. This was such an unexpected shock that he had no sooner registered it than the man holding it, an elderly, grey, bespectacled figure in a worn green overcoat, had already passed him and was now behind him. He didn't know what to do, had no idea what to say, but shouted out as loud as he could in Hungarian:

'*Kérem szépen ... izé, maga, ott!*' (Excuse me! ... I beg your pardon, er, you there!)

But the escalator was so loud, so squeaky and grinding, the whole place so full of commuters, the hall so echoey that the man in the overcoat couldn't have heard him. Terrified that he would lose him, Budai screamed out once more:

'*Halló, ide nézzen.*' (Hello! Look this way!)

The man addressed turned round, his expression astonished, as if hearing a voice from another world. He reached uncertainly towards him in the distance perhaps only to convince himself that it was no illusion:

'*Hát uraságod is ...?*' (And you, dear sir, are you also ... ?)

The rest was lost in the surrounding noise and faded in the increasing distance between them. Budai tried to turn round and follow him but the escalators were moving rather fast and were packed with people, a number of them actually rushing downwards, hurrying for trains: there was no chance – not the space or the time – of him reaching the man in the overcoat. Desperately he cried to the ever-retreating patch of green in the crowd.

'*Várjon meg a …*' (Wait for me at …)

But where the best place to wait in the metro actually was he could not think. He should at least have asked for the man's address before they swept past each other, or he could have given his. True, he didn't know the name of his hotel, nor even the street where it happened to be. In the meantime the stranger had completely disappeared in the metro traffic.

Budai was not content to let it rest there and tried to think what he would do in the other man's place, where he would wait for someone who had called out to him like that. The nearest spot was the top of the escalators, the point where they stepped off. It was just that it was no easy task getting there from where he was, on the wrong side, because once at the bottom a metal barrier prevented him from getting over to the parallel stairs leading up and he was forced by railings down winding corridors, past intersections and down even more winding corridors before he could reverse his steps. But having found his way by devious twists and turns to the bottom of the escalators, he was no longer sure whether these were the same. At the top, once he got there, another set of escalators led further up and then another so it was difficult to decide which was the very top. He scanned the heaving throng for the man in the green overcoat but he could not find him. He couldn't stop anywhere, of course, for the moment he slowed the crowd swept him on again.

But what if the other man was seeking him in exactly the same way, using the same logic, at the bottom of the stairs? He struggled back down again to the underground line he had taken before, where he had first spotted the man. That was the very spot where he should have leapt across or crawled across the two steep thick rubber handrails that divided them, only he hadn't thought of it at the time. And now he didn't find him there though he explored various draughty loud platforms. Might it be that his quarry had taken the opposite course and was waiting at the metro exit out in the street. But which exit? There were at least eight or even ten here. He continued weaving, moving between a whole series of points in the underground labyrinth but all to no avail: the single figure he was seeking among the hordes in one or other tunnel was nowhere to be found.

He was so excited he didn't think to consider whether the meeting was a good or bad sign, but even though he hadn't succeeded in talking to the man or establishing some kind of contact, in view of his utter isolation it was encouraging to know that he was not alone in a world of strangers. They might bump into each other again or he might meet another compatriot or at least a foreigner like himself. Next time he'd be lucky and would finally discover everything he had failed to discover so far.

On the other hand, once he got to analysing this strange brief encounter he found that there were certain disquieting aspects of the situation. The very fact that the stranger was holding a copy of *Szinházi Élet* for instance. The magazine had ceased publication over thirty years ago as he recalled. The old man couldn't have been living here that long, could he? And if so, had he settled here? Or had he found himself abandoned in the city much as he himself had been? How did he get here? By what means? What form of transport? And if he had brought the magazine along as reading matter, why that very number? And had he held on to it since then? That might have accounted for the look of amazement and incredulity on his face when he turned round on hearing Budai shout after him. It would have been like hearing an echo of his own voice. And the fact that he addressed Budai as *uraságod*, an old, unfashionable tag, hardly ever used nowadays! And what did he mean by the wonder implied by the question *Hát uraságod is ... ?* Did he mean that the pair of them comprised a single category? Was it simply an allusion to the fact that they were both Hungarian, or, the worst thought of all, was it a sign that, like him, the old man had been vainly trying to leave the place, only in his case for over thirty years?

He spent days tortured by the thought of a missed opportunity, blaming himself, going over the events, wondering what else he might have done. And like a criminal returning to the scene of the crime, he kept going back to the metro station, hanging about for hours in case the man in the green overcoat came by again, that is if it was his customary route. This time, just this one time, let him catch his eye. And though he did not meet him again it bred a suspicion that somewhere in the eternal crowd filling the streets and the metro there might be someone else who might understand him, maybe more than one – but how would they know each other?

Working at the halls and undertaking his regular watch on the specific metro station soon gave his day some structure. Usually he ate at the self-service buffet before then walking home. On the way back he would walk past the skyscraper in construction, to which eight storeys had been added since his arrival, the builders having got to the seventy-second. How high was it planned to be? Once in the hotel he looked for Pepepé and if she was on duty they would get together; if not he'd just go to his room depressed since it was there he felt most desolate and the time passed most slowly.

The room was always punctiliously cleaned, the bed nicely made up, the towels and tablecloth regularly changed. He had no idea who carried out these duties or when because he never saw anyone. When he stayed in – even for days at a time – they did not call. One morning, out of sheer curiosity, he pretended he was leaving but took care to hide round the corner and watch the comings and goings but he saw nothing all morning. Another time when he only popped out for some fifteen minutes he returned to find his room had been tidied.

What he chiefly missed was reading, the sight of familiar words. At home he spent half his life or more in libraries among books, occasionally as much as eighteen hours in a day and he was not prepared to break the habit and give up. Out of sheer desperation he took out the volume of short stories he had bought at the second-hand book market. He leafed through it again without understanding a word, contemplating the title page with its picture of the harbour and that deep blue sea, its palms and the little white houses twinkling on the hillside. Then he gazed at the photograph of the author on the flap, that full-faced figure in his pullover with his crew-cut hair and his faintly mocking expression and he still looked familiar. He wondered where he might have seen him, who he reminded him of, why he was drawn to him. Was it the ironic look? That lazy watchfulness in his eye? One evening he returned tired from his work at the market and caught sight of himself in the bathroom mirror just as he was suppressing a yawn and it suddenly became obvious: the man in the photographs reminded him of himself. Maybe that is why he found him sympathetic, why he had picked his book out among so many others. Was it that he found his own face attractive?

And time and again the same most terrible of questions returned to torture him. What about his family at home? Time would not have stood still for them either. Were they well and in good health? Were they alive at all? And if so what did they make of the extraordinary fact that they had heard nothing from him or about him for close on three weeks? It was pointless trying not to think of it, his entire nervous system was full of such thoughts. If only he could send a message to them, however short, simply to say that he was alive even though he had no idea in what part of the world ...

He hadn't seen a post office anywhere but they clearly had to exist. Maybe he had passed them by without spotting them. Nor did he see any post boxes, not in the hotel lobby or in the street nearby. He tried looking for postcards and stamps at the stalls in the hotel lobby but there was nothing on display and from the shopgirls' speech and gestures he surmised that they either hadn't understood him or that the articles he required were to be found elsewhere. But where?

He tried taking a plain piece of paper, folding it into the shape of a letter and addressing it to his wife though the mere writing of the letter upset him. His emotions ran away with him. He tried to ignore them and took the trial letter down to the reception desk and gave it to the clerk on duty. But the man just turned it round and round in his hand and stared at it, clearly not recognising the Latin script. Or perhaps he had no idea at all what to do with it. Maybe it was not part of his duties. He certainly did not want to be left with it because he pushed it back across the counter with a few short polite words. Thinking the lack of a stamp might be the problem, Budai took out some money and tinkling it in his palm, offered it to him, asking him to take what was necessary, then putting a few coins down in front of the clerk with a questioning look as if to ask whether that was enough. The man – an older, respectable looking chap – must have misunderstood him, taking it for a bribe of some sort for he snapped out a few sharp words and swept the coins away before turning away from him altogether and attending to the next in the queue.

Nevertheless Budai did not give up on the idea. Surely it would still be worth writing a letter. He could just leave it on the counter at reception when someone else was on duty, along with more than enough money to cover the cost of postage then quickly disappear before it could be returned. If there were the remotest chance of the letter reaching his wife the post office at home would be able to work out where he was and when he wrote it from the stamp or the franking, but he kept delaying the task even while he was weighing up his chances for neither his mind nor hand was up to it. Maybe he simply couldn't find the right first words that would enable him to tell her what had happened to him. However he put it, he was incapable of summing it all up.

So he turned his attention back to the telephone in his room. He dialled at random wherever his fingers happened to land and rang unknown acquaintances he had rung before. It wouldn't matter now if they presented him with a bill this coming Friday, he couldn't pay anyway. When somebody picked up the phone at the other hand he shouted down the line, the same words each time, for hours on end, forcing himself to be patient: he kept repeating the name of his home town and his home phone number as well as the six numbers he could at last manage in the local language. He did so in the hope that at some point he would hit on the exchange where long-distance calls were connected. Or if not precisely that perhaps he might come across some other utility that would be able to transfer his call if only he kept repeating the number often enough or obstinately enough. But however much he shouted all he got by way of answer was the muttering and harrumphing of various men, women and children, nothing at all to indicate that anyone had understood. He spent the whole evening doing this until, seized by a sudden helpless fury, he smashed down the receiver and, sweating profusely, cursed his fate and beat the wall with his fists so the neighbours knocked back. What insanely ill luck had landed him here? Why him? Why should fate have chosen him for this? Why, why, why, why?

Having calmed down a little he stared – how many times had he done this? – at the oil painting above the table, that winter landscape with its snow-laden fir trees and those delicate fawns bounding away into the distance. He knew every detail by now to the point of boredom but it was his only reminder of nature, the world beyond the town that was holding him prisoner. That was if that world existed anywhere beyond his imagination.

He still hadn't discovered from Bebé what her shifts were, where she went after work, what her telephone number was, where she lived, where she might be found and so forth. Although the girl was remarkably adept at picking up some things, she seemed to have no idea when it came to questions like this. Either that or she was pretending not to understand. Nor was he any more successful when he attempted to observe her entering or leaving the building or indeed at seeing her anywhere in the building apart from in the lift.

He did, however, know her well enough to try to ask her to take him to a railway station or an airport. But when the opportunity presented itself – on the eighteenth floor again – and Budai attempted to suggest this, even drawing the relevant means of transport Etete showed no inclination to help him but grew sad and tearful. Why should it upset her so much that he wanted to go away? He tried to console her by stroking her but thanks to his clumsiness the movement came out all wrong and he found himself like an idiot clutching her elbow, not knowing what to do with it. The linguistic chasm between them was too wide however much they both wanted to cross it. And now the lift was being called again. There was never enough time: they never had a moment to themselves.

The same night, just when he had bathed and was preparing to go to bed, the light in the room went out. He took a peek out into the corridor and then through the window: there was darkness everywhere. Not even the streetlights were on. All he could see was car headlights streaming through the black air. There must have been a major fault at the power station, something that affected the whole district because there was no light to be seen, not even in the distance. It didn't particularly worry him. He did what he had to do. He was accustomed to the layout of the room and felt his way to bed. He had nothing to read anyway so, though he was not a bit sleepy, he crawled in and made himself comfortable.

There was a faint knocking at his door. He stopped to listen in case he was mistaken but then somebody carefully opened the door. He must have forgotten to turn the key when he checked the corridor. Whoever it was stepped in, quietly closed the door and stopped, breathing quietly. It was only now that Budai realised he had actually been expecting this, that this might have been why he had unconsciously left the door unlocked, why he felt so awake and alive despite a day of hard work. Even if he hadn't thought it through, some part of his brain must have been aware that if there was no electricity anywhere the lift wouldn't be working either ... Simply to confirm then, and before the other had a chance to speak, he whispered:

'*Bebebe?*'

The girl answered with an embarrassed giggle showing that she too felt a little confused. She corrected his pronunciation:

'*Djedje ...*'

Or it might have been *Dede* or *Tyetyetye* or *Tete* or even *Tchetche* because he still couldn't quite tell what it was supposed to be. The girl did not come further into the room but continued standing by the door. It was of course perfectly understandable that she should feel awkward having entered at all. Budai had enough sensitivity to recognise this despite his own confused feelings. He got out of bed and made his way over to her in the dark. He was wearing his only pair of pyjamas, the ones he kept washing, but it was dark now and they couldn't see each other. He bumped into her as he felt his way forward, his hand just happening to land on her breast. He quickly snatched it away, terrified that she would think him too forward. but at the same time a hot flush ran through him. It was as if the heat of Pepe's body had transmitted itself through her bra. Her breast was firm and pert as a girl's. It was as if he could feel her heart beating in it.

They found themselves by the bed. Where else was there to go in this tiny single hotel room, after all? She lit a cigarette and sat down beside him, her face illuminated for a moment and all the stranger for that, her hair brushed differently, neatly smoothed down. She was turned away from him, not looking at him. Suddenly she snapped the lighter shut. Maybe she thought the dark more appropriate. From that time on it was only the red glow of the cigarette that brightened as she drew on it, her outline barely visible in the glimmer. The room was slowly filling with smoke.

But the girl can't have smoked her cigarette right down to the end. She fumbled a little and ran into the bathroom in her stockings. He could hear her moving in there as she found the tap then came the bubbling stream of water. In the meantime he locked the outside door and got back into bed.

Edede smelled of fresh soap and cologne as she got in beside him, her skin cold from the water, her whole body slightly shivering. Budai tried to warm her, grasping her frozen feet between his thighs and embracing her shoulders. Then he did all that a man should do in the circumstances, all his instincts and experience guided him to do. Veve did not resist or argue but only slowly relaxed and then not entirely. She clearly took pleasure in the act but it was as if for her too it was more important to give pleasure than to receive it. Budai was, however, the sort of person who required the full participation of the other and took little pleasure in solitary satisfaction. And he did finish a little soon. Having spent so much time alone he couldn't contain himself.

He felt a touch ashamed as he lay beside her in the darkness. The girl broke the silence asking something as she propped herself up on her elbows and, strangely enough, he guessed immediately what she was saying: she was asking him if he did not mind her smoking. She drew the covers over herself before lighting up: she was still embarrassed by her nakedness.

And then she began speaking again, quietly, with periods of silence, timid and halting, stopping every so often to tap the ashes from her cigarette into the ashtray that Budai fetched for her from the table. Her speech became more confident as she went on. She was telling him some extended story that she might long have been wanting to tell him, something about herself or her circumstances, though she, if anyone, must have known how little he understood of her language. She became ever more animated and emotional, ever more broken, though she retained the gentle refinement of her normal voice. No sooner had she finished her cigarette than she took out a new one and lit it: whatever she was talking about must have been of a highly personal nature. Might she be talking about some specific person? But who could it be who so upset her and why did she choose to tell him now? Might it have been her husband?

Budai sought out Epepe's hands in the darkness, first the left, then the right, tapping at her long fingers to see whether she wore a wedding ring. There was nothing there of course. He would have noticed it in the lift if she had one. She too must have guessed what he was thinking because she flicked her lighter on and reached into the handbag she had left on the bedside table. There was the ring.

Now he too asked for a light and in so far as it allowed he examined the ring, turning it this way and that. It looked to be made of gold in the usual round shape though there was no inscription inside it. The outside was engraved with thin blue lines, which was unusual for a wedding ring though it might have been one for all that. He thought he might have seen rings like this as fashionable accessories. But if that was what it really was why did she carry it about in her handbag?

Or could it be that this was the chief clue to interpreting her strange behaviour, the reason why she was so patient and willing to answer all his difficult questions, that is, apart from those that pertained to herself, meaning where she lived and her family circumstances? It might be a bad marriage that she now resented. Maybe she wanted a divorce. Was that why she did not wear the ring on her finger?

He tried to bear all this in mind as she was speaking now and, sure enough, the words suddenly seemed clearer. He could almost follow her speech, the rough drift of it anyway, the rest of it – the details – probably being pretty commonplace ... It was all coming out now: her life at home, how unbearable it was, how crowded the place with relatives, dependants, uncles and aunts, not to mention the two children from the husband's first marriage. Then the co-tenants and sub-tenants, and the invalids of whom one could never be free, those helpless sickly widows and widowers, the screaming neurotics, the filthy and intolerable drunkards, the women with their shady occupations as well as all their kids too, all of them crammed together in a tiny flat. The eternal noise, the fuss, the bickering and the chaos with not a moment's rest – but then where to go, where else was there? The block was already full to overflowing just like every other block, there being no better flats available, only those at prices no one could afford or through some exceptional personal contact, and even if it were possible to move away, what would happen to all those invalids and old people? No marriage could survive such diabolical circumstances. Few did. Then he starts drinking, seeking consolation in liquor. He becomes ever more impossible; soon the relationship goes cold, they hardly spend any time together and are separated in all but name. She too looks to escape because even working in this madhouse, in that narrow, ugly, airless lift, is better than being at home. That is why she does not wear her wedding ring, it is why she has never wanted to talk about herself. Even now she feels guilty for betraying her husband. Nevertheless, she would like to explain to Budai what she is doing in his room because she would not want him to think of her as some loose woman of easy virtue, which she most certainly is not. But she just had to tell someone eventually. That is, if that was what she was saying and not something completely different.

She had practically filled the room with smoke by now but was clearly feeling a little calmer for having unburdened herself. But when she reached for another cigarette on the bedside table she upset the glass of water he had left there. She made a grab for it but the sudden movement resulted in her rolling off the bed and when Budai had to try to pull her back up they both ended up off the bed. The water was dripping on their necks. Bebe burst into a fit of giggles so infectious that he started laughing, the unstoppable laughter bursting from them. Soon they were both on top of each other, utterly breathless. Neither of them could stop for if one quietened down the other would start laughing again, setting them both off once more. They were tittering and rolling around so much, that having got into bed the girl almost fell out again, and what with one thing and another, desire overcame them.

There used to be an amusing booth at the funfair in Budai's local park with a title something like Get Her Out of Bed! A fat, bosomy lady in a lacy nightgown lay between huge duvets and pillows. The player was given a rag ball and if he succeeded in hitting a certain target the bed tipped loudly over and the fat lady rolled off and turned a somersault to the great delight of the audience. Having once thought of this, he couldn't forget it now. It was such a funny memory it made him feel much better about things. So of course he wanted to share it with Vedede too and almost despite himself began to tell her all about it. She cuddled up to him and listened, nodding and chuckling, making little noises of encouragement, and ended up laughing with him as loudly and as wholeheartedly as if she had understood every word.

Naturally encouraged, he started to explain how he had got here, how and why he had boarded the flight, how he had lost his luggage, how they took away his passport and all the rest. He added other things too, as and when they came to him, in no particular order: how he had had himself taken down to the police station, what he saw from the top of the big church, how he had narrowly missed a fellow Hungarian on the escalator. Then about things at home, about his dog, how clever the old dachshund was, how it would look for old paths in the snow so you could only see his nose and the tip of his tail in all that white like two dark moving dots. How he used to ski in the mountains of the Mátra or the Tátra, and how he preferred the less-explored routes, the gentle winding slopes of the mild, serpentine woodland paths where the silence was so dense, how it was all green and white and soft with fresh deer tracks in the snow. And how, when he reached the edge of the precipice, the depths would draw and suck him in with the ecstasy of leaping, the temptation of allowing himself to fall, skis and all, the intoxication of weightlessness, the loss of self-awareness in the drop ...

She heard him through in sympathetic silence, drawing closer to him on the bed. Suddenly Budai stopped and raised his head.

'You understand?' he asked.

'You understand,' she answered.

'You understand?'

'You understand.'

'No you don't, you don't understand!'

'You understand,' she repeated.

'You're lying, you don't understand!' he snapped back in growing irritation.

'You understand.'

'How could you understand? Why do you pretend you understand, when you don't?'

'Understand,' Debebe obstinately insisted.

Budai seized her shoulders with a sudden fury and shook her, accusing her:

'You haven't understood a single word!'

'Understand.'

'Liar!'

'Understand.'

'Do you hear me?'

Shocked by his own violence, he felt his mind clouding over: he slapped Pepep on the jaw. But still she carried on muttering the same words.

'Understand. Understand.'

He no longer knew what he was doing. He lost control. He tugged at her, pushed her, hit her, wherever he could, on her face, her neck, the back of her head, her breast. She did not defend herself, only raised her arms to shield her eyes and wept quietly in the darkness, barely audible. Her passivity only made him more furious. He thrashed about wildly, grabbed her hair, beat her with his fists again and again like a madman in utter confusion, forgetting everything and thinking only: she must pay for this, she must pay ...

Then he suddenly collapsed, exhausted, panting, his heart loudly beating, utterly lost. He embraced her, pressed her, kissed her hands and pleaded shamefully, entreating her:

'Forgive me! I am a fool! Don't be angry, forgive me, I am not myself. I am a fool, a fool ...'

Tchetchetche's eyes were still full of tears, her face burning from the blows. Budai would have given anything to comfort her:

he covered her with his body, stroked her, kissed her time and time again, kissed every part of her body, knelt down beside the bed laying his head in her lap, whispering in a choked voice, mumbling endearments. The woman's skin was on fire, her hands dry and hot, as she reached down to him, stroked his hair, ran her fingers through it and drew him up towards her.

Ebebe gave herself to him completely this time: she was tender and attentive and did things for him she clearly never did for her husband. Now she could rise with him to a full climax. It was not so much the moment of pleasure that was important but that they were at one with each other, that there was nothing that was not them, time and space having melted away, leaving them the last people on earth. There were moments at the height of passion when Budai was tempted to ask whether everything that had happened to him so far was the price that had to be paid for this, and even if it was the price, whether it was not worth it?

And then, as if by way of epilogue, the lights came on, both the wall-fitting and the bedside table lamp. After such long darkness the light cut into their eyes: the woman blinked, turned away and leapt from the bed. Well, of course, if the electricity was back on the lift would be working again and she had to attend to it. She quickly dressed, lighting another cigarette as she did so. Budai continued to lie there, his hungry eyes following her every movement, watching as she drew on her underclothes and fixed the suspenders to her stocking-tops. By now he was so much in love with her that he could only stare transfixed, fearful yet happy in the recognition that he could not possibly live if he lost her.

He would have liked to give her something, at least to offer some token but there was nothing in the room except a little low-quality cold meat and the heel of a dry loaf on the windowsill. Pepet refused them, quickly adjusted her hair, applied some hasty lipstick, smoothed her blue uniform and was off. Using a mixture of words and signs, they arranged that she would come again tomorrow night at the same time. Then she was gone, having left her cigarette still glowing on the ashtray, the room thick with smoke, though Budai did not open the window, not then, nor later.

When he woke in the morning his first thought was to calculate the hours to their evening rendezvous. Wanting to make decent preparations this time, he ran down to the shops. He had some money since he had worked quite long hours at the market so he spent the entire morning queuing up in groceries. He bought cheese, cold meats and fish, boiled eggs, salad, fresh bread, butter and some sweet pastries, adding to this, since he had neither tea nor coffee to offer, two bottles of that ubiquitous sweetish alcoholic drink.

By the time he returned his room had been cleaned, tidied and aired. Even the bedding was changed. In other words it was Friday again. Another week had passed, the third since his arrival, though to him, naturally, it seemed much longer. Would there be another bill in his box at reception, a reminder that he hadn't paid the last one? He still had a lot of time on his hands. It had been late, almost midnight, when Bebe had knocked at his door, though that was merely a guess since he had no clock. He was so impatient he found no rest anywhere, certainly not in his room, so he set out again with the excuse of looking for some kind of present to give her.

He did not once see her in the lift. Was she off-duty today? Or was she working a later shift? Or was she free for the day and coming in later only to see him? Nor was there anything in box 921 downstairs, though maybe there would be in the afternoon ... He set out to explore the so-far unfamiliar streets behind the hotel. He racked his brains – what kind of present he should buy: a bracelet, a necklace, some other ornament? A cigarette box, a lighter? It should, in any case, be something that she would always carry around with her.

He was surprised to discover an ice-rink not too far away. It was relatively small, a few metres below the level of the surrounding square so that one could look down on it, and indeed there were many people gathered at the rails. The rink was full of skaters, chiefly older people as it happened: the fat and the lanky, ladies of a certain age together with bald, paunchy gentlemen, gliding and turning, messing about on the ice in time to the slow music. It was strange and haunting the way they took each other's arms, the way they were enjoying themselves, some even dancing in the dense crowd. Budai stopped to gaze. He listened to the music, mesmerised by the ebb and flow below him and by the delicately swaying old people. Soon he too began to sway to the rhythm of the slow waltz.

He realised he had missed a golden opportunity last night. Now he had both time and opportunity to communicate with somebody and to ask them to guide him to ... where? To a railway station? An airport? An embassy? No matter, anywhere would do as long as it led to some familiar territory. He knew it would not have been tactful to discuss this with Etete, especially not then, recalling how she had reacted when he first began to sound her out there on the eighteenth floor, and how it was soon after that she had come into his room. Tonight though, one way or another, he had to explain it to her and overcome her objections as tenderly as he could. He simply could not delay it any further.

The really strange thing was that the person most likely to be able to help him should be the one who most tied him to the place. He felt rather confused about it in fact: did he want to leave now or did he not? He tried to think it through but was too excited and expectant. His mind was out of kilter. Maybe he should ask Dede to accompany him to the appropriate place, that being the most important thing. Having been there once, he would know the way back and then he would have more time to think and plan his departure.

Suddenly he felt anxious; maybe he misunderstood, maybe she had arrived earlier and had been looking for him. So he hurried back to the hotel, thinking he would probably be able to buy some present there at the lobby stores. First though he had to check his room which meant standing in the queue again to pick up his key.

But when he got to the desk and handed over the slip of paper with 921 on it as usual the clerk looked round then spread his palms to indicate his key was not there. And indeed his box was empty, no key was hanging on the hook. This had never happened before. Could they have hung it elsewhere by mistake? Or was the chambermaid using it to get into his room? But they had never done this before and in any case the room had already been cleaned. He had to investigate. He pushed the slip of paper back over the counter. The clerk was an elderly grey-haired man in a dark uniform who looked familiar though he had seen so many clerks here they were a little mixed up in his memory. Or could this be the man he had come across that very first time when the airport bus dropped him at the hotel? Whatever the truth, of that he treated Budai in a somewhat offhand way now, shaking his head and muttering, clearly indicating that he could not help him. When Budai persisted he brought out a large official book, leafed through it, showed him a page and pointed – fat lot of use it was him pointing like that – to something, then slammed the book shut and immediately turned to the next guest in line who had been observing Budai's attempts while shuffling his feet and tapping his fingers with undisguised annoyance.

Understanding nothing but sensing the worst, Budai took the

lift to the ninth floor, hurried down the corridors and stopped at his room. The door was shut but when he carefully put his ear to it he thought he could hear someone moving about inside. Having waited a little while, unsure what to do and unable to think of anything better, he knocked and opened the door a little. A middle-aged woman in a headscarf appeared in the gap, took a peek out then immediately closed the door behind her. He checked the room number to make sure he was in front of number 921. It seemed they had given his room to someone else. Others had moved in. So it was for them the sheets had been changed that morning.

That immediately gave him something else to worry about. What had they done with his belongings, with those minimal items of clothing he had brought with him, with that single case he had been carrying when he arrived? He knocked again but this time no one answered. Someone turned the key inside the room. He was not content to let this go but started shouting, beating the door with his fists and kicking it until they opened it again. This time a thin, blotchy-skinned man in shirtsleeves and braces appeared in the crack, glaring furiously, shouting in a high feminine voice and would have slammed the door shut again had Budai not stuck his foot there and pushed his way in.

It was the smell that hit him first, a piercing, steaming, oppressive, living smell. Then the number of people in the tiny room; besides those already mentioned, a little old woman muttering or perhaps praying in the corner, some children, four, five or even six of them – you couldn't tell precisely in the half-light because the blinds were pulled quite far down – more people lying on the bed with a pram beside them, and others on mattresses on the floor, not to forget a child carry-basket on the table. To top things off, two cats were slipping here and there among the lot, leaping onto the windowsill, on and off chairs, on top of the wardrobe, terrifyingly large, dirty feral-looking tabbies, their shabby coats uncared for. And not only these but angora rabbits too of the kind he had seen in another room, in cages and baskets. The rabbits must have been one of the chief contributors to the combined stench. It was incredible that a hotel should tolerate this kind of thing. The room itself has been rearranged so it looked nothing like the one he had been staying in: the sofa was up against another wall, the lampshade had been removed, there was a playpen in the middle of the room, underwear was drying on the backs of the chairs. The floor was littered with personal belongings, blankets, packages, feeding bottles and chamber pots.

All the while he was observing this, the room's new residents kept up a continuous chatter, arguing and aiming remarks at him, trying to push him out of the room. He was still looking to locate some of his personal possessions but to no avail. He could see nothing of his: no clothes, no pyjamas, not his case, nor his notes on the writing desk. He glanced into the bathroom too, but the few minor items he had brought from home had disappeared to be replaced by two clothes-lines with freshly-washed nappies and rubber pants. After that he allowed himself to be shoved outside: even the children were crying and pushing at him. He could never return here. Not that he had any desire to do so and in any case it would be embarrassing to disturb or eject a family as obviously poor and needy as this. Nor would the hotel have put them in here just so that they should throw them out again to suit Budai.

Well, yes, but where would he stay? He set out to find Epepe again in case she might be working one of the lifts but to his despair she was nowhere to be found. He returned to the ground floor, struggled through the crowded hall and stood in the queue for reception to explain his predicament, pointing to the keys and asking that he be given another room. The clerk must have been bored to death of his endless demands, having to deal with this one troublesome customer all the time and paid him little heed, looking over his shoulder to the next in line. It was pointless going on. He was simply ignored.

So he tried further on at the desk with its variously labelled counters but had no more luck here since the women who worked behind the counters could not understand him and refused even to listen to him, quickly turning away. Next he returned to reception and, having waited in the queue once more, the wait exhausting for both his body and his nervous system, he tried to communicate the fact that if he was no longer desired as a customer they should at least return his belongings to him so that he might seek somewhere else. And his passport too, naturally, since without it, no one else would accommodate him. To his surprise the desk-clerk seemed to realise something for he asked for the slip of paper and took out a fat dossier. He searched in it, then waved two stapled documents, put them down in front of him and addressed him like a teacher, as if to say he had already explained that.

'*Tuluplubru klött apalapa gróz paratléba … Klött, klött, klött … !*'

Listening to this Budai could make out the expression *klött,* which he had earlier established to be a mode of address. And *gróz,* if he was not mistaken, was their word for the number 2 … He studied the two sheets of paper. The top one seemed familiar and he quickly came to the conclusion that it was a carbon copy of his last hotel bill, the one he had received last Friday, the one he had not yet settled. Next to it was a similar form with a similar rubric complete with notes, differing only in its bottom-line figure which was a little less than the other one – presumably the bill for this week.

The speech he had just heard must therefore have meant something like: First you must settle the two outstanding bills, yes you, you! … In other words: We are keeping your belongings and passport as surety, you can have them back once you have paid up. That was if he was guessing correctly and the clerk was not saying something altogether different.

Budai did not have enough money, of course, not nearly enough; after all his morning shopping he only had a little change left. He realised that the arranged meeting with Devebe would not take place now. What bothered him most was that she would be knocking at the door of 921, all set for their rendezvous, only to confront the new occupants of the room. What a shock it would be. And there wasn't even a way of leaving a message for her. This, above all, was unbearable, maddening, agonising. The blood rushed to his head: it was like a cloud hovering over him. The storm was inside him. He wanted to hit out, to break things, to murder someone. He no longer cared about anything. Quite beside himself now, he stamped and groaned and screamed in his mother tongue: no matter if no one else understood him, he could not contain his despair.

'Scandalous! ... Absolutely scandalous! Crooks and bastards the lot of you ... filthy swine, bastards!'

He was making a proper scene, causing an affray. A curious crowd gathered round and surrounded him. Then the fat doorman in fur collar, gold braid and peaked cap appeared – he must have been called over – grabbed him by the arm and started dragging him through the throng in the lobby, determined to throw him out. Budai was not yet in control of himself, his whole body was shaking, quite incapable of resistance. When they reached the door the doorman opened it and indicated that he should scram. When Budai did not move he gave him a rough shove and might even have kicked him on the backside. In any case Budai found himself out in the street.

Feeling dizzy, he swayed all over the pavement without knowing what he was doing and it was a good while before he thought to pull himself together. His hat had rolled away but he found it. His coat was open. He had lost two buttons and the shoulder was frayed. He hadn't the least idea what to do. He drifted with the flow of the crowd and eventually found himself by the ice-rink he had discovered that afternoon. It was dusk already, the streetlamps were coming on, the skaters were weaving circles in the harsh light to equally harsh music. Later he arrived at the skyscraper in construction and felt obliged to count the floors again. There were seventy-five now, three more than before.

Filth and mess everywhere – had it been like this from the beginning or had he simply not noticed? When the wind blew, as it was doing now, it lifted and carried the discarded wrappers and other rubbish with it; a newsstand was caught in the gust, a thousand newspapers were swirling about his feet. He noticed how many old people there seemed to be in town: lame, crippled, halt and half-paralysed, they stumbled, lurched and staggered on sticks through the crowd that pressed against them and separated them. Waves of alien humanity regularly washed over them. Frail old grannies, sickly frightened little sparrows, struggled against the overwhelming crowd, dragging their helpless bodies along, trying to cross at traffic lights, trying to board and squeeze themselves on to buses, constantly being shoved aside, squashed and trodden on in the mêlée. What power maintained them? What strength enabled them to go on living here? Why did they not move into the outer suburbs, into a more amenable environment, to some estate? Then there were the crazies, those who wriggled and babbled, who talked and muttered to themselves, the furious who screamed and roamed the streets uttering terrible cries, madmen who rushed about with knives threatening people who cleared a way for them. Then the mumbling beggars thrusting tins in front of passers-by, the moaning, the insane, the paralysed, the skeletal, the subnormal crawling on all fours – all of them full of the desire to live, all pressed together, each of them brushing past another, covering every inch of pavement like a flood, blocking the traffic, their myriad lives impatient to possess and mob the world.

It occurred to Budai that he might have been evicted on account of

Bebe! That it wasn't the unpaid bill, no, that was a misunderstanding, it was their relationship that had been discovered, the fact that the woman had been with him. And this puritan attitude would not have been based on any formally ethical or religious code or because relations between guest and staff were forbidden. There must be a deeper reason, namely that sexual contact might result in a child, a new being, thereby adding to the already overcrowded population. Maybe that is what they were accusing him of! It might be one of the most serious crimes against society: the wilful exacerbation of a demographic crisis.

It was growing darker: there were lights in the sky, white, red, lilac and green. Some glowed steadily, other spun or alternated or swayed or sparkled; some seemed to swim slowly away, others to appear suddenly out of the darkness only to disappear again as mysteriously. What were they? Stars? Aircraft? Signals on towers or on tops of skyscrapers to prevent aircraft crashing into them? Were they rockets? Spaceships? But he didn't feel like speculating about such things now, it was his appointment in the evening that mattered most, for the hour was approaching when he was due to meet Petebe. He hurried back to the hotel.

But the doorman who had till now greeted him so courteously, opening the swing door for him, now stood in front of him as soon as he saw him, his fat, wide body blocking the way. He wasn't a mere dummy after all it seemed, nor a robot as Budai had earlier suspected: the man recognised him, remembered his face and the incident that afternoon. And he stood before him now utterly immobile, with as expressionless a face as before, his stupid little eyes blinking. This time though his arm was raised in rejection instead of invitation.

Budai did not go away but merely moved a little to the side. Where should he have gone after all? However humiliating the behaviour of this ridiculous lump of lard might be, there was no choice for him, no other option but to try his luck here. His plan was to wait for an opportunity to sneak in when a larger group arrived and the doorman would salute them with a touch of his peaked cap. Budai carefully sauntered up to one such and joined it as though he were of the company. But the doorman was alert to that: he let everyone through but when Budai tried to enter he quickly stepped forward and blocked him with his enormous belly. It was no use: however he schemed and plotted the doorman was too alert. At his third or fourth attempt Budai went at it with such determination that the pair of them came right up against each other and were struggling in the doorway, each trying to shove the other out of the way. Budai was no weakling and thought he could handle a mound of blubber like the doorman but the latter proved to have much more stamina than he thought, and in any case he had propped himself against the doorframe which gave him an advantage. In the end they reached a stalemate and the two of them stood there, back to square one, neither of them having gained an inch. This effectively meant defeat for Budai since it was he who had wanted to advance. Now he had to retreat.

But wasn't there a side entrance to the hotel? There might be. It was possible that Tyetye entered through a door reserved for staff. He set off to find something of the sort, turning the next corner to take a tour of the building for surveillance purposes. Surely he would come across it. Yes, but it so happened that the hotel was stuck in the middle of a group of other buildings of various sizes, the roads behind it winding either side so the side streets led him away from his intended route or towards a road-up sign that forbade entrance. After a while he realised he was lost and had no idea whether he was still in the area of the hotel as he had planned or somewhere else altogether.

Then he found himself in front of the ice-rink once more, the third time that day. They were just closing it, or rather were aspiring to close it but the skaters would not leave. However those in charge shepherded them towards the stairs, however they pushed and tried to corral them with the wide brushes they used to clean the ice, the crowd swarmed back in, surging between and around them, squeezing or sneaking in somehow, crowing in triumph as they did so, covering the ice once more so the whole process had to start from scratch.

This was quite entertaining and Budai would have been happy to watch it for a while but suddenly anxiety seized him: what if, right now, while he was wasting his time here, Dede was arriving at the main entrance? He was hungry too, not having eaten anything since the morning. What had happened to the packages of food he had left on the windowsill of his room? He had forgotten those when he pushed his way in and now he felt deeply annoyed about it. Could the big family have consumed it all? Or had those ugly cats scoffed the lot?

If he went into the self-service buffet now or bought something in a shop that would mean standing in a queue again and he feared missing her. So he refrained and worked his way back in the direction from which he had come to the main entrance of the hotel. He arrived at the precise moment that the usual priestly delegation was emerging from a big black car. The doorman swept his hat off with ostentatious reverence, greeting them and bowing low as the bearded, purple-vested, gold-chained ancients entered. Budai tried mingling with them, hoping the fat nincompoop would be too absorbed in the task to notice him. But the man still spotted him, grabbed him and pushed him out: he was not to be fooled.

Was the doorman never off duty? Though now that he took a careful look at him he was not at all sure that he was the same man he had seen earlier. But even if it was someone else, he resembled the first one so closely, not only in his uniform of fur-collared coat, flat peaked cap and gold braid, but in the dull blinking of his tiny eyes, the way he squinted. There was the same puffed up, characterless, empty, buffoonish, primitive expression on his face as on the last.

A long time passed, it might have been hours, hours when nothing changed except the weather. It started raining. Budai took shelter in the awnings before the entrance. The doorman did not mind this and seemed to pay him no attention at all, but Ebede failed to appear. There was no sign of her. Was there any hope of her turning up at all now? If his guess had been correct and it was the relationship between them that had led to his eviction, his partner-in-crime was also likely to have to face the consequences! Being his lover, she might have been dismissed or disciplined in some other way. Was it possible that he would still be waiting for her this time next year?

He was almost dying of hunger by now as well as being faint with exhaustion after the stresses of the day. After all that walking he still had no clue what to do. He leaned against the wall for support. But there must be something – he roused himself – something he had not yet tried! What was it? Maybe he could distract the doorman the way children used to by pointing to something behind him or by throwing some object so that he turned away and momentarily became defenceless. But what distraction could he devise for this vast heap of lard? Lesser distractions would be useless: there was no point in throwing a pebble or a screwed-up piece of paper at him, he was too suspicious to be taken in by that ...He had to make a sacrifice, to take chances, he had learned that much. There was a price to be paid for everything in this town.

With a bitter sigh he dipped into his pockets and fished out a fistful of change, and when there was relative quiet in the street and no one was passing the hotel he threw the change on the ground in front of the doorman. It was done with an easy sweep of his arm and executed from a certain distance. He didn't have much. The coins hit the road with a sharp chink and did not roll away in various directions. He had calculated correctly. The fat pig's ears pricked up, he bent down and looked around curiously to see what it was. Budai had planned to use just this moment to sidle in behind him and to disappear quickly into the building.

He had all but reached the swing doors and seemed to be practically inside when a large group pressed forward from the hall towards the exit – the same door being used for both entrance and exit, a rather eccentric and incongruous feature in a hotel as busy as this. There were a lot of them, tall slender youths, some Africans among them, all in bright pink track-suits, laughing, gesticulating, chattering incomprehensibly, larking about. They looked to be sportsmen of the kind he had seen in the enormous stadium. They were packed together in a solid mass so he was unable to work his way between them, and by the time they were all outside, some twenty or twenty-five of them, the stout Cerberus was back on guard, as alert a watchdog as before.

Desperately disappointed, Budai set out to collect up the coins so he might try again but the doorman put his enormous foot down over most of them so he could recover only the lesser amount. He thought the doorman was joking but it was useless pushing at his foot or trying to shift it, useless making noises to suggest he should raise it, the man did nothing of the sort. Budai turned all his fury on the nincompoop and kicked him on the ankle as hard as he could. The doorman blew a loud whistle. Budai ran away.

Only on the next corner, once he had recovered his breath, did he reflect on why he had been so frightened. No doubt the sound of the whistle had reminded him of his adventure with the police and he had no wish to get mixed up with them again. And it was likely that, having attacked him, that idiot of a doorman would in fact have been whistling for the police. Whatever else happened now at least he had the satisfaction of having given the idiot a good kick and taken it out on him ... He felt terribly sleepy and could hardly stand up, and as for his hunger it was worse than ever. The trouble was he did not see any way of getting back into the hotel tonight. Even if he did get back in, he couldn't move into his room and they would not give him another one where he could lie down. That much was clear from the doorman's behaviour. He'd end up cruising the corridors or sitting in the lobby.

His usual bistro was open and he quickly ate his way through a few sandwiches. And now? What should he do? Where should he go? So far he had at least enjoyed a degree of comfort, a tolerable bolthole where he could lay his head, hide, bathe, rest and gather his thoughts. But what was he to do without any of his possessions, with most of his remaining money under the doorman's heel? Where could he stay? Should he, by some chance, stumble across another hotel – though he had no idea just then where he might find one – he would not be allowed in without his passport and other documents. And Gyegye? How would he find Egyegye again?

It was still raining. Little by little his hat, coat and shoes were being drenched through. Being near the metro entrance he instinctively slip-slopped his way towards it to seek shelter. It was the route he took when he was working as a casual labourer at the market. Down on the platform he took the usual train out of habit, too weak and numb to think of anything else.

As he already knew, work at the market continued right through the night, the ramp at the side entrance always being busy. But he did not come here to work now but to find somewhere to lay his head, any crude approximation to a bed where he could lie down and stay dry. In this respect he was just like the tramps he had seen earlier who, after work or a few drinks, always found a corner to curl up in. Pretty soon he found himself quite a comfortable nook at the back, near the end of the ramp where there was less bustle than elsewhere, a place full of empty crates piled into towers behind which a man might sleep without being noticed. There were a few old sacks on the concrete floor. The space must have been used as a refuge by others before him. Wet through as he was, he lay down and covered himself with his damp coat that smelled of the rain, made a crude pillow of sacks and, overcoming his inbred disgust of anything unhygienic, turned over and fell into a deep exhausted sleep.

He woke feeling hot, dizzy and shivering, not fully awake, in fact less than half awake. It was dark. Rays of lamplight filtered in from outside, as did the sounds of porters, the vibration of truck engines and the squeaking of the conveyor belt. Was this the same night or the one after? He had a fever, there was no doubt about it. He must have got chilled through in the rain, hanging about for hours like that in front of the hotel. Maybe it was flu. Cold shivers ran through him. He might even have contracted pneumonia.

He hadn't been as low as this since leaving home. He felt utterly bereft, lost without a doctor or medicine: in his present condition he couldn't even think of stumbling down to the clinic where the dentist had pulled his tooth. Not even a dog would take notice of him in this god-forsaken hole. No dogs were sniffing around him. Nor was he interested in anyone else. All he wanted to do was what mere animals did, to hide and be left alone with his troubles. He sank into himself and stayed there, his mind wandering at the rock bottom of his consciousness. The sickness numbed his body and spirit: he tossed and turned in his own heat, his own perspiration.

He was in a twilight condition with very few needs and, in so far as he had any will left at all, it was to reduce his needs still further since there was no way of requiting them. There was no food but then he had no desire to eat. A cup of tea might have been nice for his dry throat and to mask the bad taste in his mouth but what to buy it with? Best not to think about it; other matters were still less pleasant to think of though they were desperately urgent. A few days ago he had discovered a filthy latrine at the back of the market, though some people, it seemed, preferred to conduct their business by the wall. That was something he had to attend to. But first he had to raise his body and get over there, tasks that seemed to be beyond him now. Nevertheless, he was determined not to soil the spot he currently occupied. He could not imagine doing so, not while he had a spark of consciousness left at any rate.

It took considerable effort to get to his feet: for a full quarter of an hour he kept encouraging himself to get up but postponed the moment because the task seemed so difficult. After a number of failed attempts he got as far as sitting up but felt so dizzy that he immediately collapsed again and lost consciousness for a while, drowning in a dark red mist. Once he came to his senses he tried again, obstinate, cursing, He would not resign himself to failure. If he gave up the attempt, he insisted to himself, he might as well throw it all in.

So he kept trying, struggling and cursing his helplessness until finally he succeeded in standing on his feet. Surely with such determination he had to succeed. He took one step at a time, his hand on the wall, feeling his way like a blind man, fighting for each yard with brief intermittent losses of consciousness at which point he had to grasp something not to fall. He was forced to stop from time to time, resting on a bale or a crate for a few minutes before continuing. The short journey there and back took over an hour and at the end of it Budai was utterly exhausted. By the time he dropped on his mean improvised bed again he had no reserves left.

He tossed and turned in the confused hinterland between wake and sleep, the two blurred, sometimes all but inseparable. One time it seemed he was seeing rats. It was as if they were running over his legs though he felt no fear of them. Afterwards he could not tell whether it had really happened – as it well might in a place like this – or if he imagined it. He tended to dream a lot in any case and even more now that he was feverish. The dreams were usually about finding someone, someone with whom he could talk. It was a different person each time, a different occasion under different circumstances. The figure tended to appear in the metro, but the man in the green overcoat, his fellow Hungarian, turned up in other situations too. In one dream he was struggling with the fat doorman, in another he was sliding awkwardly between a group of skaters, occasionally falling over. He dreamt he was on an aeroplane, on a train, on a ship, even on a horse though he had never ridden one before. They were galloping down a damp sandy field, the soft soil behind them clearly showing the horse's hoof prints.

Images of his more recent experiences got mixed up with memories of home. Even if they were looking for him they would not find him here. He had neither accommodation nor address now. He was a homeless vagabond like the others: who could possibly know where he was? ... That was the one thing that could still bring tears to his eyes. It was what others would think of as his disappearance, the way he just vanished off the map. He wept quietly to himself on his bed of sacks behind the crates. All this might just be bearable if he had no ties, no family, no workplace, no friends, no dog. Or wife. He missed his wife most. She was the most powerful and deepest loss. They had lived together so long and so intimately, she was so much part of his own being, that the pain she must be feeling at home was his pain too. He would, if he could, have taken a scalpel to his own heart and cut her out of it.

No, he must not feel sorry for himself. He knew that even in his confused state, even as he was tossing and turning in his fever. Self-pity would not get him anywhere. There was no one else to pity him here. Self-pity would only be a burden, a handicap ... His thoughts eventually did what they were bound to and ran to a natural conclusion, to the possibility that underlay every thought. There was hardly anything he needed to do in his current situation. He had simply to let go, to allow the thin thread of hope that had so far sustained him to slip from his hand and he would sink, or rather fall headlong, into a happy oblivion: that was, after all, for the time being anyway, the easiest course.

But he delayed it, put the thought away, refusing to let it preoccupy him. He could give up any time he chose. That was probably the chief reason he resisted: there was no urgency about giving up. The thought of escape, of flight, remained even if only as an idea, not a concrete plan. Despite his helplessness, despite his sick and muddled mental state, there continued to burn in him the small flame of defiance, an indescribable and indeed hopeless fury at his predicament. It was the fury that would not allow him to surrender and end up a loser. Simply grinding his teeth and cursing even at the worst hours of a crisis was evidence of struggle. Some particle of his consciousness would always resist the power of vacuous darkness. It was a kind of obduracy, rogue's honour, an irrational, perhaps even ridiculous holding fast. It was a fellow-feeling with oneself when there is nobody else to turn to.

Pepe started to appear in his dreams. He came upon her in various situations always with an associated feeling of anxiety and guilt. He couldn't forgive himself for having hit her. He kept returning to the event: was that why she did not turn up again? Might she have felt too angry afterwards? Whatever the answer it was not something he could reconcile himself to. He had to make up for it, to provide some recompense for her, to explain and let her feel he regretted it. That was another reason he had to get well as soon as possible: he had to go back to the hotel and find Bebebe. He could not live without having put things right and he certainly could not leave without doing so.

He no longer had any idea how long he had been mouldering there in that miserable corner. His sense of time was gone: night and day ran into each other. The next time he woke and painfully teetered out to the latrine he saw that the market hall was empty inside, the various stands and booths locked up, shuttered, bolted, fixed with iron bars, though there were still workers at the side entrance operating loud machines and cranes. It must be Sunday again as it had been the first time he had come here. It was on Friday that he had been ejected from the hotel so he must have spent two nights here.

He was feeling a little better, his temperature must have dropped too. He was too weak to leave his shelter yet. His recovery was too slow. He needed two or three more days. His appetite had returned though he could find nothing to eat apart from a few partly rotting apples that must have rolled from their baskets. He tried to eat the whole, albeit with a certain disgust, but it was better than nothing.

After all this time he felt so dirty he wanted a good wash. He swayed about looking for water until at last he discovered a tap at the far end of the ramp. There was a long queue for that too with jugs, bottles, even buckets. He joined them while wondering who they were: stallholders, customers or casual labourers like himself? Already there were others behind him so he had no time to do anything except to drink from cupped hands. No sooner had he rinsed his mouth than he was shoved out of the way by those following, the sheer weight of them pushing him on.

He thought it best to return late in the evening once the stalls were locked up, when only the side and rear stores were being replenished, while the empty crates and bundles were taken away – a process that went on right through the night. There were far fewer people waiting for water now, just four or five tottering drunks, and he was soon alone and undisturbed at the tap. The water ran less freely now and he had no soap but it still felt good on his hands, face and neck. He put his head under the cold water to cool his overheated brow and splashed and rinsed his hair. He would have liked to wash below too but what was the point if he was only to put on the same dirty underpants soaked through with perspiration? There was no point in even starting.

Eventually he did get better and since he had to eat and to live he set about finding work again. Fortunately there was always a need for porters so it was up to him now, depending on his strength and mood, how much he took on and when. When it was food they were carrying he could grab the odd fistful, much as the others were doing since it all went unchecked. There were carrots, onions, fruit, raw vegetables and sometimes crackling or the odd stick of sausage when the storeman was looking the other way. And if he needed something else he could buy it right here with the money he was earning.

His life had changed enormously, of course, compared to what it had been before and now that he was no longer sick, it was not only more difficult to resign himself to, it was all but unbearable. The few belongings he had brought from home had remained in the hotel along with the little intended presents. His first task was to procure some soap, a toothbrush and some toothpaste, articles he could buy in the market hall, though the toothpaste tasted sweet like everything else here. He didn't buy a shaving kit partly because it was expensive and partly because buying one would have proved too complicated, involving separate items such as razor, razor blade, shaving brush, shaving foam or cream and so on. Why shave in any case? For whom? He hadn't been to a barber since he first landed in town and though he really didn't give it much thought now his chin was stubbly and hairy, his hair was an uncombed mess and the nails on his fingers and toes had grown long and hard. Having no sewing kit, his general appearance had become steadily less respectable: he had lost buttons, his shoelaces were broken, his suit had rips and holes in it and everything was dirty. They were the clothes he both slept and worked in. On one occasion, having wandered a little further away from the market hall than usual, he saw his reflection in a shop mirror and hardly recognised the bearded, ragged tramp staring back at him. It was his eyes especially that frightened him, the dark, jaded, hunted-and-confused look of primitive man in the thin, worn, sallow face ...

He missed the change of underwear most. There was nothing clean to put on. Even if he had possessed a change of clothes where would he be able to wash the set he had taken off, where could he have dried it or, indeed, simply kept it? Clothes were scandalously expensive here as he had noted in the window of the department store he found in the outer suburb on the day he had wasted his time trying to find a cinema. He simply didn't have the money: he would have had to slave away for ages before scraping enough together. He would have to postpone the idea. Until then he could do no more than imagine a new being for himself, one that was distinct from his clothes, from his skin too if that were possible – indeed from his entire neglected body.

As he grew more feral so his homesickness grew less insistent. He had practically stopped keeping track of how long he had been here. Did they still remember him at home? Had they given him up for lost, written him off, perhaps even forgotten him? The home he had left behind, his old life, was fading away. All that remained of it was the desire to get away, far away from here. It no longer mattered where, in what direction, simply away, away, away.

Once he felt a little better he took a metro back to the hotel. He was pretty sure they wouldn't let him back in and he was right. The fat uniformed doorman barred his way again, raising his arm to indicate no entry, but why after all should he admit such a suspicious-looking figure who might be a beggar or something even worse? Or was it just that he remembered their last encounter when the fellow had ejected him from the hotel and did everything to stop him going back in? ... Budai felt weaker now, less able to stand up for himself and, after three or four half-hearted attempts, simply stopped trying. The doorman stood at the ready, automatically blocking the entrance each time Budai reappeared. The man was clucking something from beneath his fat fleshy nose as if he were talking to him. Budai leaned closer to try to catch what he was saying and make sense of it. It sounded a little like:

'*Parataschara … Kiripi laba parasera … parataschara …*'

The man was repeating the same phrases he had used before when Budai asked him about a taxi, a phrase Budai had later concluded was a form of greeting. Might he have been wrong? For it wasn't very likely that the doorman would be uttering such things while getting him to clear off. Or could it be that the phrase had another meaning too depending on the occasion, that it meant both you are welcome and to hell with you, the way the Latin adjective *altus* could mean both deep and high, and *sacer* both blessed and cursed, in other words, precisely opposite things?

As he stared at the hotel from the street it seemed to him a lost paradise from which he had been banished. He regarded it with the most intense nostalgia but was almost incapable of conjuring up any part of it or even imagining that he once had his own room, his own made-up bed, his own writing table, bathroom, basin and shower. And that Edede was there each day … Was she still riding the lift up and down, pushing the buttons? If the authorities had discovered their relationship, as he feared they had, and it was regarded as a capital crime, it would be the same for her as for him; their vengeance would seek her out too and it was pointless looking for her. On the other hand, he admitted to himself, he would be ashamed to be seen by her in his current state.

His capacity for action had drained away, his mind was dry and barren and he had little appetite left for renewing his battle of wits with that lump of lard. He hung around the entrance for a while longer but nothing changed, no new stratagem or scheme occurred to him. For a few moments he wasn't even sure whether he wanted to enter at all. Some time later, without having made a decision as such, he set off back towards the metro station. The skyscraper on the building had grown another two floors since he last passed that way: it had reached floor seventy-seven.

He was familiar by now with the faces of some of the market labourers though he had no desire to make their acquaintance. Since there was a fairly rapid turnover of workers there were always new faces at the loading area and it was noticeable how many of them were coloured, more here than elsewhere. Those who, like him, had no accommodation tended to seek out any available place in the market come dusk, on bales, on heaps of coal or next to the wall, generally drunk. Every so often a policeman would stroll over the ramp, moving on those he spotted, though no-one discovered Budai's hiding place. Once the policemen had gone those he had disturbed returned to their places and lay down again.

Having finished work Budai too took to the bar in the next street. He made a firm decision to get used to it. It was part of his current way of life, after all, much more so than a clean shirt. Where was he to wash a shirt? His lack of resources also had him choosing between clean underwear and getting drunk, and it was in perfectly sober mood, after considerable thought, that he opted for the latter. His situation would have been simply intolerable without alcohol.

The bar was normally solid with customers and served no more that two or three different kinds of drink. He was unable to discern a significant difference between even these: they all approximated to the syrupy-sickly liquid you could buy anywhere and which, in his estimation, was pretty high in alcohol content. The dirty, stuffy, loud, smoke-filled room was patronised mostly by market employees, casual porters and the like, lowlifes and underworld types as well as a few tired, sluttish women of dubious appearance. The patrons would lean on the bar for hours on end, glass in hand, engaged in long debates that, Budai suspected, were conducted in mutually incomprehensible languages, so that, like all drunks, they simply held forth notwithstanding. Occasionally the conversation would grow heated and suddenly an argument would break out, reaching a pitch of fury that sometimes resulted in a fight. When this happened the barman, a powerfully built, bald black man in a green apron, would usher the troublemakers out through the door or sometimes physically throw them out.

Budai was kept amused by little things there. It was how he filled his time. He drank until his money ran out or until he felt woozy and had lost all sensation to the point of collapse but still had just enough alertness left to stumble back to his shelter where he was overcome by sleep. He would wake next morning with a bad headache, a foul taste in his mouth and a burning sensation in his stomach but that wouldn't stop him returning the next evening.

His nerves though were being worn to tatters. He was constantly tense, charged with a nervous electric energy. Passing this or that figure in the street, it didn't matter who, it would only take an irritating gesture or an annoying face and he would suddenly be overcome by a terrible blind fury. The sober part of his mind would know the fury to be perfectly unreasonable but he still could not resist: everything went dark and he cursed and swore at the person. He would imagine hitting or kicking him and using his face as a punch-bag. Once he was gazing at a good-looking slender creole boy dressed in a slightly over-elegant fashion with a bracelet and a chain around his neck. He was chewing gum to judge by the rhythmic movements of his jaw. The sight of his blazer, of his delicate fingers absent-mindedly plucking at his lips, filled him with such indignation he wanted to smash his fist into the boy's face and beat him to death and would have done so had he not feared the consequences. For days after that he felt ill just recalling the moment.

It was the old, the ailing, the feeble that particularly irritated him. It was wrong and unfair as he well knew but he couldn't help himself. On one occasion he found someone had taken his spot behind the crates. It was a puny, graceless figure who was asleep there. The fellow's hair was grey, his face had fallen in, he was hardly bigger than a child. His blue canvas trousers had patches on them. Budai was seized with a terrible anger. The blood rushed to his head and he dragged the tiny unresisting figure to his feet and tossed him aside ... Later, in a fit of conscience, he looked for him everywhere, hoping to earn some forgiveness by buying him a drink but there was no trace of him. Like so many others that he had met in the city, he simply disappeared.

Wherever he wandered in town – and now he was deliberately crossing roads against the lights – he strewed rubbish, trod over floral borders and generally sought to break as many rules as he could. He had convinced himself that such rules had nothing to do with him, that he did not belong here, that he was simply a foreigner, an alien. If someone pushed him in the crowd, as often happened, of course, he craftily kicked the person back, or hit him with his fists, or if he lacked the opportunity to do that immediately, kept following the guilty party until he caught up with him and was able to exact full revenge by beating, slapping, punching and tearing at him. When he passed an empty telephone box he would enter, tear off the receiver and crush it under his heel. He would kick over the rubbish bins people had put out in front of their houses and enjoy seeing the rubbish spill out. He would throw stones at windows at night and smash streetlights.

But he never stopped making excursions, exploring ever new directions from the market. He had not yet given up the hope of spotting a railway station, a post office, a bank, an airline or tourist office, or of bumping into another of his compatriots like the man in the overcoat carrying a copy of *Szinházi Élet*, or indeed anyone else with whom he might make himself understood in one of the many languages he was capable of speaking ... Sometimes he felt he was so close to realising this dream, found the prospect of it so real, he would not have been surprised to meet someone round the next corner. At other times though, he felt he had lost all hope and was resigned to spending a year, two years, or even five or ten years here if only he were assured that he would find his way home at the end of it. He needed something to wait for, something to measure, a reason for counting the days, weeks and months.

Or was there to be no return from here? Was this to be the end of the road, his *ultima Thule*, the place he had to reach sometime whichever way he turned, whether in Helsinki or some other place, the place where everyone wound up?

Spring crept on day by day. In the morning as he opened his eyes a sharp, oblique clot of light would explode all over his little nook. He had been so used to seeing the city in bad weather, under dense cloud, that at first he thought the source of light must be electric and it was only slowly, with a fluttering of the heart, that he realised it was the warm rays of the sun.

There was a strange stirring in the air. There were always a few stray dogs rambling about the market hall but now they were running about, restless, barking, whimpering, howling, romping together in packs. A gentle light spilled across the ramp. The loading stopped for a break. He could hear music in the distance: drums, cymbals, trumpets.

He set out in its direction, drawn by the hullabaloo and soon enough reached the wide street he had come across on a previous scouting mission. There was an even larger crowd here than usual, onlookers gawping from both pavements while a procession of infinite rolling length covered the roadway.

The procession included children, school-age pupils, girls and boys in wind-cheaters and other brightly coloured uniforms, carrying batons, twirling yellow-white-black plumes of feathers, some in coherent masses, some all mixed up. Some groups proceeded by dancing, others on roller-skates, still others threw balls in the air or kept them bouncing. Some held balloons. There were flags, signs, banners too, all in the local, incomprehensible script. And images, representations whose significance Budai found it impossible to grasp; heraldic devices, symbols composed of various elements, caricatures, bulls and foxes with human heads, birds, an ape brandishing a fly-swat, an old woman who seemed to be dropping from a tree, a fat figure with the ice cracking beneath him, a baby with a wrinkled face shorn of its hair. Who were they? Who were the people being mocked? Then came the drummers, a band of girls in sparkling silver costumes, every one of them with a drum, and then the horn players, a bunch of metro conductors in dark uniform. An entire marching band of firemen clattered by, lads in red helmets with the red fire engine following them at a stately pace, the engine fully manned, the ladder extended.

Horsemen arrived at a stately clip-clop, hussars in mourning-black boots and collars followed by throbbing motorcycles with sidecars, their riders in one-piece cycling gear (once more Budai pondered what organisation they might be part of). And trucks full of infants bawling in reedy voices and waving flags. The trucks were drawing an enormous cylindrical object painted grey that must have been almost forty metres long at the sight of which the crowd stirred and rumbled, though Budai could only guess what it was: a bomb, a torpedo, a rocket, a spaceship? Then more musicians, this time playing xylophones and instruments that looked like vibraphones, mobile choirs grown hoarse, giving their all. Then a solitary, rather overweight, middle-aged woman in a brilliant yellow dress and a wide floral hat who was received with applause and general muttering to which she responded by smiling at everyone, this way and that. Nurses clad in white pushed wheelchairs laden with the paralysed and crippled. Other disabled people hobbled past on sticks and frames. There were even a few carried on stretchers.

There were clearly a lot of organisations involved: sportsmen, cyclists, weightlifters with bulging muscles, acrobats, clowns, masked figures, though the latter can have formed only a minor part of the revelry and were probably marching on other main routes too ... The most astonishing and most populous group in the parade was composed of prisoners in the regulation stripes, their wrists handcuffed together, their heads bowed. They were escorted by rows of guards on either side wearing brown canvas one-piece uniforms like the motorcyclists before them. This peculiar procession of prisoners did not seem to want to come to an end. Ranks of women followed the men wearing similar outfits, then came children, even tiny ones, eight- to ten- year old boys and girls, all in the same prison dress, also handcuffed. Could they too have been taken from jail? Children? And where were they going? Or was it all a masquerade, a game, possibly a protest or demonstration. But against what? The guards were armed but seemed to be enjoying themselves, laughing, relaxed and waving at the crowd who waved back.

A distant humming signalled the arrival of the next attraction. Birds rose and wheeled above the road. It was a long time before it became clear what was it was. There was a large truck with some cages on it piled very high and as the vehicle proceeded ever more cages were opened to allow birds to fly out. They were not pigeons, more like starlings, their wings whirring as they circled in dense flocks, chattering, whistling, crying out in joy at being able to fly free again. They settled on telegraph wires, screeching loudly, then, suddenly roused, would take off once more into the vast blue sky. This was the most popular show, everyone whooping as they passed, and Budai too watched them, enchanted, his spirits rising with them, waiting to see what would come next.

But the nature of the procession changed at this point. Four solemn and bearded old men, wearing dark suits, marched past at funereal pace, slow and full of dignity followed by a noisy but loose group of what must have been ordinary if colourfully dressed people, happy, it seemed, to be led by the town elders. Spectators began to filter in among them, blending with the procession, swelling it into a flood. Budai too was swept along though he would willingly have joined them anyway.

Ever swelling, ever moving under its own weight and momentum, the crowd pressed through the street without a visible head or tail as if no-one knew quite where they were going or why. Here and there a flag or banner emerged above them. There was some chanting of slogans too, with people forming improvised choruses, singing a variety of songs all at the same time. A brown-skinned, gypsy-looking man in a sweater marched beside Budai, bellowing through a paper trumpet, his voice occasionally rising harshly above the general babble. A little further off a group of women and girls were screaming with laughter and teasing everyone. They tried to involve him too. One of them kept tickling his neck, giggling away with her brightly coloured plume of feathers. Now and then a wave of anger passed through the ranks like a gust of wind.

This endless torrent of confusion eventually fetched up in a large circular open space that must have been filling up from other directions too since it was already almost full. There was a fountain at the centre with a stone elephant that was supposed to spout water from its trunk. It seemed familiar from his earlier walks though the fountain wasn't working now. A young, flowing-haired man had climbed between its tusks onto the base of the statue and was busily gesticulating. He wore a black shirt buttoned up to the collar and was haranguing the crowd. Judging from the rhythmic movements of his arms and a genuine euphony in his words he seemed to be reciting verse. The massed crowd watched him, gently shifting and arranging itself, some voices shouting back at him in agreement, others repeating the refrain or chorus of the poem along with the performer. That is if Budai had properly understood what was happening. The youth in the black shirt was ever more caught up with his performance. He shook his fist in the air, he raised his finger to heaven and closed his eyes. When he finished people applauded and cheered him as he leapt off the pedestal.

No sooner had he vacated it than someone else was helped up into his place, a frail, elderly, white-moustached man with thinning grey hair. He was visibly trembling, his legs hardly supporting him. It took two people to anchor him and his voice too trembled with passion. His prominent cheekbones and his broad bulging brow were flushed as he quietly stuttered something from a sheet of paper. The square had fallen silent as they heard him out, deeply moved. The old man was visibly delighted by the respect they afforded him, and it was only when he took a break and looked up that the crowd broke into loud, indignant agreement. He must have been specifically chosen to read out a series of declarations or demands. The excitement of doing so had exhausted him to the degree that his voice almost failed at times and he could hardly bring himself to whisper but kept coughing into his handkerchief, his face bright red, so that eventually he had to be helped down and led away.

It was the waist-coated, bowler-hatted black man in the chequered jacket that climbed up next. He spoke no more then six or seven words, then pulled a mocking face, slapping the elephant's trunk as he did so. What he said must have been amusing and clever because it was greeted with a great deal of laughter. They didn't want him to get off. He kept bowing and pulling faces, thanking the crowd for their appreciation. Even Budai was laughing: the whole thing was so funny he simply couldn't help it.

The next speaker was a soft, smooth-faced figure in glasses. No sooner had he started than he was greeted with whistles and cries of fury. He waited till they calmed down a little, then continued. He must have been giving some kind of explanation and though he was mocked and shouted down time and again he rode the crowd's disapproval, pleading with them to at least hear him out. The more it went on the more he seemed to be begging and promising things and the more angry the crowd grew. They cursed him, waved fists at him, warning him to leave off, even throwing empty bottles at him. His voice was drowned out in the noise. Budai too was indignant, fed up with the idiot's smooth line of argument and was shouting as loud as he could with the rest.

'Get down! Enough! What do you want! Go on, scram, kick him out!'

Eventually he was dragged from the pedestal and chased away by some youths. He should be glad to escape a good beating!

Other speakers appeared, among them the big woman in the bright yellow dress whom he had noticed in the procession. She was carrying a basket on her arm from which she distributed badges and cockades. People greedily grabbed them, practically fought each other for them. Budai was standing too far off to get one. The only thing he understood in all this was that the badges reminded him of certain ladybirds, the black ones with red spots or the red ones with black spots. The woman pinned one on her own breast and the crowd once again cheered and grew merry, crying loud huzzahs and drumming their feet on the pavement. And they fell to singing again, all of them together.

Then a priest ascended the pedestal in full cape and mitre, very like the one he had seen in the church with the dome. He unfurled a flag, one with red and black stripes, the same colours as on the badges and cockades, bearing the central motif of a bird with outstretched wings – might it have been a starling? – the flag so enormous, so wide, that he was unable to extend it himself without the help of two ministrants in surplices. The priest said a brief prayer, then was passed a censer that he swung in the direction of the flag, letting it swing to and fro, enveloping the flag in thick white smoke that might have symbolised a blessing or a consecration ... The crowd was overcome with veneration, many were deeply moved. Some people were in tears and those who could get near enough kissed the edge of the flag while others fell to their knees in worship or threw themselves to the ground in front of it.

Sirens suddenly started wailing from various directions. Ambulances? Fire services? The police? Hearing the sound, the entire crush began to break up, running off this way and that, filling up the surrounding streets again. The section in which Budai was trapped made for the wide gates of the great buttressed castle nearby, gates normally reserved for cars, and flowed through. Whichever way they went, shops brought down their shutters. Traffic was at a standstill, buses and cars parking at the side of the road, the passengers spilling from them to join the ranks of those who had been part of the procession. Bells were ringing in the distance and a horn was constantly sounding, the kind of horn that normally brings an end to a day's work at a factory.

He found himself at the building site with the skyscraper, the one whose floors he had so often counted, but he had no time for that now. The construction workers had in any case started to leave the building as soon as the remnants of the procession came into view. They were descending by lift and ladder. Cranes and all other machinery stopped working: the high steel frame, the walls, the platforms emptied. Everyone engaged on the building joined the mass below, coming just as they were, in paint-stained overalls, with paper hats on their heads and so the wave of humanity swelled and grew. What was this? A general strike?

Posters still fresh and wet on the walls bore messages with huge letters. Groups read and debated in front of them. The human flood swallowed them too and was soon joined by residents of the wayside houses and the hordes emerging from the steps of the metro with its yellow barriers. In the meantime someone was rasping something through a microphone, the voice cracking and babbling as if it were trying to communicate urgent instructions. It met with a hostile reaction. The protesters grumbled, cried out in hoarse voices, turned disorderly and started pushing and shoving. Another stream joined them at the next crossroads. There were bottlenecks and vortices, lines got mixed up, people cut across each other, trod each other down in the confusion. And still the amplified voice crackled on.

Budai's heart leapt for a moment: he thought he saw Epepe on the other side of the road. It was a second or two, no more, perhaps less than that. Her blonde, blue-uniformed figure stood blindingly clear of the crowd, Or was it simply the blonde hair, the blue uniform and the familiar build that made him think it was her? Was it someone else? No sooner had she appeared than she was gone and however Budai struggled to reach her, he couldn't see her anymore, nor anyone who looked the least bit like her, though it was perfectly possible that those on her side of the road had been shoved aside.

The failure did not crush him. He had not given up hope that he might catch sight of her again in the crowd despite its arbitrary turns and shifts. Hope spurred him to action, encouraging him to take real part in whatever was going on here, to go where the others went, to do as they did, to share their fates, adopt their causes, to fight tooth and nail with them.

He tried to grasp and learn the songs they were singing. Most of the time it was a stirring rapid march, one he had heard before so not just the melody but even the words had stuck in his memory, that is in as far as he could make it out. It sounded something like:

Tchetety top debette
Etek glö tchri fefé
Bügyüti nyemelága
Petyitye!

The last word tended to come out snappish and short accompanied by either fury or laughter. They song was defiantly repeated as if to threaten or annoy, as though the singing of it had long been forbidden. There was a very thin young man with an abundance of hair who kept it going: if others stopped singing it he would start it up time and again, conducting them with his long arms until everyone near him took it up. It became intoxicating after a while: people were drunk on their own voices as though they felt – and Budai felt it too – that they were accomplishing something important by singing it. This happy confidence bubbled through them like the fizz in soda: together, they felt, they could overcome anything: nothing could stop them, they were all-conquering heroes. And this led them into ever wilder excesses of joy. They embraced strangers, they kissed each other, they danced and clapped and shouted: they seemed to float on its energy.

Next to Budai a silver-clad girl with golden-brown skin and a head of woolly black hair was beating a drum. She must have been part of the procession when it was at its orderly stage, one among many girls in silver who only later melted into the crowd. She can't have been much more than fifteen but she beat her drum tirelessly, her face transfigured by a passionate enthusiasm, so much so that she was almost beside herself, the whites of her eyes prominent, her gaze fixed somewhere above. Budai could not help thinking that though still a child she would have no hesitation in offering up her life if it became necessary.

A little way down the road they were building barricades. They had taken up the paving stones and gathered furniture from the nearby houses, continuing to bring out sideboards and pianos, also building a small hill of sand and pebbles as wide and high as they could on top of which they fixed a flag.

A line of uniformed men with guns were waiting in riot order on the next corner, blocking the side-street, their uniforms consisting of those ubiquitous canvas overalls and tunics. The crowd recoiled but a bunch of young women started teasing them. They approached ever closer, clapping and dancing, however much the officer in command yelled at them, taking no notice of him but pinning flowers in the young men's berets and when they raised their guns, planting one in the barrel too. This encouraged others to come forward, offering them cigarettes, embracing them from front and from rear, slapping their shoulders, shaking their hands and smiling, loudly explaining the state of affairs to them. Within a couple of minutes of this display of friendship the soldiers had been unarmed. The side street that had been blocked off now lay open and the crowd swept down it, carrying Budai with them. Soldiers who a few moments ago were barring their way joined them now, men in tunics marching along, laughing and singing with the rest. Here and there you could see a member of the crowd carrying one of the official rifles.

Reaching a narrow street, they merged with a boisterous crowd already there. A large anonymous grey building looked down on them, all the windows of its four storeys full of curious faces. There was a great deal of coming and going in the smaller houses opposite. The whole street felt like an ants' nest. Budai tried to push his way through and saw that the gates of the grey building were locked, its great iron doors barred and reinforced with bolts and straps. A tank sat in front of it, blocking the entrance with its weight of metal.

It wasn't clear to him quite what was happening so, following a hunch, he walked into one of the houses opposite and though the gateway, the stairs and internal corridors were already packed with people no-one asked him where he was going. He reached the top floor without any difficulty and went through an open door into a flat facing the street front. There were a number of people already in the various rooms. Clearly they could not all be living here, in fact the tenants themselves might be elsewhere. He stepped out onto the balcony and looked down on the seething masses as waves and counter-waves of them flowed to and fro. He also took the opportunity of observing the neighbouring houses and assumed they were as packed as this one was.

Opposite him in one of the first-floor windows of the grey building people were setting up a loudspeaker to address the street. The crowd below watched this suspiciously, a little quieter now than before, every so often shouting something in mock encouragement. A buzz and crackle signalled that the loudspeaker had been switched on. The set started to whistle and fizz. Once the interference was gone, a female voice was heard gabbling something very fast, followed by a few seconds heavy with silence, followed by the striking of a gong. Then a deeper, more resonant male voice addressed the crowd in ceremonial fashion:

'*Tchetchencho …*'

But the very first word roused a chorus of disapproval, whistles, boos, and general grumbling. Even the slim black girl leaning on the balcony railings next to him shook her fist in anger. The voice repeated slightly less certainly:

'*Tchetchencho …*'

This roused such an explosion of elemental rage the speaker couldn't go on. A brick sailed over the street. It must have been thrown from the very house Budai himself was occupying. It only succeeded in hitting the wall of the grey building where it shattered and fell to the ground. The second struck the window-frame, the third hit the loudspeaker full on. The loudspeaker fell silent. The people gathered in the windows of the grey building vanished: the onlookers drew back. In front of the gate the tank started up, its turret swung around, the barrel extending menacingly from the closed metal box. The people in the street moved aside but not very far, remaining close to the tank, chanting slogans at its invisible crew, raising their arms in oaths of allegiance. Then they sang their anthem again:

Tchetety top debette
Etek glö tchri fefé …

In the meanwhile others continued to throw bricks so that eventually Budai felt anxious enough to leave the building. On his way out he came across great piles of bricks in the yard that served as an ammunition store for the besiegers who had formed a human chain to convey the bricks to the front line.

Just as he reached the gate a few trucks appeared at the end of the street full of uniformed men. They advanced together blowing their horns, forcing their way through the crowd that was not at all keen to let them through. A tall, muscular man leapt on top of the leading truck – he must have been an officer though he wore the same uniform as the others, without insignia. He spoke sharply, clearly, in a voice that could be heard a long way off, a voice used to command that rose over the shouting and yelling. He spoke briefly in a clipped military tone, his gestures decisive and harsh, waving his arms: he was probably calling on the mob to disperse. But he was shouted down by the impatient and ever more hostile crowd and soon enough a brick was flying in his direction too. Though the brick passed within inches of him, the officer showed no fear. He cast a contemptuous eye in the direction from which the brick had come and swung from the truck in a manner that implied impending danger.

Uniformed men leapt off the truck and formed a cordon to cover the whole width of the street. They started to press the crowd back but there weren't very many of them and their combined physical force was nowhere near enough, not even after repeated efforts. Then they tried using the fire hose, aiming jets right and left. Those in front who were struck directly crept back into the ranks, drenched and dripping, but one well-aimed brick struck the hand of the soldier holding the hose and broke the hose in the process.

Next the soldiers started lobbing smoke bombs. This was more effective: the crowd did begin to break up and were forced back, then had to run away to avoid the white billowing puffballs. The smoke did not reach Budai but he was caught up with everyone rushing this way and that. Some turned down the crossroads directly behind them. Budai followed, then skipped over a nearby park fence and scampered down to the next corner.

As he stopped to get his breath he spotted a half-lowered set of awnings under which a lot of others were ducking and vanishing. He joined them to see what was going on. There were steps leading down into a kind of cellar lit only by naked light-bulbs, the place lukewarm and smelling faintly of hemp. It must have been the storeroom of a rope and canvas shop as there were rows of folded sacks beside the lime-washed walls with great rolls of canvas and rope piled over them from floor to ceiling. Other shelves were packed with balls of string and straps. And then there was the crowd, a great mix of men, women and youths. Budai could not decide at first what they were doing here: could they be examining the rope?

A smaller alcove opened to the left and people were crowding into it. He had to stand on tiptoe to see what was happening. A tall, jaundiced-looking, droopy-moustached man in a leather jacket was distributing machineguns from a box, exchanging a few words with whoever was next in line, then shaking hands before handing the gun over. Some people were wearing uniforms, those of the kind he already knew: conductors, boys and girls in green waterproofs, a lot of common canvas tunics. There was even a fireman among them. Others were wearing various forms of combat gear, a mixture of the civilian and the camouflaged military, as well as boots, felt waistcoats, earth-coloured raincoats, shoulder straps and ammunition belts as well as fur hats or peaked police caps. There were even a few in striped prison outfits, convicts with shorn hair, of the sort who had been in the procession in the morning. Could they have been part of the parade or were they just protesters in fancy dress? And if they really were prisoners, what had they been imprisoned for? Were they criminals or political enemies? And how, in any case, did they manage to get free?

Budai seemed to have stumbled on one of the cells of the group in command of the district, possibly the whole city. The continual coming-and-going bore witness to that. Later people brought drinks too, some of them rolling a small barrel down the steps. It was received with cheers and whoops of joy. The barrel was immediately seized, a hole sprung and the contents emptied into jugs and bottles. He was invited to take a swig from the flask that was doing the rounds: it wasn't the sweet-sickly swill that was measured from taps in the bars but a genuine, strong, head-splitting brandy.

Another group arrived at the same time as the barrel, among them a strange, bent-looking girl with a machine gun. Her posture was so bad she might have been genuinely crippled. Her neck was short, her brow low, her face flat and simian. She looked almost simple, her eyes shining with a peculiar light that looked as though she might be suffering from cataracts. She did not drink with the rest, nor did she speak or laugh, she just examined everything, sniffing around, in constant, slow, soft, mysterious motion, checking everybody with a sly look, as if she were seeking someone in particular or waiting for someone to arrive. Perhaps she felt that her hour had arrived now she had a rifle on her back. Where did they get her from?

Just as everyone was drinking and having a good time a blond young man entered, at first almost unnoticed. Silence settled around him: slowly all conversations stopped. He simply stood on the steps, without moving or saying a word until his eyes got used to the dim light. He might have been about twenty-five, with thin pale lips, his eyes were icy grey. He was wearing a tattered cap, stout boots and a dirty green tracksuit top with a gun belt. He rested his right hand on his holster. When everyone had fallen completely silent he descended a few steps and still without saying a word knocked the flask from the hand of a boy who was just about to drink from it.

The brandy spilled on the floor. When the boy made a grab for his flask the newcomer slapped him across the face.

Strangely enough, the boy he had hit looked to be the stronger of the two and he too had a gun but he did not think to strike back or even defend himself. Nor did anyone else so much as mutter. The people in the alcove drew back and even the monkey-faced girl stood stock still ... The blond youth tightened his belt a notch and said something to break the sudden silence. He spoke very quietly in a flat, passionless voice, breaking the words up so clearly that for once even Budai could almost make out what he was saying. It was something like this:

'*Deperety glut ugyurumba?*' He looked round questioningly. People did not look at him, in fact most of them lowered their eyes. '*Bezhetcsh alaulp atipatityapp? Atipatityapp?*' The man with the droopy moustache and jaundiced face who was dispensing machineguns wanted to say something but the blond shut him up and calmly dismissed him. '*Je durunty ...*'

He spoke for two or three minutes in the same flat tone while everyone listened intently, standing in a circle round him, hardly breathing. He ended on a question, though even then his voice hardly rose.

'*Eleégye kurupundu dibádi? ... Dibádi, aka tereshe mutyu lolo dibádi?*'

'*Dibádi! Dibádi!*' they all roared back at him in high spirits.

No-one bothered with the drinks anymore. They swarmed into the street. Tanks happened to be passing at that moment, rumbling by, deafeningly loud. The turrets were open, uniformed men looking out of them. Those who had issued from the cellar store quickly surrounded the tanks and mounted them, led by the blond youth in the green track-suit top. There was a replay of the earlier scene: much debate with the civilians explaining matters with wide sweeping gestures. The uniformed troops were visibly confused by the sudden onslaught. The tanks came to a halt, the helmeted figures clambered out. One, who first removed his headphones, presumably the commanding officer, raised his arms for silence and asked something. He received a hundred replies, hats being waved everywhere, in response to which he ducked back down into the tank. After a short interval he stuck his head out again and simply said:

'*Bugyurim.*'

The crowd burst into cries of joy, cheering and welcoming him. Someone produced a flag, the one Budai had seen before, with red and black stripes, and to more loud cheers fixed it on the leading tank. The tanks then set off again, rumbling on, now laden with troops and civilians all heading in one direction, back towards the grey building. Soon enough they reached the end house. There it had grown dense again: it seemed that attempts to clear the area had not been entirely successful or that others had since come along to join them. The windows of this building too were crammed with onlookers, once again a mixture of troops and civilians, much like outside. Budai tried to stay close to the blond youth and keep his green tracksuit top in sight. The bent-backed girl with the machine gun and idiot eyes seemed to be following Budai, sticking close to him, constantly pattering along behind him.

Now there were shots, a few stray volleys and some longer rounds. It was hard to tell from where Budai was whether it started from inside or outside the building. Perhaps there had been a few warning shots from within and the besiegers had replied with a show of force. Or it might have been the other way round. But it hardly mattered who started it. There were so many guns in the street and the mood was so tense that something was bound to happen. People might have been shooting from the roofs too. The rattling of guns was soon underscored by another deeper, more compact bass noise that sounded like thunder. It must have been the tanks firing.

One section of the grey wall fell away and collapsed into the street, leaving a great gaping hole.

Automatic fire opened up from inside the building, spraying the street. Panic broke out. The crowd broke up again and people fled in terror, everyone seeking shelter wherever it could be found, in nearby doorways, behind advertising pillars, by parked cars, by dustbins or simply lying flat on their stomachs by the walls of locked shops. As the roadway cleared a good number remained lying on the ground, motionless or waving and crying out in pain, some rising and reeling about in search of shelter. A wounded woman was weeping and pleading for someone to help her but then another round of automatic fire from the floor above them swept across the street.

The small group Budai had joined sought cover by the blackened pillars of a ruined house. His whole body was shaking with a mixture of fury, frustration and helpless desire for vengeance. Hatred rose in his throat like a fist. He cursed and swore at the hidden enemy along with the rest, calling them 'murderers, bloody murderers'. But after the next volley he felt so frightened he took to his heels, scrambling past the sooty, angular walls of the ruin, desperately looking for a way, any way, out. He needed to get as far as he could, somewhere he could no longer even hear the sound of gunfire.

It seemed an earlier catastrophe had overtaken the house. The ruins suggested that it was not simply fire, for the blackened plaster bore traces of bullet holes and shell fragments. It might have been destroyed by bombs, by heavy artillery and hand-to-hand combat, and only after that set on fire. But what was the occasion of the catastrophe? What had happened? Was it a siege? A war? A revolution? And who were the combatants? Who fought whom and why?

He had discovered a way out. There were just a few stairs he needed to run up and at the top there was an open corridor that surely led to freedom. But someone called him and snatched at his coat. It was the blond youth and when Budai turned around in fear the youth beckoned him with his finger. Budai stopped in his tracks, not knowing what to do, not understanding where he should go and why. The boy extended his hand, offering him a revolver and now that both of them were still, pressed it into Budai's hand. He suddenly felt ashamed: that icy-grey gaze could clearly see straight through him. He would have liked to explain himself but how, and in any case there was no time. So he merely weighed the revolver in his palm and nodded in confusion as if to say, very well, I am with you.

They stole through the ruins as far as the first crossroads that ran to one side of the grey house to the left of the main elevation. On the opposite side there rose a modern, light-coloured round building like a tower and they ran into it. Inside, a spiral ramp some four or five metres in diameter led up to plateaus on various levels, each packed with ten to twelve cars. It was a multi-storey car park, a light construction into which many cars could fit, though currently there was no-one going in or out. There was a large mass of men there too, armed, like themselves. The battle had spread over the whole district. They were firing from windows using the barriers to the ramp, the parked cars, or anything else they could find as cover.

Budai and the youth made their way up the inner edge of the spiral ramp a little back from the firing positions, then up an extra set of stairs. Gunmen had set themselves up there too as best they could. There were ammunitions dumps, relays, notices written in various hands, arrows pointing out directions, even some first-aid stations in the corners for the wounded. The youth in the green tracksuit top briefly consulted with various individuals, then directed them to the top, floor and beyond that into the roof, vaulted with a series of wave-like forms, from which opened a series of what might have been tiny, circular air vents overlooking the street. From here, they could shoot down at the roof of the building opposite.

The silent ape-faced girl immediately took up one of the positions and began firing.

Also in their company were the young man who had earlier been slapped across the face and the man with the leather jacket and droopy moustache. Just as familiar was the fireman in his red helmet and one of the convicts. This little improvised group was joined by a few uniformed troops in tunics who had transferred their loyalty and some nine or ten civilians with rifles or machineguns who had attached themselves to the cause somewhere along the way. There was another woman there too, a stout, older black woman who was unarmed, her face wreathed in an enormous permanent happy smile. There was no argument about who was the leader, it was the blond young man in the green tracksuit top. He directed operations with a confidence that exuded authority and gave each one of them their specific tasks.

They spent the whole afternoon and evening up in the roof firing at the grey building opposite. Having had no experience of such things Budai was shown how to use and recharge his revolver. Most of the time he was firing bullets blindly with no great sense of purpose. The enemy had in any case withdrawn from the windows on the far side, reappearing only for the odd second to take better aim but still kept up a constant exchange. The chances were that there were a great many of them too, and probably just as mixed a company as was to be found on this side – it was not a battle between ethnic groups.

So many other things happened that evening it was hard to tell where one stopped and the other started. They fired and rested and fired again from different vents. Food was brought, a cauldron of soup a little like goulash, slightly sweet, with herbs and bits of meat. There were also loaves of black bread that normally served as military rations. Later, one of their number, a young man in a raincoat, was wounded and suddenly fell back, his face gone pale. He made no noise but you could see from his tight lips and desperate looks that he was in pain. He was taken away on a stretcher.

Budai managed to sleep for a couple of hours. They had created a temporary resting place out of bits of polystyrene in a corner of the loft. The crazy girl seemed to be close to him as he slept, at least from time to time. She did not address him – no one ever heard her speak, she might have been genuinely dumb – she just fixed him with a blank look that was plainly insolent, leaning on her elbow next to him, never without her machinegun. What did she want from him? She made Budai nervous even when he was half-asleep: he felt tense and anxious not knowing why she was there. How come they had been thrown together like this? What had he to do with a half-wit of the underclass? Later it seemed she was holding him in her arms, embracing him closely with a shameless sexual pleasure though he was all the time as aware of the foul smell of her perspiration as of the battle going on outside. He was also frightened of the severe youth in the green tracksuit top. What would he do if he caught them in this dim corner? It was of course possible that he was imagining all this, that it was an illusion based on acute anxiety. Later still an enormous explosion shook the loft, perhaps a bomb or a grenade – or was that hallucination too?

The evidence suggested it was no hallucination for when they left the multi-storey car park at first light of dawn and looked back, they could see that the wall had gaping holes in it and that the cars parked there had been more or less shot to pieces. The grey building opposite was in a still worse condition with what might have been tank damage: a wide crack ran across the elevation and one corner had collapsed right up to the fourth floor. There were a lot fresh scars and holes.

The little group found its way back to the front gate of the grey building. That obviously had been the chief point of the attack. The burnt-out turret of the tank that had been guarding it was lying on its side and the tracks of the vehicle had become detached, half twisted off. The most daring attackers now used it as cover, firing from behind it, then put their weights to the great mass of steel and with an enormous effort and loud cries pushed it ahead of them for use as a battering ram, thinking to break down the gate which was barred and bolted but shot full of holes now and therefore buttressed on the inside with sandbags, struts and beams.

It did not give easily: they had to shove the great armoured tank against it ten or fifteen times with constant encouragement and a deal of shouting. The thick iron doors kept bowing and bending but they always sprang back. Then the assailants started throwing grenades at it so the whole thing creaked and shrieked and was covered in smoke until finally they succeeded in loosening it from its hinges. Once the grenade smoke had cleared, they tried another push and the gate gave, the whole lot simply falling away. The crowd pressed through with cries of triumph, those behind pushing and encouraging those ahead, hoping for an unobstructed route into the building.

But the gap behind the gates was quickly filled by ranks of men in tunics, the same tunics as worn by many in the crowd – or might there be some difference in the head-to-toe uniform that only Budai hadn't noticed? Those who had swarmed in noticed the automatics and machineguns and stopped in their tracks for a moment. Budai was not right at the front but close enough to take a brief survey of the terrain. From inside the building a hoarse, choking voice was screaming above them, almost certainly giving a last warning. But even if they wanted to heed the message there was no way back since ever more people were arriving behind them, pressing them forward: there was no option but to rush the defending lines ...

A volley of gunfire. Cries, protests, chaos. Commands screeched, almost sung out. A second volley, practically next to Budai's ears. There was no stopping now. People forced their way in. There could be no resistance as they pushed forward, treading over the wounded and dead, over those with guns, over everything and everyone. Another wave of the living collapsed following the third volley; the blond boy was next to Budai, drenched and impassioned, fighting his way through the mêlée of bodies, clutching his revolver, waving his companions on with his left arm, his voice loud, lost in the general noise of the struggle so that only by the movement of his mouth could you tell he was calling. Budai followed him in a red haze, a kind of dream in which he was no longer afraid of anything, an ecstasy of movement in which the only aim was to get through. The twisted, ape-faced girl at his side grabbed at his shoulder and fell but he was no longer concerned with that: he was driving and ploughing on, wrestling down machinegunners, hitting out, screaming with the rest in a voice so strange he had never heard anything like it issuing from his own mouth.

Suddenly there was a great lurch forward and they found themselves inside the narrow little paved courtyard. They had broken through the line of defence. As Budai looked back, the gate was completely filled by a dark mass of insurgents: their numbers were overwhelming. There was no defence left now, it had quite vanished and the victorious crowd was roaming here and there through the building, intoxicated with its own triumph. A staircase led up from the corner of the yard. Budai ran up the first and then the second floor with others, excited and curious to see what they would find when they arrived at the top. But there were only hallways, doors, rooms and office furniture. The mob was everywhere, kicking things over, shoving things aside, searching through desks, throwing books and files here and there so that paper covered the whole floor. People ran round wildly, some in uniform, some in civilian clothes, the armed and the unarmed. Some of them were wounded and wore bandages. Budai couldn't tell insider from outsider, nor had he any idea what purpose the building served and why it was necessary to occupy it.

Some people were dragging a man down the corridor. They were led by two men with automatics with many following behind, all of them, including anyone else they passed, trying to get to the captive, to kick him, hit him and beat him down, screaming at him with hatred on their faces, so that even the armed men could not defend him. The captive was a tall man of military bearing, his boiler-suit uniform practically torn off him, his face and his shirt completely covered in blood, his arm raised to his eyes to ward off further blows. A thin girl, who looked like an angel with her long blonde hair, cleverly slipped through the ring around the man and spat directly in his face.

Others had been captured too and were also being hauled down towards the main gate. One woman was being pulled along by her hair. People were tugging and tearing at it. She fought and struggled using her nails and teeth but was soon forced to her knees. She protested and wept, spreading out her hands, begging for mercy. They tore off her skirt, then her pink knickers too so she was forced to slide along on her naked rump as they dragged her all the way down the stairs.

Budai was caught in the whirl and found himself back at the gate. There were terrible scenes of accusation and vengeance. One after the other individuals were brought down and given over to the lynch mob, most of the victims already badly beaten, hardly able to support themselves, others half-dead. What Budai couldn't understand was how they were identified in the general chaos. Many of them were wearing canvas tunics but a lot of the accusers were in similar outfits. It bothered him. What was the difference between them? Civilians were being brought to judgment too, more women, then another group of uniformed men. There must have been an element of pure chance in the selection, the product of a moment of fury or a sudden urge in sheer blind mass hysteria.

It was as though the combatants themselves had changed: he couldn't see anyone he had fought with. On the other hand, there were ever more mysterious, suspicious-looking figures, some of them demagogues of the first order. Take that dissolute, bearded man with the pockmarked face who looked strangely familiar: he was halfway through directing the hanging of one of the prisoners. The unfortunate victim had little if any life in him but they stripped him half-bare all the same, pulled off his boots, tied his ankles together and hanged him just like that, upside down from the lamppost in front of the gate with everyone cheering, cursing and laughing.

A few armed men tried to resist. You could see that they did not approve and wanted to cut the corpse down. A student who looked saner than the rest tried to dissuade those around him from more killing and used his own body to defend two middle-aged black women who looked as though they might be cleaners. He had little success. The furious mob shouted him down and the bearded, pockmarked man turned on him, pushed him aside and shouted:

'*Durundj!*'

Now Budai remembered who the pockmarked figure was: it was his cellmate at the police station, the failed opera singer, the man with whom he could not get a word in edgeways, or if it not him then someone very like him. He was a proper guttersnipe this hangman-in-chief, clearly enjoying the atrocities, waving a metal bar around, bringing it down on a captive soldier's head. As the soldier collapsed, the man leapt on him, knelt across his chest and stabbed him several times in the neck and in the balls too while the other was still kicking. Then they brought petrol, poured it over him and set it alight so the body blackened as it smoked, giving off the smell of roasting flesh. Nor was this the last of their terrible deeds.

In the meantime the young blond man in the green tracksuit top appeared running out of the building with four or five companions as if he had been told what was going on outside. As soon as he appeared the bloodthirsty crowd hesitated. It wasn't clear whether that was because they regarded him as their leader or because his sheer presence commanded respect ... He hurried over to a group of prisoners who looked resigned to their fate, pushed the gathering mob out of the way and kicked the bearded man on the backside so he fell on his face. Everyone laughed. He picked out the uniformed ones among the prisoners and arranged them in a row with a few sharp words of command. Slowly and reluctantly they obeyed him. He sent them to stand by the wall. The crowd drew back and fell silent.

About a dozen captives were lined up, tensely waiting. Most of them were already wounded, their arms in slings, their heads and brows swathed in bandages. A middle-aged, greying man who cut an elegant figure even in his torn tunic was being supported by the man next to him. He was smoking quite calmly and watching the roused mob without any sign of fear. The blond boy mustered them with a glance of his blue-grey eyes, his lips clamped tight, expressionless. He spoke softly to them and they all raised their hands. Once they had done so he took a machinegun from one of his companions, fiddled with it, examined it and even took a look down the barrel while the uniformed prisoners stood with their hands in the air. There was no fear on their faces, simply a look of incomprehension or confusion as if they didn't quite know the best way to behave in the given situation. One of them blew his nose without lowering the other arm.

The blond boy stood sideways on to them and shot from the hip. He fired a long round right and left, scything through them. They fell on top of each other, some stiff, others still moving their limbs, even rising a little. The grey-haired man took one more drag of his cigarette, flicked it away and only then did he sit down on the pavement with a glance that looked sleepy, faintly bored, as if he had acted voluntarily, even setting his arms on the ground so he could rest his head on them. On the far side of the line two people were still moaning and groaning. The boy in the green tracksuit top, lightly blinking, fired another round that way. Then all movement ceased.

Budai saw three more rounds of executions that morning. He did not even flinch at the third. He could bear to look on; he had developed his immunity. If there were a God, he thought wearily, he would ask that his heart should never grow cold to pity.

He was tired and hungry. He drifted through the crowded streets where tumultuous waves of people pulsed and swayed, their ranks, if anything, even denser then before, all excited by the prospect of what might happen next. Small knots of them were gathering together in debate, collecting around ad hoc speakers. There were aeroplanes humming above and beyond that a constant slow, deep rumble of a city under siege. From time to time trucks would speed by full of armed men. Here and there people were singing and whenever someone came by with the latest news he was immediately surrounded and questioned. The walls too were plastered with announcements, not only printed posters but hand-written messages. Ever more were going up.

Further on, one neighbourhood lay utterly in ruins, all the buildings collapsed and shot to pieces, the street piled high with rubble. One or two fragments were still smoking: there must have been a fierce battle here. A lot of people were clearly moving on, carrying bundles and packets. Families suddenly homeless were pulling carts with bits of salvaged furniture and other miscellaneous possessions. A ragged, long-haired figure stood in the middle of the road, bearded like a prophet, his mad eyes turning this way and that as he flung his arms about and cried the same phrase over and over again like a curse:

'Tohoré! Muharé! Tohoré! Muharé!'

Budai felt sick without quite knowing what was wrong with him. It was partly nausea. There was a nervous feeling in his stomach that he put down to hunger, but even after he had managed to grab a bite – a cheap corn and flour mush he bought at a stand – the nausea persisted.

In the afternoon it started to rain. It was a heavy spring shower. The distant rumbling suddenly grew louder and closer too, ever more frightening. A peculiar restlessness took hold of people: they were running this way and that, keeping close to the walls, sheltering in doorways and abandoned shops, searching for cover as the growl became a threatening roar. Crowds were mumbling and muttering together, some women weeping and screaming in terror. A little further on people were unfurling an enormous black and red flag bearing the symbol of a bird. They stretched it between two windows so it was flat against the wall. Together with a few other pedestrians, Budai took shelter in a china shop on the corner and watched events through the broken window, waiting to see what would happen.

New formations of troops arrived in armoured cars and tanks, on motorcycles, heavily armed detachments. Their uniforms were different from the ones he had seen before: a pale, off-white drill. They wore camouflaged helmets. Two tanks stopped directly in front of the shop and uniformed men stuck their heads out, pointing and shouting to each other – the language they spoke was as strange to Budai as the rest had been.

The upshot of the brief discussion was that they aimed the bigger guns at the large flag and fired. Immediately a cloud of smoke and dust swirled up and most of the wall collapsed. The next shot so shook the building that plates, trays, vases and glasses in the china shop tumbled to the ground and smashed.

Budai ran on, his heart almost giving way. The shower had become a downpour and within a few minutes he was soaked through. He was somewhere he had not been before, a working-class district, he supposed, an estate with enormous, bare tenements, ugly, awkward masses with countless tiny windows, the buildings arranged round a cobbled, oval-shaped open space. Further motorised detachments were rumbling through the streets behind him but even in the rain the open space was full of people. It was only after a while he noticed that the crowd was exclusively female, old and young women, matrons and girls, many with umbrellas. There were at least ten occasions when he thought he saw Bebé among them.

The soldiers arrived and the women surrounded them all talking together, making broad gestures. The soldiers made no answer, staring ahead with stony gazes, their expressions unfathomable as the rain beat on their helmets. Budai couldn't tell whether they were silent because they spoke a different language and did not understand the women or because they were forbidden to answer. Eventually the women broke into the familiar anthem:

Tchetety top debette
Etek glö tchri fefé
Bügyüti nyemelága
Petyitye!

Having pronounced the last word like a challenge, they cried out bitterly and attacked the white-uniformed men who even now did not react. But the crowd had been changing: ever more men had joined it. They appeared to be doing no more than drifting towards the armed cars out of sheer curiosity but Budai saw that some carried guns under their coats. As their numbers grew, they exchanged significant glances. The women meanwhile were carefully drawing back as if this had all been arranged, part of a strategy.

The whole thing started with the sound of a whistle: suddenly the square went mad with battle cries. Guns suddenly appeared from under coats and opened fire on the tanks. Hand grenades were thrown as well as bottles filled with some explosive, possibly a household liquid. At the same time a mass of other men emerged through the tenement doors and entered the fray, similarly equipped. Over a hundred of them were now swarming around the soldiers. They ran about in strange formations, zigzagging and turning sharply, now this way, now that, only to straighten out and lob their explosives before immediately throwing themselves flat on the ground.

It was far from enough. The soldiers in the armoured cars ducked back down, pulled down their hatches and fired their guns while those on motorbikes let loose volleys of powerful machinegun fire. The ranks of attackers dissolved and pretty soon the open space was covered with the bodies of the wounded. The tanks started up unexpectedly fast and ploughed into the heart of the crowd ruthlessly crushing those who got in the way. They moved like macabre grinders, accompanied by the most desperate screaming and rattling. The cobbles were turning red.

Budai was watching from a little way off, seized by the awful fear of death and, as he ran away, treading over the bodies of the living and the dead, he kept thinking a tank was specifically following him, catching up with him, grinding him under with its metal jaws. His pistol was still in his pocket and he would have been glad to be rid of it but did not want to throw it away in case he attracted attention by doing so. A lot of people were sheltering under a yellow-colonnaded pavilion at the far end of the oval-shaped open space so he joined them.

Everyone was fleeing: crowds were breaking up and scattering chiefly into the surrounding buildings. But even there they refused to give up the fight, firing guns from open windows or from openings in the roof. Now the helmeted soldiers leapt from their vehicles and pursued them up the stairs and soon the battle was raging inside the tenements, gunfire drumming and flashing on ever higher floors and up in the loft. The drama ended with a body falling from on high and landing with a terrifying clatter on the wet cobbles, followed by another and another, some figures waving arms and legs and crying out as they fell, then more and more, one landing on another, blood mingling and running together in the puddles in the rain. It was impossible to watch: Budai gathered all his strength and pushed past people ever deeper into the pavilion. Suddenly he realised that the little yellow structure he took for a pavilion was in fact a metro station or an entrance to it. He managed to dispose of his gun in a litter-bin in the concourse. There were people moving up and down the steps and through the passageways and a great many more waiting and sitting on the platform though there was clearly no service. Only an indifferent voice issuing from the loudspeaker continuously gabbled an endless stream of information. It was close and hot below ground. Steam rose from Budai's damp clothes. Not having slept for two nights, he found a corner and curled up.

He was woken by the same noise to which he had fallen asleep, the distant, continuous croaking of the personal address system. Down here there was neither night nor day and a great many people were still coming and going, falling asleep or swaying about the corridors and platforms. He stumbled up to ground level but found the gates locked and barred so there was no way in or out and saw that a few white-uniformed soldiers were standing on guard outside with guns at the ready. All he could see through the bars was that it was grey outside – was it dawn or dusk? – and that the oval space, and all the roads leading into it, was completely empty with guards posted on each corner. There must be a curfew, he thought, and went down again to sleep some more.

The next time he woke he could tell by the rumbling that trains were running again and he even felt the familiar draught of their approach. The way out was also open. It was sunny and breezy outside. The street and the square were packed with people exactly as they had been before the fighting started, the road too was just as full of cars as before. The dead had vanished, there was no evidence left of the battle, its effects having been covered over with hoardings and fresh layers of paint. Budai joined the crowd and walked down to the china shop where he had taken shelter. Its windows were boarded up but the shop was open for sales again though the choice was limited. The building next door across which the flag had been hung, the walls of which had collapsed as a result of heavy artillery fire, was covered over with matting.

There were even greater changes in the ruined neighbourhood where the homeless had been carrying away their possessions. The wreckage had been gathered up and taken away. The earth on which the buildings had stood had been rolled flat and smoothed so it seemed it had been a vacant site for a long time, the spaces between the buildings like missing teeth. Where there had been barricades they had not only been dismantled but the broken road surface itself had been repaired. Further on he saw that the building whose progress he had often stopped to note but which had been abandoned by the striking workers was once again firmly in construction: the builders had already reached the eightieth floor.

He found the grey house where fighting had continued through the night. It had suffered too much damage to be easily patched up but the damage was hidden by scaffolding. Perhaps they were pretending it was only normal renovation. The wrecked tank had gone from the entrance. Had Budai not been a party to the events, he would hardly have guessed from the condition of the city that anything had happened at all.

A park extended on one side of the house. Those were the rails he had run past to escape the smoke bombs. The sunshine had tempted people out. Children were chasing each other across the grass, there were boats on the lake and sunbathers were relaxing by the water, taking off their shoes and dipping their feet in. Could the insurrection have been a fairly regular run-of-the-mill event? The black broken walls he had fled among certainly suggested earlier conflicts. Might it be that such outbreaks were a necessary product of the way of life here, that from time to time there were revolutions that channelled people's furies? Were they a way of reducing the population?

Spicy sausages were being sold again and since he had enough money to buy one he stopped and queued at a stall: the food tasted better than before. Children were playing around him, kicking balls while lovers embraced, others ate and sang or listened to loud pocket radios. Everywhere people were sunbathing, sleeping, skimming pebbles in the lake, enjoying the fine weather. Could they already have forgotten the battles and buried their dead? It seemed a betrayal of trust, but the thought did not depress him. As he lay on the grass and ate he was filled with hope, happy that people were so greedy for life. He felt very much at one with them. He might even have been happy himself. He scrunched up the paper in which the sausage had been wrapped and threw it into the lake.

It was a moment or two later that he noticed the ball of paper had drifted away. At first he thought the wind must have carried it, but no: the leaves on the water, the tiny bubbles under the surface, those thin stalks of reed and sedge were all proceeding in the same direction. The water was moving! The movement was slow, very slow indeed, but there was a definite current. He tried again. This time he threw a little twig into the water and it too was swept away.

It was a moving discovery and it raised his spirits. Because if it was really the case, if the water was in motion, the tide would have to lead somewhere. He started walking through the park, intending to circle the lake. It was an irregular shape no more than two or three hundred metres across. A marble fountain fed into it on one side and further off there was a wide terrace with tall sturdy columns and an equestrian statue prancing against the cloudless sky. The boats – light, colourful, flat-bottomed beach canoes – were gently bobbing in the waves. They were mostly occupied by young people, boys and girls paddling here and there, shouting to each other.

He discovered the draining-off point opposite the fountain. A little wooden bridge arched over it. The stream was quiet and small, more brook than stream, snaking away between the denser clumps of park trees. It was not only slow but shallow too and so narrow that two strides would have taken him across it, but however insignificant and modest a stream it was, it would, sooner or later, feed into a river, into some main current and that would eventually lead to the sea. And once he had arrived at the sea he would find a harbour, a ship, a route to anywhere.

He did not want to think of himself as he had been five minutes earlier: it was as if that person had never existed. All he had to do was to follow the stream and never to lose sight of it, to walk along its bank or maybe hire a boat, or steal one. A boat would be produced from somewhere! He could practically hear the low moan of the sea and smell its salty tang; he could see it, dark blue, as it seethed and sparkled, its foam like marble, the wind forever drawing new shapes across its restless surface and the seagulls plunging into it time and again ... God be with you, Epepe. He was full of confidence. He would soon be home.